CW01646988

It's an Ill Wind

Pam Keevil

Book Cover by Ken Dawson
www.ccovers.co.uk

A Peverel Press Publications Book

Book One in The Gloucestershire Chronicles; a Detective Mulroney Mystery

The Black Beasts of Gloucestershire are reputed to be panthers or black leopards, released into the wild or escaped from private zoos. So far, no-one has managed to obtain good video or photographic footage.

Contents

Chapter 1

October 2020

Late evening

The yowl stops me. This could be my lucky day. One photo of the beast will set me up for life. Nobody's got anything except a grainy image of these big cats. I switch on the night vision camera fixed to my lapel and move towards the undergrowth. I know it's there, somewhere. I take the torch in my left hand just in case. Its beam would scare off the four horsemen of the apocalypse if they turned up unexpectedly. On a clear night like tonight, the pearly light of the moon is all I need. Hunter's Moon it's called. Helped the poachers in years past. Well, it can help me now. I step away from the road towards the trees at the edge of the wood. Further in, the ground is covered with brambles and nettles. Just what these creatures like. The musty smell of damp leaves wafts upwards as my feet crush them.

A headlight strafes the tree trunks. A van squeals to a halt. I turn as the driver leaps out, goes to the back and opens the double doors. 'Out,' a male voice shouts. 'Get the hell out of here.'

I crouch down as one, two, no, must be half a dozen men with rucksacks or carrier bags obey and without warning run towards me. I hold my breath as they dash past, heading towards the open fields and the town beyond. I stay still, breathing slowly, deeply, trying not to let my breath disturb the still night air. The driver glances round, goes to the back and slams the door. He is about to get in the driver's seat when he too hears the yowl. It is coming from somewhere behind me.

'Who's there?' he calls.

He switches on a torch. Its beam lights up the track along which the men have run. He moves it in an arc as he comes closer. I know he'll see me. The beam shines straight at my eyes. I flinch and the movement makes me stumble backwards.

'What the fuck?' he says as he drags me out. I am on my knees, looking up. I can't run away and my voice is no more than a strangled croak.

He pauses for a moment. Will he let me go?

'Stupid bitch,' he says as the torch is raised high in the air. Something as soft as a whisper of wind or a flutter of a leaf wreathes through the night air. I'm not sure what. It sounds like *I'm sorry.* The head shakes, the eyes soften before screwing up tight. I have no time to protect myself except cover my face with my hands. I can only pray it does not hurt too much. The crack splits the silence. The pain in my head, jaw and face strips the breath from my body. I sink to the forest floor and close my eyes. All I want is the hurt to end as something damp slides down my face. I lick my lips. It has a metallic taste. An engine starts; tyres kick up the gravel from the roadway. I close my eyes. Let me sleep.

****

I open my eyes. The light is too bright. I close them again.

'Rachel?' I open one eye. A figure bends over me. The voice is slight. It is a woman but she has a mask so most of her face is obscured.

'I was the last time I looked,' I say. It's a pathetic joke. It's the most I can manage. Her scrubs are not covered with plastic so it can't be a Covid ward.

'How are you feeling?' She takes my pulse, scribbles something on a clipboard and adjusts some dials behind my head.

'Like I've been run over by a bus.' I shift my body to get a look at my surroundings. Yep. It's a hospital ward.

Senja, the name is written on her scrub cap, turns and looks at me again. 'Is that what happened?'

I shake my head and regret the move. Shards of pain. I wince. 'Bloody hell.'

'Lie still,' she says.

I have no wish to disagree. 'How do you know my name?'

A smile crinkles her eyes. 'Your phone does not have a lock. It's something the police checked straight away.'

'Police?' This time I ignore the pain and lift my body away from the pillow. I grimace. Shouldn't have done that.

Senja is bustling round, checking dials, smoothing covers before she pulls back the curtains. I am in a small four bed bay and we are spaced apart, with a chair and a bedside unit for each patient. The walls are a pale green and the screens are made from a green and orange leaf print. The window blinds are up and outside it is bright and sunny. The golds and browns of the nearby trees glow.

She returns to stand at the foot of the bed. 'The dog walker who found you called the police. That's why you're here. You were in some bushes off the main road.'

'I was in the woods,' I say and sink back.

'Later,' Senja says. 'Lie still and get some rest, unless you need the bathroom?'

'My rucksack? My cameras?' I glance wildly around. 'Please say you found them?'

'In the cupboard. All safe. Your clothes have been taken by the police and they said something about checking the camera on your lapel.'

'Why?'

'Information that might lead to an arrest. Whoever did what they did should be strung up.' She slams the clipboard into its container at the foot of the bed and mutters something in a language I don't understand. 'Get some rest.' She turns and leaves.

I glance round the room. The other beds are full of elderly people. There is a nod and a smile from the white-haired lady sitting by her bed and knitting. No one else takes any notice. I think they must be sleeping. I doze and drift into a semi-drugged sleep. Images of wild animals, running figures and staring eyes jostle, fade and return on an endless carousel.

****

I don't know how long I've been asleep. A cool hand touches my arm. I jerk awake. Senja is back. Her dark eyes may seem stern but they are wreathed in laughter lines. She's older than I'd thought. 'How are you feeling?'

'When can I go home?'

'You've had a nasty bang on the head. You're in here for observation but as there seems to be no lasting damage other than a bump and a gash, we might let you out later today.' Her words are clipped.

I raise a hand to my head and touch the dressing. 'Is it serious?'

'We anticipated concussion but you are a tough one, with an even tougher skull.' A faint smile plays around her lips. Perhaps she isn't so unfazed as she seems.

'You said someone found me?'

'A late-night dog walker called the emergency services and you were brought in soon after.'

'What time?' For some reason this is important.

'Just after two am.' She checks my chart at the end of the bed. 'Are you ready for some questions? The police are very insistent,' she says.

'Better let them in and you can get back to your proper job, not nursing fakes like me.'

'There is nothing fake about possible concussion.' She tilts her head on one side as if checking me out. 'Can you walk? We've set up a video link in the consultation room off the corridor.'

'Video link?' I ease my body into a sitting position and swing my legs on the floor.

'No visitors are allowed. That includes the police,' she says and offers me an arm.

I shake my head. 'I'll be fine.'

The floor is cool to my feet. The ward is quiet and few of the beds in the other side rooms are occupied. Of course, routine operations have been cancelled. I suppose I was classed as an emergency. I need to get out of here and let them get on with the important stuff. Isn't there a national emergency? I walk beside Senja and she shows me into a small room. It is painted in the same insipid colours. The blinds are down and the lights are bright.

'Here you go.' Senja points to a small tablet propped on a white table. I sit in the brown fabric upright chair and use the chrome arm rests to lower my body. For some reason I am exhausted by these few steps. I adjust the screen. Senja closes the door behind her.

'Rachel Thomas?' A face peers out of the screen. 'I'm Sergeant Mark Mulroney. Can I ask you a few questions?

I shrug. 'I can't remember much. There was a van, a man and a belt on the head.'

'Let's start at the beginning, shall we?' he says and smiles. His eyes are green and he's got reddish grey hair. A wedding ring glints on the third finger of his left hand as he taps away at his end. So much for getting swept off my feet by a fit policeman. I focus on his questions and tell him everything I can remember.

'Was there anything about the van?'

I shrug. 'It was a white transit and I couldn't see the number plate or the make. They all look the same to me.'

'Would you recognise this person again?'

'Like I said, he wore a mask, like a lot of people today and it was dark. A beanie hat covered his hair. There's not much else to say.' I pause. 'Except for one thing.'

Sergeant Mulroney pauses too. 'Yes?'

'His eyes. They were dark. And… he said something as if…as if…' Words dry up. 'Sorry.'

'Take your time.'

I place my head in my hands. There is something I need to tell him. I shrug. 'Sorry,' I say again.

He shifts in the chair. The interview is over. 'If you do remember anything, you can get in touch with me at the police station.'

I nod. 'I promise I'll do that.'

'You might find when you're at home, something comes back… you know… an image… a sound… a smell… anything like that can help.'

'What is the chance you can catch him?' For the first time I'm scared. What if he comes back to find me?

Sergeant Mulroney stares from the screen. 'You'd be surprised how the smallest detail… an accent… part of a car number…We have followed up some unusual leads in our time with amazing results.'

That is what I want. To catch him. I must remember everything. 'I'll do my best,' I mutter and I will.

I am rewarded with a smile. 'You do that.'

'There is one thing.'

'Yes?' The eyes are warm yet checking me out all the time.

'Do you think he'll come and find me and…' I want to add *and finish me off* but it sounds so melodramatic.

'We'll be putting extra patrols in your area, but as you are certain you don't know him it is unlikely. Where would he start looking?'

I feel slightly better. 'When will I get my camera and clothes back?'

'The camera is being checked for images. Once we've downloaded them all, it's unlikely we'll keep it.'

'No pinching my pictures of the big cats. That's for David Attenborough.'

'Big cats?'

'I'm a nature photographer,' I say. 'That's why I was out at night.'

He smiles. 'I wondered what you were doing.' The smile fades. 'Once more, please let me know if there is anything you remember at a later date.' He logs off and I am left staring at nothing.

I walk slowly, checking each foot is secure before lifting the next. I am in hospital clothes and yet I feel naked. I pass the nurse's station. Senja looks up. 'You shouldn't have walked on your own. Let me help you back to bed.'

I shake my head. 'When can I leave?'

She flinches as if I'd startled her. 'Leave? You can discharge yourself but we don't recommend it.'

'But I can do it?'

I watch as her lips purse together. 'As I said, we don't recommend it. What if you are taken ill or there are complications?'

For a moment I am scared. 'What complications? I had a bang on the head. I was knocked out.'

'We never can be too sure…' her voice fades away. She knows she cannot hold me here.

'I can stay with a friend. She's an ex-nurse.' I am lying. We've all done a basic First Aid course at school.

Senja's shoulders drop slightly. 'In that case, I can arrange for you to discharge yourself.'

'Please do it,' I say. 'I can be looked after and it will free up beds for others.' I indicate the elderly clientele.

'Very well.' She returns to where the other nurses have been listening and watching. One raises her eyebrows before tapping at a screen. Why do I feel guilty? I shuffle away.

When I get back to my bed, I rummage in the small cupboard. My phone has some power left.

'Tashi? Can you pick me up?' I say. 'I'm not staying one minute longer.'

I want to get back to being Rachel and not a victim. If Sergeant Mulroney is right, I might even be able to remember more and get that bastard put away. A draught from an open window chills my bare arms. 'And bring me some clothes, please.'

Chapter 2

Sergeant Mark Mulroney shuffles the papers in his hands. He'll type up the notes later. All he has to do now is download the images from Rachel's camera and go through them. Not that he expects much. He's had a quick glance and it's all blue tits, ducks and blackness. Not like the images you get on the nature programmes when you can practically count the whiskers of endangered species.

'The boss wants you in her control room,' the desk sergeant calls out. 'It might be a long one.'

Mark goes up to the desk. 'Me? Why does she want me?'

'Better go and find out.'

Mark takes a deep breath, keys in the security code that gives access to the back rooms of the station and heads along the blue and grey painted corridor, past the kitchen, full of dirty cups and half eaten microwaved meals, the toilet block and cloakrooms, past individual offices and the wider spaces allocated to CSI and special crime teams. He has been summoned to the large open plan room at the end. The wall and door are half glazed and inside a meeting is taking place in front of the white board on which is pinned a map of the area, photos, dates and times. DCI Eve Fletcher, referred to as *Ma'am* to her face and *the boss* behind her back, is holding court. Mark feels like he did outside the headteacher's study; scared even though you know you've done nothing wrong. He hesitates, places his hand on the door handle and opens it.

'Ahh there you are. This is Sergeant, soon to be Detective Sergeant Mark Mulroney, I hope. I've asked for him to be seconded to my team while most of our people are dealing with the County Lines. Sit down.'

Mark looks around. This is not a good move. He'd be regarded as her protégé and he'd only recently completed his training to be sergeant. There was a shifting of seats and a young woman pulls out a chair. She is in uniform, like him. He joins her. He feels more secure here. The others are all in their own clothes and exude confidence, or is that just his stuff?

'Welcome,' she says and whispers, 'We're not as bad as we look.'

'As I was saying.' Eve glares across at the young woman. 'We've had it all this summer, raves, illegal gatherings, more domestics than you can shake a stick at and drug use has gone through the roof. Now we've been landed with a potential people smuggling gang.' Mark senses eyes turning on him. 'This gang has been of interest to Bristol for a while. God knows why they've come up here.'

'Out of the way of the big pockets with plenty of cash. Everyone knows rural forces are stretched.' There is a murmuring of assent.

Eve ignores the voices. She turns to Mark. 'That's your brief with Cassie here. We've got dribs and drabs of sightings but nothing that suggests people smuggling, just the results of lockdown and people going a bit crazy. Start digging and see what you can find out.'

Why me? Mark wants to ask. He remains silent as Eve turns back to the board and draws a large circle. Inside she writes *Attack on Rachel Thomas* in capital letters. Lines like the rays of the sun fan out from the circle. Each line ends in a question; *link with people smuggling? who? why? does she recognise her attacker? other suspicious sightings? liaise with serious crime squad in Bristol?*

There is silence as Eve allows them to read and digest the questions before she holds up a printout from a newspaper blog. The name of the newspaper is clearly written on the top. The headline sends shivers up Mark's spine; *Innocent woman attacked and left for dead.*

'And I want you to discover which toe rag snitched this to our wonderful press so early.'

Chapter 3

'Get in quick.' Tashi leans across the seat as I scramble inside her car, pushing away packets of tea-lights and a box of diyas. She's getting ready for Diwali early. 'We can't hug but imagine I'm giving you one,' she says.

I clutch the rucksack with my cameras, lie back against the seat and fasten the belt in time before she sets off. 'Thanks for this,' I mutter. 'I'm sorry if I'm an inconvenience.'

'Never say that again. It's just with all the nonsense about tiers and what you can or can't do it would be my luck to find some jobs worthy sneaking round and spying. If he or she does, I'll claim you're in my care bubble. Mamaji will back me up.'

'How does she know?'

'Wait till we get home. You'd better have your big girl pants on. Close your eyes and pray to whatever god you fear we don't get stopped.'

We continue in silence, broken only by the satnav squeaking and directing the car down a myriad of backstreets I didn't know existed, until we swerve into more familiar territory and stop in front of the three-storey semi overlooking the park. Before I can move, the door flies open and Mamaji in a red shalwar with a long black cardigan is at the side of the car.

'Come, come,' she says and helps me out. She clasps my arm and I feel her cool skin next to mine. 'Poor girl,' she whispers. 'Some of my home cooked food and plenty of rest will set you up. Soroush will check you over when he gets home. I don't trust some of these new doctors.'

I know better than to protest and allow myself to be swept along in a ginger, jasmine cloud of warmth and love. Within ten minutes I am ensconced in the spare bedroom, the children banished with a threat of never having a story from Aunty Rachel again unless they let me rest. I am sipping sweet chai, resting on a bed covered in mirror cushions and velvet throws in jewel colours when Tashi creeps in with a printout from the local newspaper website under her arm.

She plonks her slim frame on the side of the bed and looks at me under her long dark fringe through eyes the colour of Brazil nuts. 'Are you up for this?'

I shrug. 'If it's the local rag it'll be about two lines of a hit and run in a country lane.'

'You wish.'

'I'm fine. Let's see what they've dug up this time. If it's anything like the Tik Tok balloon battle that was reported as internecine gang warfare, I'm ready for a laugh.'

Tahsi clears her throat and holds out the newspaper, folded to page three. *Talented amateur photographer found injured* screams the headline. There is a photo of the road side where I was found and one of me, presenting prizes to the young winners of the Cotswold county show photographic competition. My face is clearly visible and the smaller strap-line text says it all. *Local teacher and talented amateur photographer, Rachel Thomas, attacked by unknown assailant.* There is speculation I might have recognised my attacker. Interestingly the police are not mentioned. How the hell did they get this information? Did I blab in my sleep? Was it the dog walker? Except how would they know me?

'Why don't you stay here for a while until this all dies down?' Tashi says.

I hand the paper back to her. 'A few days of Mamaji's food and some hugs from my surrogate nieces and nephews will set me up,' I say. Am I breaking some rule? Who cares? Aren't we supposed to protect the vulnerable? Today I am vulnerable.

Chapter 4

Finn Driscoll studies the message.

You said you hadn't been seen. Find out what she knows and deal with it before we deal with you.

He types.

> *I hit her before she'd got a good look at me. All she could really see were my eyes and as we don't yet have a police data base of iris recognition, I think we're in the clear.*

The reply is almost instant.

> *We need to be sure. A big drop is imminent.*

Finn sighs. Why the hell had he got involved? Except he knows why. It's easy money and he needs all the money he can get his hands on or the farm will go tits up and his brother will take control and sell everything.

> *I'll find out what I can.*

He returns the phone to its hiding place and closes the barn door. The night will be cold. He breathes in the freshness and stares up at the sky, peppered with stars. A warm, golden light filters from the curtained windows of the farmhouse. How could his brother want to get rid of all this? The dump by the canal wasn't worth much. Arable land goes for sod all and there'd be no chance of building on it. His brother was welcome to the cash, but this place?

He heads back to the house, checking the barn doors are padlocked and the main gate is secure. A lolloping black and white collie cross greets him. Before he closes the kitchen door Finn looks at the silhouette of the barns against the night sky. This was and is his home. He'll do anything to keep the place. He crouches down and rubs the dog's ears. 'How can I arrange a meeting with a young woman without raising any suspicions?'

The dog wags his tail and wanders off to stretch out by the fire. Finn pours himself a single malt and sits down on the faded chintz sofa. He opens his laptop and types in her name. Rachel Thomas, adding wildlife photographer. If she's a teacher, she might even have a local watering hole near the school. A few questions in some of the local pubs might provide interesting answers.

Chapter 5

I open the front door of my terraced cottage. For once, no one's curtains twitch. That's the trouble with living in a small town; there is no isolation, mentally or visually. People know what you do and where you go, even if they don't know you. For the moment I am pleased with the lack of interest. I thought I'd feel normal. I don't. After the busyness of the last few days, I relish peace and quiet. At the same time, it unnerves me. I'll be fine when I get back to work.

I unlock the front door and step over a pile of flyers from the local takeaways, catalogues with the names of the old couple who lived here before me and several envelopes that look more formal. I'll deal with them later. I sniff. The air is musty and is that damp? No, probably just the dusty, sour smell of an unused home. That will soon change. I walk along the hall and into the kitchen overlooking the scrubby patch of land the estate agents described as a patio garden. The wall around it has the remnants of the summer's sweet peas clinging to life after the recent gales. Next year I'll make it better.

I cannot believe it's only been a week since I was last here. No. Four days? Yes. One night in hospital and three with Tashi. I sniff. Jesus, didn't I do the washing up? A plate congealed with my hurried ready meal is in the sink. I open the fridge. I won't get fat on a small piece of cheese, a wrinkled tomato and half eaten jars of jam and marmalade. I'll need to go shopping. At least I don't drink milk. I fill the kettle and pull a mug from the rack; bone chain patterned with butterflies, a present from my mum as a house warming. My eyes fill. What would I give to be able to hop on a plane and be with them both? No chance. Spain's in lockdown too. At least it would be warm and I could stuff my face with paella.

While I wait for the water to heat up, I have to decide what to do with my clothes. I have two carrier bags and my rucksack. The rucksack I place carefully on the kitchen table, the bag of Tashi's castoffs I place for washing by the machine. What about the clothes I was wearing when… I grab the carrier bag, race upstairs and throw the whole thing into the back of the small cupboard where I store the stuff I rarely wear. I can't bear to chuck decent stuff away but at the moment I can't bring myself to touch, let alone look at anything from that day.

I walk slowly back down the stairs. I will feel better soon. I know I will.

I wake in the early hours of the morning. There is a noise. A rattle. Cats? There are plenty around here. It's so dark. The blackout curtains work well. I'd be grateful for a hint of brightness, like a security light. I sit up in bed and pull the duvet closer. It's cold. Even if I could afford the heating, should I? Climate change and all that? I strain my ears for the slightest sound. No cars. There shouldn't be. There's nothing to go to and certainly no reason for anyone to be out and about unless it's dodgy. Where did I get that word from? I haven't used it in years. It was from my dad. He used to talk about dodgy deals when he was buying a second-hand car. I want to see him. I never felt scared with him. I want to be a child again, safe and cosy at home. Except where is home? Number 23 Telford Drive was sold years ago and while The Brits Bar in Benidorm might be my parents' idea of home, it isn't mine. I'm stuck here.

There's that noise again. This time I slide out of the covers and creep across the floor to the window. I pull aside the blind and peer underneath. A dim street light from three houses down sheds a glimmer onto my patch of garden. The back gate is firmly closed. The bins are upright. The patio chair and table are where I left them. Nothing is wrong and yet I'm certain I heard something. I press my face closer to the cold glass and squint as far as I can. Solar lights from the Jackson's patio four doors away shed a comforting glow. A scratch and a tap tapping. I jump back, leaving the blind open. The noise is right outside. I sit on the bed, shaking and shivering. My heart pounds and I push a fist into my mouth. Tears fill my eyes, expecting at any moment to see a shadowy figure outside the window before it bursts open. What? I'm five metres off the ground, aren't I? Can't cat burglars climb drain pipes? I clasp my phone, ready to call the emergency services and fall to my knees, creeping closer. A sudden tap startles me. My heart beats faster. A thin branch whips across the window and the tap happens again. How stupid can I get? I stand up and move to the window. A loose runner from the climbing rose over the back door flaps in the wind.

The sooner I get back to work, the better. Zoom or no Zoom, coronavirus or no coronavirus, I'm going into work on Monday. Until then I'll clean the house and start clearing the back yard and that damn rose will be the first thing to go. I curl up in bed and pull the duvet over my head. I'm imagining things, I know I am. No one is interested in me.

Chapter 6

The school building is as welcoming as a 1970s design can ever be. We joke it's in Eastern Bloc style; three storey, windows along two sides, peeling, painted cladding in what was the previous school colours before we joined a wider, academy conglomerate. A few lights shine from the classrooms and a handful of cars are in the car park. At least we've got the view of the hills beyond. My hand holds the fob close to the security reader. A click and it swings open. I adjust my mask and walk through. Weird how quickly we've got used to the hand sanitiser and the yellow and black tape everywhere. I follow the one-way system to the upper school staff room. There's no one there so I check my pigeon hole and escape to my room. I call it my room; it's a specialist facility for photography with a dark room, would you believe it? Not that we bother anymore. I run up the stairs and unlock the door. I don't want to talk to anyone. I'm back. That's all they need to know. I check the room and set up the IT system for online and in person teaching and take my place behind the plastic screen.

Before the first lesson, a familiar face pokes round the door. Tashi manages to look elegant, efficient and fearsome at the same time. How does she do it? Is it the dark grey suit or the white blouse which I'm sure is silk? No. It's her general demeanour which says 'I'm in charge. Don't mess with me.' Probably why she's Assistant Head and I'm part time nobody. Even today in my smartest black trousers and tan leather jacket, I look more like an advertising executive in some on-trend establishment and not someone designed to inspire reluctant students.

Tashi comes forward. 'Heh, good to see you back in place. The room hasn't been the same without you. The kids were pretty good, and I know that Years 12 and 13 are up to date with their course work.' She pauses. 'That full time post is still available, you know?'

I shake my head. 'You know me. Still trying to get the big picture, the nature scoop that'll thrust me on *Spring Watch* before you can say Chris Packham.'

Despite the mask I know she is smiling. The lines radiate from her eyes. She smooths a hand over her neat pencil skirt. An emerald ring sparkles against the dark material. 'Why can't you take an interest in something…' she struggles to find the word.

'Safer?'

'Yes, like slugs? Slow and easily forgotten about?'

'And certainly not newsworthy,' I say.

She holds up one hand. 'You can't stop me from trying to keep the best art and design teacher we've had in years, can you?' There is another pause. Those brown eyes are watching my every move and reaction. 'Are you sure you're ready to take on Year 10 and their latest projects, which will be heavily influenced by whatever film, download or Instagram star they are following?'

'Bring 'em on,' I say and beckon to the soon to be arriving hordes.

She laughs. 'I had to ask. Duty of Care and all that.' She is about to turn and go when she stops. 'This Friday we're meeting up at The Star and Garter. It's Jake's birthday bash. We can all sit at a safe distance and he's paying for the pizzas. Shall I book your place?'

I hesitate. 'Go on then. As long as the wine is decent.'

'Good for you. I'll tell him. He asked specifically if you'd be coming.' She winks.

'So far this morning you have planned my next career move and set me up for an evening out. What next?'

She stands, head on one side, dark fringe falling slightly over one eye. 'You could try wearing your hair longer.' She ducks as I pretend to throw a marker pen at her. The conversation is over, ended by a screaming bell that says lessons are about to begin. She closes the door.

'Distance, remember distance,' I hear her saying to Year 10 who are waiting outside. They are strangely silent behind the obligatory face masks in school colours.

'Can we come in, Miss Thomas?' Ameena peers round the door.

'Yes, sanitiser on the front desk and sit in your assigned seats.' They file in, squirt their hands and rub them together as they find a place in the vast expanse of the room. That's another thing I like about this school; there is a sense of space. It makes my life easier as I can separate potential and certain trouble makers. They take their places as the screen shimmers and I invite the home zoomers to join.

I clear my throat. 'Good morning, everyone. Today we'll be exploring nature in art as a possible choice for one of your themes and to help with the study of drawing techniques. Get out your personal sketch pads and the assorted pencils in the tray below the desk.'

'Miss, is it true you nearly got eaten?' The mask is removed and Ryan stares at me. It is an ongoing battle who will win control over the class; him or me.

'At least I'd have a decent story to tell you all,' I say. 'Sorry to disappoint.'

'We saw your photo in the paper,' a short girl with long curly hair says. She has not taken off her mask. Is it Ellen?

'Not my best profile I'm sure,' I say and close the conversation down.

'Do you reckon they'll get that bloke who socked you?' Ryan again.

'The police are doing all they can.'

Ryan shrugs. 'I'd be careful, Miss. If he's scared you saw him, he might want to finish you off.'

'That's horrid,' Emily says. 'Take no notice of him, Miss. He watches too much online.'

'Just saying.' Ryan wafts a hand as if dispelling her words. 'We don't want you off sick again. That old lady on supply was useless. Didn't let us do anything interesting.'

Behind my screen I smile. 'Thank you, Ryan. That is praise indeed.' Yet his words chill me. That man coming to silence me is exactly what I have been thinking.

I fend off the enquiries from fellow staff as best I can and volunteer for lunch supervision. It's weird how quickly the kids have settled to the new regulations. They are quieter and after a recent ban on mobiles in school time, we are spared the squeals of laughter as another clip of dancing animals or bin men in hula skirts is shared.

I am in the middle of ensuring Y7 do not play *Covid you're dead* as they try to pinch each other's arms in the dinner queue when Tashi calls me over. We stand at the regulation two metres, masks covering our mouths so it is impossible to lip read in the clatter of plates and cutlery. Our voices sound too loud.

'Are you feeling okay?'

'Yes. Never better. Why?'

'A kid in Y8 bubble three has gone off sick with a temperature. We're sending the rest of them home and Mr Howe who was teaching them this morning. How are you up for covering his classes this afternoon?'

I nod. It will keep my mind off Ryan's words. He's street savvy. How much more so would a smuggler be? I vow to get home before it's dark. I am tempted to call the police but what could they do? It's all in my imagination, isn't it?

The afternoon passes easily. Mr Howe's classes are all either Year 7 or Year 8 and still apprehensive of unfamiliar staff. It was good to teach something other than art and design.

English I can cope with. I park the car in front of the house and breathe in the autumn air, a mix of smoke, decay and earthiness. The valley around the town is still more yellow brown than grey. The last beech leaves cling to the trees and a few hazel twigs still sport green leaves, as if they are reluctant to let the winter and the dark season cower them. The final few streaks of sunlight burnish the sky. It will be a cold night. I shiver and lift the boot of the car. Footsteps sound along the pavement. They are getting closer. I press myself against the side of the car. The footsteps stop. Why? If someone lived here, they'd be opening the door, wouldn't they? Could it be a visitor? No. Visitors aren't allowed, are they? Unless it's a carer, and they don't usually walk. They sweep in, park, unlock their houses, go in and disappear later. There aren't any really old people along this street. I know that by the clap for carers over the spring and summer. The road was full of young families and middle-aged couples in crocs and baggy trousers.

A dog walker? The footsteps start again. A light shines at the front of the house. Shit. He's got a torch. The fear courses through me.

A dark figure emerges from the street. The light shines. I blink and hold up my hands to cover my eyes.

'Amazon delivery for number forty-four?'

The accent is foreign. I laugh. It's not a normal laugh. The poor guy looks startled. 'Next one,' I say and point up the hill. 'This is number forty-two.'

'Sorry,' he says and disappears. The light goes ahead of him. Even in those few seconds the dark has deepened and I feel more alone.

I slam the car boot shut and scurry inside. Once the door is locked and the chain in place, I switch on all the lights and close the curtains. I resist the temptation to pour myself a glass of wine. It would be too easy for it to become two. I must get a grip. Perhaps Sergeant Mulroney would know who to talk to. I'm sure this is all a normal reaction but I don't like it.

I find the number easily enough and am put through to the sergeant on duty. She knows about the case and says she'll leave a message.

'Before you go, is there anything we can help you with?' Her voice is like melted chocolate.

'I know you'll think I'm stupid, but I keep imagining I see people watching me, lights shining where they shouldn't… I'm not making any sense, am I?'

'Everything you are describing is perfectly normal. Do you have the number for Victim Support?'

'What?'

'It's completely free, confidential and everything can be done over the phone.'

'Like counselling?' I have images of myself lying on a couch, explaining how my mother didn't breast feed me enough.

'Sort of…' There is a hint of laughter in her voice; kind, understanding and warming. 'It's not what you see on TV. Especially American TV, all shrinks and everyone in therapy for years on end. It's worth checking it out. I would.'

'Thanks, perhaps I'll give it a go.'

'You do that. The number is….' She reels off a number. 'Or you can check online for more information.'

'Thanks,' I say and end the call. I write the number on the noticeboard in the kitchen. If I don't feel better next week, I'll give it a go.

I check WhatsApp and Facebook. Nothing new. Instagram is different. There is a message.

> *Hi*
>
> *My name is Finn Driscoll and I'm really interested in photography. I saw the report in the paper. I must admit I don't think I'd have the courage to chase the Black Beasts. Owls and badgers are more my thing, unless the cows on my farm get over excited. I've been on Instagram and the images you've got are amazing. Just like to say well done and perhaps we can share a few photos from time to time.*

> *By the way, I don't have much of a Social Media profile. It was frowned upon in my last job so I took everything down. Now I'm free I'll have to start again. (Don't ask me what job. If I tell you I'd have to kill you.)* LOL
>
> *Hope to see more of your stuff online and if you've got any insider tips on how to keep animals from wandering off when you've spotted the perfect image, I'd appreciate it. I'm on a BIG learning curve.*
>
> *Finn Driscoll*
>
> *Although you know that because I started with it!* DOH

I check online. Finn Driscoll is as elusive as those damned animals I'd been hunting. Not that it is unusual round here with so many Ministry of Defence and specialist security offices practically on my doorstep.

Another message pops in.

> *Sorry if that sounded a bit odd. I'm not. Odd that is. Just how did you get into these semi-mythical creatures?* FD

He sounds okay and if he does work in the military or security, he'd be vetted to within an inch of his life and so would his family. I decide to message back.

> *I suppose we all dream of getting the scoop and appearing on TV with David or Chris. I know I do. And those cats have haunted me since I was sure I saw one and when I told my family they all laughed. For a teenager that was hard to handle.*

It is gone ten when we eventually end the conversation.

Chapter 7

Acting Detective Sergeant Mark Mulroney scans the list of unusual activities and sighting of white transit vans in unexpected places and at strange times. There are a number, but none would have justified an investigation, especially as the public has become remarkably jumpy about such things in lockdown. He reads the incident logs. There are several reports of mountain bikers, deprived of their fix, turning up in local woodland and terrorising the dog walkers. Others could easily have been people doing a midnight flit from debt collectors. There are plenty of occasions when social contact starved teens got together for a party. Some are more interesting. He prints out a list and takes a highlighter pen. There are numerous sightings of transits pulling up at odd places in the county. So far, they have the appearance of random events, easily explained. There is conjecture of possible fly tipping, assignations between sex starved lovers and young twenties, possibly students planning an illicit rave.

He is not so sure. Nothing is ever random. He checks the message he has been sent. Rachel Thomas wants to speak with him. Has she remembered anything? He'd better check it out. He picks up the phone. No. It's too late. No one wants a communication from the police at eleven at night. Tomorrow will do.

He logs off and goes out to his car. A brisk and chill wind blows over the rooftops of Moreton. Few lights shine in windows and the roads are empty. Nothing to do, nowhere to go. Most people are holed up at home or online. Funny how he thought he wouldn't miss the day to day. Give him a decent burglary or a pub fight rather than domestics. It's always the children he feels sorry for, standing watching, taking everything in and forever remembering their mother or father with a bruised face, broken tooth or worse. He presses a switch. The car purrs to life. Better get home and get to bed. If he puts the alarm on, he might be up in time to see his two kids off to school. If their classes are still open. He smiles. Them and Ginny keep him going. He swings the car out of the car park and stops at the brow of the hill out of habit. Nothing. Not even a kid in a hoodie on a bike running the dope to someone. He knows and they know he knows. That's the trouble.

He lets the silent car nose down the hill. The launderette is still open. No one inside. Not even a cat crosses his path as he drives out of town. Within five minutes he is in the small estate with the only decent, local houses he and Ginny could afford. He parks, gets out and opens the front door. Book bags are waiting on the shelf; a space for each child to stop them arguing. A drink? He goes into the kitchen and opens the fridge. No beers. Damn. Two packed lunch boxes sit on the top shelf, one adorned with dinosaurs for Andrew and one with spaceships for Emily. Funny. Eight years old and already they know what they want to do; Andrew is going to be a scientist and discover a new breed of dinosaur which he'll name after himself. Emily will be the first spacewoman to land on Mars.

He closes the fridge, creeps upstairs and into his bedroom. Ginny is asleep but she stirs as he climbs in beside her. 'Good shift?'

He curls himself into the crook of her back. She is warm and smells of roses. 'So so,' he says.

'Good night.' She turns over, pulls the duvet around her and moves away slightly.

****

'Dad, you missed hearing me read. Will you do it now?' A book is thrust under Mark's nose. He raises himself on one elbow and opens a scratchy eye. Too much screen work and not enough collar feeling.

'Did I? Sorry, sweetheart.'

'Can you do it now?' The tone is more insistent. Like her mother. Talk about chip off the old block.

'Come here,' he says.

Emily snuggles closer. 'Pooh. You smell,' she says and holds her pointy nose between two fingers.

'Sorry. No time for a shower last night. Can you put up with me?'

There is no time for her to answer. Ginny's head appears round the bedroom door. She is already dressed, her makeup on and her black hair framing her smiling face. 'I said go upstairs and clean your teeth, not annoy your father.'

He mouths *thanks* as Emily stumps off to the bathroom. 'You did promise,' she says. Has to have the last word as usual.

Ginny comes over and ruffles her hand through his hair. If only he had the same energy he had before the kids were born. He'd have pulled her into bed with him for a quickie. 'Sorry about being so late last night.'

Ginny holds up a hand. 'I married a policeman, not a nine to five clock-watcher. Get showered, breakfast is ready. I reckon you need a decent one so I've cooked scrambled eggs with mushrooms on toast. Suit you?' She sniffs. 'You do whiff a bit.'

'Late nights, bad food and even worse digestion,' he breathes out heavily.

'Urgh, morning breath.' She pulls away. 'You've got ten minutes or your breakfast will be outside where the starving hordes of crows are lined up on the fence, waiting.'

Mark slides out of the bed, makes it by punching the pillows and smoothing the duvet, before running a hand over the under sheet to flatten out the worst of the creases. In the shower he lets the water splash over him. There was something he had to do last night. What was it? He claps a hand to his forehead. That was it. Send a report on what that woman's camera had picked up. He'd given it a quick glance. There had been nothing of interest so far, except a few images of dark bushes, the bright eyes of a fox and a small deer. Still, there might be more. He'd do it when he got to work.

Eight minutes later he is sitting at the breakfast table, forking eggs into his mouth. Emily perches on his knee as he helps her decipher more stories of Kipper, Biff and Chip.

'That book's easy.' Andrew doesn't even bother to lift his head from the book he is reading. Mark remembers *The Sheep Pig*. The boy is already outstripping Emily. Poor kid works so hard too. How can twins be so different? Except were they twins? Two eggs? Two sperm? Same implant and neither of them prepared to lose either of the babies Ginny had longed for.

'Not the first time it isn't,' Mark says. 'And being rude to your sister is against house rules. Remember that.'

'Is this a warning?' Andrew looks up, a frown on his face.

''Yes.'

'Okay.' Andrew returns to his book without another word. Obviously, Dick King-Smith is more interesting than arguing with Dad.

'Hol-i-day.' He sounds out the word after Emily stumbles three times.

'Come on, sweeties. Leave Dad to eat his breakfast and we'll be off. Get your coats and bookbags and wait by the car.' Ginny shoos the children out of the kitchen.

'I should be on time today,' Mark says.

'Good. I want to talk about Emily.' She glances towards the hallway. 'She really isn't making progress and we ought to get her some help.'

'Isn't that for the school?'

Ginny raises one eyebrow. It is followed by a sigh and a slight shake of the head. 'Schools are as strapped for cash as the police. You know that. We must do something.' She kisses the top of his head. 'See you tonight,' she says and closes the kitchen door. The sound of young voices and scampering feet down the stairs is followed by the slam of the front door and silence. Sudden, unexpected silence.

Mark checks the month's cash balance on his phone. The amount left will cover bills, nothing more. How the hell could he raise some money for extra lessons? The phone rings and interrupts his thoughts. His DCI's voice shows no pleasantries.

'Get your butt over here ASAP. We have a few more leads about the attack and the possible links with a people smuggling gang. Will you go over that woman's video footage again and check for anything that might be of use?'

'Will do, except preliminary viewing shows nothing except a fox, a badger and a couple of scared deer.'

'Double check for me, and while you're enjoying your late start give Rachel Thomas a reassuring call. She's panicking. A nervous witness is never good and there's just a chance the driver of the van might be checking up on how much she knows.'

'Is she in danger?'

There is a pause as if Eve is weighing what to say. 'I reckon it's not a local person and whoever did the job has gone to ground in a big city. But I don't like loose ends. This is still live as far as we're concerned. Right?'

'Right.' The phone goes dead.

Mark calls Rachel's number. She picks up straight away. 'Yes?' Her voice is hesitant.

'Detective Sergeant Mulroney here,' he says.

There is no mistaking the relief. 'Thanks for getting back to me.' The voice takes on a more serious tone. 'Are you now a detective? Am I in danger, or have you found out something?'

'It was coincidence,' Mark says. 'We're short staffed so I got the move earlier than usual.'

'Well, good for you, I mean,' Rachel says.

Her tone has changed. 'How can we be of assistance?' Part of him hopes she has remembered something more about her attacker, perhaps a glimpse of a number plate.

'I know I'm being silly, but I can't get over the feeling I'm being watched.'

'There's nothing silly about what you're experiencing. It's normal.' Mark pauses. 'Is there anything specific?'

'Oh, I jump at the slightest sound. I think people are following me, cars slowing down, stuff like that. Is it normal?'

'Perfectly.' He needs to strike. 'If there is anything suspicious, like an attempt at contact, a call, you will let us know, won't you?'

Her voice takes on an edge. 'Do think I'm in danger?'

This is tricky. He doesn't want to appear dismissive or scare mongering, but he needs to be realistic. 'Until we've frightened these people off or preferably locked them up, anyone and everyone with any knowledge could be of interest. That's the way they work.'

He can hear footsteps. Is she pacing the room? 'I really appreciate the call. I'm going to get onto Victim Support. They might help.'

'If there is anything concrete that is suspicious, don't waste a moment, call me or the main office, 999 if you really feel scared, and mention the attack. We'll do the rest.'

'Thanks. I know I'm overreacting.' There is a hint of a sigh.

'No-one would accuse you of over-reacting. We are here to support you, remember that.' Mark ends the call. She knows nothing more. It's probably a dead end. What might be more useful is to go through those random sightings again of vans in odd places. There might be witnesses with information.

Chapter 8

I'm online for most of the week. Years 7, 8, 10, and 11 are isolating. I can understand why the older children are off sick. There was a rumble of excitement and a lot of hushed whispers about a garage party somewhere on the Woodlands estate. If that wasn't a super spreader event, what was? Years 7 and 8 should be under the watchful eyes of parents after school, except they're the ones most likely still to want to chase and play games. Their close personal contact is a thump on the back for tag, not intimacy.

I make an effort every day to dress as I would at school and that includes makeup. I haven't yet succumbed to the temptation to slob around in a shapeless onesie with body hair sprouting in unwelcome places. If I ever did weaken, a few comments from the A team of glossy and wannabee influencers in Year 10 will dent any street cred I have been amassing.

I am tired of my four walls. Any excuse to escape is grasped. A trip to the supermarket is an excitement. My morning run is getting later and later, as the light is defeated by the darkness and I still get spooked at the thought of being alone, out there, where he may be waiting. There I go again. I'm still fixated on my thoughts. What was it Roosevelt said? "There is nothing to fear but fear itself" and that was when the whole American nation, no, the whole world was facing the Great Depression. Surely I can get over this?

I focus on Friday. It will be good to socialise, unless there is another lockdown. At least under current restrictions we can sit at separate tables and enjoy a laugh and a decent drink. No one makes a strawberry daiquiri like barman Matty.

****

Friday arrives. Boots, thick tights and a dress with a fleecy jacket in case we have to drink outside or the doors and windows are wide open will stop me from shivering. Part of me always wonders if I'll meet anyone. Or if someone from work will miraculously transform themselves into someone passably decent. I've never held with all that *man of my dream's* romance.

The pub is what we regard as safe; close enough to the school to keep off the pupils and easy for staff to get to after work. Someone told me it had a ghost and was an old coaching inn on the road to Bath. Thank goodness it lacks the old-world twee style of rustic benches and tapestry cushions of hunting scenes. I prefer its scrubbed pine and stone floor minimalism. I scan the QR code as I go in. The hand sanitiser is waiting and my mask is in place. A waitress in a visor comes over from the bar. 'Have you booked?'

'I'm here for…?' What do I say? Big gatherings are banned. How has Tashi wangled this?

'The birthday group?' I nod. 'They're on tables of six in the marquee. You'll need a blanket.' She points to a pile. I select one.

'Is it that cold?'

'I've become a fan of thermals since September and I'm moving around.' She smiles again and nods in the direction of the garden. I walk through the bar, between tables with families and couples enjoying restaurant cooked food and pub drinks. What is it about them that tastes so different? I reckon it's a secret ingredient called companionship. I smile and fix my eyes on the entrance ahead. On either side are tables with yet more sanitiser between two fake trees in silver grey planters. They are festooned with white lights. Reminds me of Christmas.

That's when I notice him, sitting alone at a table, nursing a pint. He smiles. Shiny white teeth. A dark blue jumper and a striped blue and white shirt cover a muscular frame. Not a tattoo in sight. Looks a preppy type, as they'd say in the States. Nice. I smile back behind my mask and nod before I enter the seated bustle of a socially distanced birthday celebration.

'Rachel. Over here. We've saved you a seat with us.' Tashi budges along the wooden bench. Soroush, her husband, is with her. Well, he's practically staff, the amount of time he spends sorting out the place.

I sit in my allotted space. 'Good crowd?' I say and look around. Jake notices me and raises a glass.

'Someone is very relieved you are here,' Tashi says.

'I reckon Rachel is relieved to be here too after the last few days,' Soroush says and signals to the waitress. 'Drink? You are allowed one even if you're driving.'

'Small red wine,' I say.

Soroush raises one eyebrow. 'Not a cocktail? You can have a non-alcoholic version.'

'What's the point of that?' Tashi says and drains her glass. 'Same again,' she says. 'He's driving.' She jerks her head in Soroush's direction. 'After the week I've had, I need it. I reckon the government should give all teachers alcohol on tap to get us through. And don't get me started about the exams.'

'I won't,' I say. 'Shall we make this a school free bitch fest?'

'Good idea. Let's talk about something else instead,' Soroush says. 'Politics? Brexit? Coronovirus?'

Tashi punches his arm. 'Don't look now, but there is a gentleman sitting outside who is taking an interest in you. Can't stop looking this way.'

Of course, I look up and that man is watching me. 'Could be a parent,' I say.

'Jesus, he'd have high-tailed it to the hills rather than get caught up with his kid's teachers. And he's too young unless he was very precocious,' she adds.

I study my fingers and sense Tashi tensing. 'He's coming over. Act calm and cool.'

'It's not me who needs to be calm and cool,' I say. Anyone would think we were hormonal teenagers let out after the exams.

'Excuse me,' a deep voice with no trace of local accent says. 'I know it's not allowed, mixing, breaking bubbles and all that, but are you the photographer, Rachel Thomas?'

That does it. I melt. I don't care who he is, he recognises me as a photographer and not just Miss who teaches Year 10. 'Yes. How do you know me?'

'I'd hold out my hand but it's not allowed,' he says and smiles. 'I'm Finn Driscoll.'

I take a closer look. It is the same man I'd noticed earlier. His eyes are hazel. Remind me of a cat. Soft and gentle. The eyebrows have been manscaped, I'm sure. Unless he's very lucky. The dark curly hair has just a tinge of grey at the temples. I reckon he's early thirties. Should I glance at his hands? What am I looking for? A wedding ring? If he wanted to play away, he'd take it off. Others do.

'Hi. I'd accept your hand if we were allowed, unless you want an elbow bump? Like our leaders?'

He pulls a face. 'Why does it seem like grown men playing at being down with the kidz?' He slurs the ending, like a z. 'I expect them to pull on a baseball cap back to front, slouch and start to grunt like a hormonally challenged teenager.'

I giggle. 'And you know about hormonal teens?'

He shrugs. 'I was one once and I always wore a baseball cap.' He smiles. 'I'm really pleased to have bumped into you. This is my local.'

''It's ours and practically the whole school's when they can get away with passing off as over eighteen.'

'I see you've got a drink or I'd offer you one.'

I hold up my glass. 'Yeah, and I'm driving.'

'I'm walking,' he says.

For a second there is a pause. Finn speaks first. 'I don't want to keep you from your friends, but I wonder if I could pester you with more questions. I Zoom regularly for work so have an account.'

'Yes, I'd be happy. You've got my email. No.' I pull out my phone. 'Give me your number and we'll fix something up.'

He reels off his number and I tap it in. I am tempted to take a photo but that would be too cheesy. Instead, I smile. 'I'll be in touch.'

'Thanks. Do that, and there is one thing…'

'I tilt my head on one side. 'Yes?'

'Why those big cats? Why not something…' he fishes for words.

'Please don't say anything about cute animals and birds. They've been done to death.' I pause and feel my skin warming under his gaze. 'I reckon I saw one a while back and no one ever believes me. A decent image will be a life changer.

'That's a good enough reason,' Finn says and stands aside so I can get past. 'I'll look forward to hearing from you.'

I escape to the cloakrooms. By the time I get back, he has gone. Probably an evening in a bar filled with knackered and very noisy teachers is not his idea of a quiet drink down at the local.

'Who was he?' Tashi can barely contain her interest. 'Looked cute and keen. Just how we need them.'

Should I give her some ammunition to matchmake again? She will anyway. 'He's an amateur photographer who wants some tips. He's seen my work and likes it.'

Her eyes widen. 'I saw you exchanging numbers. Are you planning on meeting him?'

'Only remotely.' I watch as she deflates. 'But if he was to invite me to go for a meal or a photographic walk, I would agree. Socially distanced of course.'

'Of course.' She winks. 'Wait till the summer for the wedding though. I look better in a floaty dress and sandals.'

****

Mark Mulroney thumps the keyboard. Where the hell is that file? He could have sworn he'd downloaded and saved it. He clicks on the most recently used files and there it is — Rachel Thomas video incident number GNP 3499861. He clicks. Nothing happens. He tries again. There is a pause and a message appears on the screen.

This file is no longer accessible. Try a different name.

What has happened? He dials through to IT. 'Any problem with our server?'

The voice is clipped and curt. 'Nothing except the speed would impress a tortoise.'

'No recent glitches with lost or damaged files?'

The voice chuckles. It is now snide and patronising. 'Lost something?'

'No. Just wondering.'

'The autosave will kick in every fifteen minutes unless you closed down by mistake.'

'Thanks.'

The line goes dead. Damned file must be here somewhere. Mark searches again. There is a name but no video. He slaps his head with his hand. He'd been in a hurry. It was time to get the kids from school. He'd glimpsed a few of the images. Nothing special. The angry call from Ginny had disoriented him. He'd glanced at his watch. That's when he'd realised he should have picked up the kids half an hour ago. He must have pressed *don't save* before he closed the screen, removed the memory card, and replaced it in the camera.

Now the damn thing had been returned to the victim. Could he go round? Say there'd been an error? No. He's sure there was nothing on it. He opens the report and types.

Apart from images of assorted nocturnal animals, nothing else is visible. Battery now dead so perhaps it was fading even then. No further action.

He adds the date and time, his signature, closes the document and forwards it to his boss. No one would know or care. They had a pandemic to deal with, didn't they? And who was copping all the extra work? Him and the rest of the front-line staff. Oh yes, it's all right for the politicians to say the police would stop illicit rave parties, watch for social distancing infringements, not to mention checking queues and being on hand as neighbourhood niggles exploded into feuds. They were stretched. With more staff self-isolating as students and children mixed in classes and brought the virus home, they were even more stretched. No one would have time to bother about a few fuzzy images.

If they want to catch the people-smugglers, they need to know where the drops are taking place and when the boats arrive. He checks his watch. It won't take long; a map, a compass and a few pens are all he needs. He'll do it old school. There must be a pattern somewhere.

Chapter 9

I stretch and fling off the covers. It's good to have a whole day without bells, feeling like a jailer more than a teacher. Our social distancing protocols don't matter a jot because as soon as the pupils get outside it's masks off, crowd round someone's phone, chase, jump on each other's back and share their cocktail of viruses and bugs. I spotted them earlier in the week when I parked in the supermarket car park one evening shortly after school had ended. There were crowds of kids all milling around. What should I do? Can't shout at them. It'd be a one finger salute as some irate parent came up effing and jeffing and telling me I was stopping his kid's human rights. Let them get used to a few more human deaths. This thing is with us for a lot longer.

Strange how times have changed. I remember getting a detention for not wearing my blazer out of school on a very hot day. Seems some teacher spotted me walking across a road with the thing slung over my shoulder. What has happened since then?

Sod this for a start to Saturday morning. The house needs cleaning, the dirty washing is piled on the bathroom floor, my legs need waxing and I'm late with the monthly nature notes blog. Damn. Have I got any decent images? I wander through to the kitchen. Galley kitchen they call it. Yes. A strip of a room so narrow I can close the drawers behind me with my bum when I'm facing the oven. I switch on the kettle and reach down for a canister of ground coffee. Can't stand the instant sort. I wait for the kettle to boil and look round. At least it's dry and clean and mine. I can paint it what colour I like. Perhaps I should. The pale grey paint I'd chosen in the summer makes it feel like the inside of a submarine. Not that I've been inside a submarine, but you know what it must be like — all that riveted metal. The red kettle and red mugs were chosen to create splash of colour. Who said? Grey must be the most depressing colour after institutional green. I spoon coffee grounds in the cafetière and add water. The spicy smell of Monsooned Malabar wafts up. I drop a slice of sourdough into the toaster and take a near clean plate from the sink. That'll do. With toast, bitter orange marmalade, real butter, and decent coffee I'm ready to read the papers. I open my laptop. A message has pinged in from Finn. He must be keen. Or desperate? I hope it's the former.

I read it through slowly. What's the subtext? Or am I being paranoid?

I was so pleased to see you in person last night. What a coincidence. Who would have thought it but I suppose with all the new restrictions and warnings, we've all become more local? I wonder if we could meet up on Zoom or something? I'd really like your take on some challenges I'm having with my images. You just seem to get the knack of knowing when to click. Me? I spend ages and the moment has gone.

A few months ago, or should that be last year, it would have been a meet-up somewhere for a coffee or a drink at lunchtime or even brunch. Brunch? Even the word makes my teeth clench. I want my life back. I want the freedom to pop in for a coffee and not worry or to meet up for a theatre visit before going on for a late-night drink where the wine is cold and the music loud. Are we all being super cautious? What was the new government advice? Stay Safe? Is that what we are doing or is he simply someone who likes to keep his distance?

Great idea. Anything to take me away from the grind of cleaning and washing, not to mention preparing next week's lessons and the numerous adjustments in case the class are self-isolating. I'm around this afternoon and tomorrow morning.

I don't want him to think I'm a real no-mates. On the other hand, are we allowed to go out so much? Well, he's not to know I'm not a fanatical gym bunny or have an elderly grandparent to deliver the week's groceries to, is he?

I refuse to sit around waiting for a reply so close all social media and concentrate on the news instead. Donald Trump with Covid 19 screams the headlines. I wish I hadn't bothered. That's the trouble today. The news is always full of the same things; Brexit, Covid 19 here or anywhere in the world or platitudes about celebrities. I look back with fondness to a good scandal involving a politician with his pants down, uproar over young people getting awkward about climate change, even a drubbing of any English sports team by a foreigner can bring out a slightly amusing xenophobic rant. I finish my toast and coffee and switch to a playlist of uplifting songs and head to the shower.

I'm swathed in towels, my hair a frizzy mess and checking the eyebrows for signs they should belong to a caterpillar when there is an alert on my phone. An email with a high priority tag. Please not another change to schools? No. It's Finn.

How about this afternoon? 2.00pm. I can set up a link?

I don't know what it is, but I feel an icy finger run up and down my spine. What is he really up to? Or am I so used to being messed around by assholes, I always think the worst? There's only one thing for it.

2.00pm sounds great. I will get my cameras and lenses set up and we can start from there.

I go back to my eyebrows. Can't look like a Zoom Zombie, can I?

Which is why I have spent two hours cleaning and rearranging my small study area. Okay, a space under the stairs, but it suits me, with a few specially chosen books arranged spine outwards behind me. I can't be the only person who checks what's on people's shelves and the photos they have on display.

I keep hoping I'll come across *How to win friends and influence people* on a politician's shelf…or perhaps…*Good to be Great?* Or even a well-thumbed copy of *Fifty Shades of Grey*. I select a Stephen Moss, a David Attenborough and a couple of collections of photos; Imogen Cunningham and Elliot Porter would look good. And Eric Hosking's book on owls which changed my life when I came across a battered copy in my sixth form library. Every time I looked at his images I felt I was a neighbour, a voyeur even, privileged to get a close-up glimpse of these wonderful yet deadly killers.

That will do. I've chosen a pale blue silk shirt, which looks good with the jeans I'm wearing. I can't look too posed, can I? At least my hair is sleek and smooth for once, and I've even added some makeup. I check in the mirror, adjust the collar and select a pair of pearl earrings that once belonged to my grandmother. I feel as if I'm going on a date. Perhaps I am.

The email with the link arrives at ten to two. He's like me, so on time I'm before time. I click on the link. The small window in the middle of the screen acts like a mirror. I can't be the only one who adjusts their hair, checks their teeth, tilts their chin up or down to get a more flattering and thinner outline before settling on chin up, eyes down. Not that I can keep this up for long. I end up going boss eyed. The side bar tells me I am in Finn Driscoll's private meeting room and the host will let me in soon. I'm Oliver Twist. Except I'm asking 'Let me in.' Not 'Can I have some more, please?'

The side bar changes. My static Gmail image sits above Finn's intense face. He's adjusting something. I click on *join with video, gallery view* and *full screen*. We lock eyes and I do the Zoom wave, all jazz hands, and check I'm not on mute. He looks up and smiles. The hazel eyes are greener today. Must be a reflection from the green sweater he's wearing. Very preppy again. A cream collar sits above the neckline of the sweater. I hope he's not wearing green cords. Or even yellow. Please don't let him be a county type, escaping down here from the city to stay with

Mummy while he sits out the pandemic, making and losing millions at home instead of in Canary Wharf. I want him to be ordinary, like me.

'Hi, Rachel. How's the connection?'

It beats, do you come here often as a chat-up line. 'Great. Clear and crisp,' I say.

'Not like King Wenceslas?'

I frown. 'What?'

Finn holds up one hand. 'Sorry. Like the old cracker joke. What type of pizza does King Wenceslas like?'

'Deep and crisp and even.' We both say the words at the same time.

'You know it?' Finn is teasing me. I know he is and I feel at ease. He likes goofy jokes and I suspect he's feeling more nervous than me.

I decide to take control. I'm not a teacher for nothing. 'So how can I help you?'

Two hours later, three reboots of Zoom as we over run time and we've talked, laughed and even sung some old Beatles' refrains. (His mum and dad were fans, like mine.) I feel I have found a friend. We've even explored our respective bookshelves and I got a glimpse of black trousers. Does he wear slippers? *Come on, Rachel, you're not marrying the guy*, I scold myself except some things are pivotal. I've never understood how any woman could share her life, let alone her body with someone who doesn't keep his toenails neat and tidy, has hair in his ears or wears his trousers for so long before a wash they get that greasy, shiny look. Or am I too fussy? Is that why I'm single. That will do. His reading tastes are more eclectic than mine. Stephen King nestles next to a yellowing copy of *A Hitchhiker's Guide to the Galaxy* and the whole series of Dickens squats beneath a range of modern crime and thriller writers I do not know.

We agree to meet in person for Sunday lunch. He tells me he'll definitely get a table as he's an old school friend of the owner and chef. It's in an old coaching inn on the common. We end the meeting with more waves and for a moment there is silence and stillness, like the first snowfall of winter when everything is fresh, new and exciting, tinged with awe at this spectacle of nature fluttering from the heavens. In that moment I'm sure we both connect.

Chapter 10

Mark Mulroney moves the children's school work from the top of the desk. Ginny hasn't spoken to him for two hours. He'd been late collecting them and the expression on the teacher's face, even hidden behind the mask, said it all. Where are you? I've got as much stress as you have. I've got kids of my own to look after.

The children were standing on a painted circle on the grey playground. At least it wasn't raining. A weak sun peered through the grey clouds pressing down on the red brick of St Augusta's Primary School. Its high windows decorated with coloured rainbows do not stop the overall effect of a prison. Still, that's what the Victorians wanted, wasn't it? Good, docile, and amenable workers who accepted their lot at the bottom of the heap. He felt his anger rising. He pushed it aside but Socialist blood coursed through his veins as it had done in his parents, grandparents and great-grandparents before him.

The teacher thrust a pack of printed paper at him. 'Suspected outbreak in Years 3 and 5. All children are asked to work at home with blended learning for the next few days until the test results are back.'

He nodded. What he wanted to say was what the hell is blended learning and just because Ginny wasn't a key worker, she had to stay off too. Less cash at the end of the month. No let-up in bills either. Instead, he had nodded. 'I know the drill,' he said. 'Online and at home as from tomorrow.'

The teacher's shoulders sagged in relief. Poor woman must have got it in the neck from a number of parents.

'Thanks for being so understanding.' Her voice cracked. 'Anyone would think I've been going round infecting them deliberately.'

'Come on, you two.' He cuffed Andrew's hair. He knew better than to touch Emily's. She was already a diva. How had that come about? 'Good day?' he said.

'S'all right,' Andrew said and skipped ahead, kicking at the nearest stone and dribbling it with remarkable skill along the pavement.

'I got a team point for reading and a team point for helping Mrs Bates stack the tables at lunchtime,' Emily said. 'Bet I won't get ten this week for a super sticker.'

It was her dream to earn ten team points in one week and get one of the headteacher's super stickers.

'Why is that?'

'Because we're not at school this week now, are we? I can't get team points at home, can I?'

There was no doubting the frustration in her voice but when had she learnt to be so cheeky? His dad would have pulled him up sharp. Should he? He knew the answer. He wouldn't and couldn't. He was hardly at home. The last thing he wanted was to nag them when he was. 'Heh, what if your work at home is sooo good, they have to give you team points?'

Emily looked up at him. 'Will you help if I get stuck?'

'Of course, sweetheart.'

'And you won't tell Andrew?'

'He's your brother. He won't mind.'

'He will.' Her lower lip wobbled. 'He says all the brains were given to him.'

'Well, he's wrong. You are just as clever. Different, but just as clever.'

She nodded. The red pompom on top of her hat bobbed up and down. 'Don't tell him, though?'

He did a zip movement across his lips. 'Sealed forever.'

Emily placed a small hand in his. He closed his fingers round it and his heart squeezed as if it would burst. Is that why she was difficult? Cheeky? It must be hard for her with a clever brother like Andrew, and he was her twin. They're supposed to be the same. If only she could get some extra help. More money. That's what they all needed. How to get it was another matter.

The kids are in bed, Ginny is watching a medical programme and he's excused himself saying he wants to do some research. He takes a deep breath and spreads out the map. It's a bog-standard Ordnance Survey, Landranger style, with the symbols he remembers from his youth; the little cross to show a church, *sch* for a school written over a shaded block, and the vast expanses of green, dotted with trees to signify woodland. He ordered it at work, justified by being an essential research tool, and customised the area so it took in the docks and the places close to where some of the drop-offs had been spotted. The boats could have slipped into small wharfs under cover of darkness. No one worked in these places 24/7 and yacht enthusiasts had been put off by all the Covid rules and regulations. He'd visited one a few weeks ago when they'd received sightings of an unusual trawler like vessel. A few hours afterwards a shipment of heroin was discovered in a white transit a few miles away. No one could prove a link. There was one, though.

He selects a highlighter and marks all the places with sightings of unusual behaviours or people. Could there be a link? Did they smuggle people as well as drugs? So far, all the hot tips had fizzled out. He puts a big cross on the wharf by the canal entrance and joins up each sighting with a straight line. He turns the map on its side. Weird? It looks like a kid's drawing of the sun with the rays fanning out like wheels on a bike. He checks with a ruler. Most are a similar distance from the wharf as the crow flies, not according to journey times. The spokes too are regular, at an angle. Less than 45 degrees if he was guessing. He needs a protractor. The kids' pencil cases? No, they are too young. He opens up his laptop and searches. There is a good image of a protractor. If he prints it and cuts it out it might work.

The printer hums and spits out the image. A few snips and it will do for a protractor. He places the centre on the wharf. Oh, hallelujah. Some of the sightings are twenty degrees apart, roughly, while others in multiples of twenty. The test would be the woodland where that woman had been attacked. He marks it, draws a line from the wharf. It is slightly further out than the rest but fits the pattern. Whoever is behind this, if it is one person, they are remarkably organised and methodical. With any luck, that might be their downfall.

He stares at the map, the intersections of roads, the blue meandering lines of the rivers and stream and the clusters of houses in the many small villages and hamlets that dot the landscape where once, thousands of years before, the sea would have smothered the land. The next question is where might they land next and when. There must be another pattern. He writes out the dates and times of the sightings on Post-it notes and places them on the map at the end of the lines. Like bunting, they flutter as his breath catches them.

'Sorry I snapped earlier.' Mark looks up. Ginny is leaning against the door frame, her dark skin contrasting with the cream painted wood that frames and forms a backdrop, like a Medieval painting of a Madonna in a stone niche. He'd paint again when he had the time. If.

He shakes his head and holds up his hands. 'My fault too. I got so caught up in this new case, it all went clean out of my mind.'

She comes closer and leans over the map. Her slim figure nestles against his arm. The baggy jumper slips from her shoulders to reveal a lacy bra strap. 'Looks interesting. What are all these lines?'

'There's a pattern here, I'm sure. What really bugs me is the timings. They seem… odd. I'd have expected weekly or fortnightly drops. Smugglers are creatures of habit.'

Ginny places one slim, cool hand on his shoulder. Her breasts rest against his back. The other hand traces the dates on the Post-it notes. 'Every twenty-eight days, give a day or two, and either late at night or in the early hours of the morning.' She pauses for a moment. 'Tides. High tides. I reckon these all coincide with a high tide.'

Mark slaps his head with the flat of his hand. 'Talk about the obvious. Why didn't I think of that?'

She kisses the top of his head. 'Because you are a Townie. Not a city boy, living close to an exciting river like the Tyne or the Thames and not a country type with a boat borrowed from his uncle. You are a true, concrete jungle lad, more interested in the skate park than anything else.'

He pulls her onto his lap and envelops her in his arms. 'How did you guess?'

'I know you so well.'

'There was a canal in Birmingham,' he says.

Ginny kisses the tip of his nose. 'Canals don't have tides that reveal dead bodies, crashed cars, shopping trolleys. We used to scavenge on the mud flats at low tide, me and a couple of hundred others. Proper treasure seekers we were.'

'Ever find anything?'

'Bits of pottery, old bones… I was there when a guy found a Roman coin.'

'Genuine buried treasure, eh?'

'Right, now come to bed. I need an early night and so do you.'

'Is that a proper sleeping early night or an early night?'

'What do you think? It's mid-month. Perfect for baby making.'

Mark tenses. After all the trouble they had conceiving the twins, did Ginny really want to go through that again? 'I thought we'd agreed. No more children. The twins are enough.'

Ginny's face clouds over. 'I want another baby.'

'Why, for God's sake?' He runs a hand through his hair. 'We can't afford to lose your wages and if you want extra help for Emily, where's that money coming from?'

Ginny pouts. 'Two children do not make a family.'

'It is in my bloody book.'

Ginny gets up and flounces off. The door slams behind her.

Later that night in bed, she curls closer. 'Okay. No baby. But that doesn't mean we can't have sex, does it? I'm sorry.'

Even as she speaks, she strips off her t-shirt and throws it on the bedroom floor.

'You've talked me into it, just this once,' he says and draws her warm body closer.

Chapter 11

Finn removes the phone from the dented filing cabinet he found in the barn as soon as he'd taken over the house after his father's death. It was obvious why the place had gone tits up. He'd had to spend all his savings paying off creditors. How had his father let it get to this state? The piles of yellowing copies of *Racing Post*, heavily marked in pen, were the clue. He'd burnt the lot and paid off the runner who'd placed the bets and let his father get into thousands of pounds of debt. The guilt rankled. He should have realised and done more. It was too late for that. At least he'd make a go of the place. Jeremy had already put the house and land by the river up for sale. Not that he needed the money, but Dad had left it to him. Perhaps when all this was over he'd go and see him. Dubai was an all-round holiday place, wasn't it? And he hadn't seen his nieces and nephews for a couple of years. Still, it would be a pity when the land was sold. That guy's little girl must enjoy exercising her pony in Upper Meadow. As long as the place was kept secure until the sale went through, he'd let her have some fun.

He sits on a bale and the crisp stalks from last summer's hay press into his trousers. He breathes in the dusty, musty smell of dried grass, clover and the different meadow grasses he wished he could name. It would be good to get the barn up to standard and keep a few ponies for the children to pet. He'd add that to the spreadsheet of costs. He takes the phone from a canvas bag. Sure enough, there is a message; it is terse and to the point.

What have you found out about the girl?

He texts back.

She hasn't a clue who I am. I'll do what you asked and then I want out.

Someone is monitoring the number. There is an instant response.

You wanted in. We cut you in.

Finn texts.

What if I go to the police?

The reply comes back.

HaHaHa! Find out how much that woman knows about you and deal with her. Then perhaps we'll talk about getting out. But no rushed bodged job. An accident. Set it up.

Finn waits. The conversation is at an end. He stows the phone away. In the meantime, he has a date. Time to turn on the charm.

Chapter 12

Sunday morning is always a treat. An excuse to do nothing. Today is different. I am meeting Finn again. In person this time, although we had bumped into each other on Friday night. I didn't count that. It was more of an introduction. I get out of bed. The wood effect floor is cold. Please don't let it be time to put on the heating. The air is cool, not chill. I will last out a few more weeks or at least until the clocks change. So? Exercise? Food? Shower? I check the clock. Nearly nine. Plenty of time for a run, food, get ready and be out for twelve-thirty. I have no idea how long it will take me to get to The Coach House on the common. Twenty minutes? As a massive worrier, I will of course be there early, probably too early, and panic even more. No, I'll take my camera, no lenses, use the macro function and pretend to be nonchalantly snapping at odd pieces of flora and fauna. That will also give us something to talk about. Except if yesterday afternoon was anything to go by, we'd be fine.

I fling open the wardrobe and pull out my running kit. I sniff. Not too musty. Must stick it in the wash when I get back. I skip down the stairs, my feet clattering on the bare wood. Could I afford carpet? Not yet. I stop by the front door and open the small cupboard under the stairs. The previous owner created some shelves, perfect for shoes and boots. I select a very muddy pair of running shoes and tie them on. Keys, phone, no water. I slam the door behind me and grimace. 'Sorry,' I whisper to anyone I've woken up. I go down the small path across the patch of land called a front garden and stand, arms on hips, breathing in the autumnal air. Which way? Down the hill to the park. It's not too isolated. I'm still jittery.

I walk for a few minutes before stopping and pretending to do some stretches. I should be more professional. I'm not. I am a slob, really. I pick up my pace and trot, I cannot call it a run, through the sleeping town, past Tescos and the river. It is deserted. Once there would have been anglers, camped out on the wooden platforms. Or has the fishing season begun? Or stopped? Or isn't it allowed?

I pass a dog walker. The mutt sniffs before he is pulled to heel. 'Sorry,' the woman says.

I smile. 'Nice dog,' I say and jog past.

There is another dog walker ahead of me. The run becomes a jog. My heart pounds and it's not because of the exercise. I am walking so slowly I'm practically at a standstill. That coat. It's a Barbour. Not the usual type. This is dark with the collar like a roll of cord up to the chin. It's the same as his. I remember now. Except for the colour. This is navy blue. His was green or brown. Sludge like. Reason takes control again. It isn't him. Part of me knew that all along. I wait for the palpitations to subside. Are more details locked away in some part of my mind?

I must get back. Email the sergeant or whatever he is. It might help. I turn and retrace my steps. The town is still deserted. What's the point of going out? People are still scared. Infections are rising. A few months ago, these streets would have been busy on a Sunday. There'd be brunch with the family or friends. Perhaps there would be a festival going on with venues opening for the first event of the day, queues of keen theatre goers, jazz enthusiasts, book lovers, food lovers, film buffs. They were special days when we went out to satisfy our cravings for entertainment and friendship; cravings that cannot be satisfied by a small screen.

I reach the house, shower, and sit with a cup of coffee at the kitchen table. I find Mark's card from my bag and type in his email address. How do you start an email? *Dear Mark* sounds too mundane. *Hi there,* is too friendly. I ignore salutations.

I know this probably isn't much use, but today I remembered that his jacket was a waxed one but not like the usual type. This had a collar, done up as if it was a roll neck, nearly up to the chin and it was in a sludgy brown/green.

I'm hoping more details will come back as the fear fades.

Rachel

I'm not even sure about the Rachel bit so in brackets I include my surname. I don't know if it will do any good. I lean back in the chair and take a sip of coffee. It's good to be proactive.

At twelve forty-five I am ready, parked and my hands are sweating. What if Finn doesn't turn up? I'll pretend I only came up here to take some photos. Except that wouldn't fool anyone. Why am I in full make up and dressed in jeans, leather jacket and boots and not bare faced in an outfit that would suit a dedicated bird watcher? I pick my way over the puddles in the car park and cross the small road towards the common land. I won't go too far. I still want to be able to see the road. The turf is springy under my feet. It drains well on these limestone hills. I lift my camera and adjust the settings. I want a wide view of the brow of the hill and those beyond, with acres of sky above. I put the camera to my eye and peer through the view finder, moving, shifting till I am happy with the shapes I can see. For a moment there is only sky and land. A hang glider swoops from the heavens, hangs in the air before he tugs on some cords and swings away again. My fingers have clicked and continue. There must be a decent shot here. I go closer to the brow of the hill. I hadn't realised the escarpment was so steep here. On the level below, wings like giant dead butterflies spread out on the grass. Men and women in padded jackets and all in ones like skiers bustle around, checking their equipment, the only thing that is between them and death once they have left the land. Some are stretched out, sipping hot drinks from flasks, like the discarded chrysalis or pupa that still have to metamorphose into their final, dazzling forms.

I watch from a distance as those securely strapped wait their turn before running along a short patch of grass and launching themselves away from land, trusting in the laws of thermals. They must have an incredible understanding of wind direction, lift and thrust. I take some photos. For the first time in days, I feel calm and relaxed. Is it because for a while I have forgotten what happened or I am happy when I see life through a lens?

'Rachel?' A voice disturbs me. Who is it? I turn. 'Thought it had to be you with a camera. How these people have the courage to fling themselves off a cliff attached to a bit of wire and flapping material I have no idea.' His face crinkles into a smile. 'Finn? Finn Driscoll? Or do you need to see me through a screen?'

He is just as charming off screen as on. I'm looking forward to this. 'Hi. Thought I'd get a few photos. I never go far without this.' I hold up my camera. 'I can show you over lunch,' I say.

'I would hold out my hand or even offer you my arm to escort you to lunch, but in these strange times we might be spotted by the thought police and strung up before the House of Commons for insurrection.'

'I wish,' I say and stop. Is politics a dangerous topic for dates? I pull myself up short. This is not a date, or is it? Why did I dress so carefully and extricate the last of some Marc Jacobs Daisy to dab on my neck?

'What say we eat first, share photos and then think up evil tortures for any politician. Perhaps we can come up with the ten we'd least like to get stuck in a lift with?'

He holds out his arm. It is not a request for contact. More like a teacher shepherding the children into class. I follow at a social distance but on a level with him. It's the best of both worlds.

Once in the entrance to the pub we sanitise and the visor wearing waiter shows us to a table overlooking the common and with a good aerial view of the sky and the occasional hang gliders floating above.

We are handed a menu. 'Any drinks?' the waiter asks.

'I'm for a pint of Long Tom. What about you?'

'Half of Buddings,' I say. It will help me keep a clear head and I don't want to appear a typical cocktail, Prosecco or Pinot Grigio quaffing female.

'A fan? Of Stroud Brewery?'

'Of course. I used to love their Thursday evening pizza and fund-raising nights. I've had some laughs there with the school crew.'

Finn leans back in the chair. 'Aah yes, the school crew.' He pauses. 'I feel so sorry for you, with all the closures in the spring, online learning, and cancelled exams. And now? I know what I would have been like, playing tag and shouting Covid instead of fleas.'

'The boys at my school when I was a kid used to do the same. Except they didn't shout out Covid. It was fleas and then later VD.' Am I sounding flustered? I take a deep breath.

'That was me. I was hardly the model pupil,' he says as the waiter arrives with our order. 'Drinks are served.'

The waiter places two glasses in front of us. 'A few more minutes before you decide?'

'Please,' Finn says and lifts his glass. 'To photography, good food and new found friends.'

I tip my glass against his as he smiles and looks at me over the rim of the glass. His eyes are warm and they remind me of something. I don't know what. Or who. But there is something. Yes. They remind me of a cat's eyes. Golden brown, like the beer in his glass.

'To all those and more,' I say. The glasses clink and, in that moment I know here is someone special.

'Let's check out what's on offer today,' Finn says as he picks up the piece of paper and reads. 'I know the steak is good. It comes from my neighbour's farm.'

That is when I notice the hand holding the menu is reddened and scratched. I have to ask. 'Are you a country dweller? I know you said you live in Meadow Cross but that's quite built up, isn't it?' My memory of distant journeys to London and the passage after the tunnel before we enter the valley is one of houses clambering up the steep hillsides, interspersed with narrow, twisting pathways, and roads barely wide enough for a car.

'Yes. I own or rather have been left Wayside Farm. We've managed to convert a couple of the barns to holiday accommodation and still keep a number of rare breeds. Sheep, goats and alpacas.'

'We?'

'My brother's working in Dubai and so I copped the job of making the farm work or…' His voice tails away.

'Farming's tough, right?'

'It will get better. We just need to weather this passage. Hopefully, when he sells his share of the estate which is some land and a few buildings by the river, we can invest a bit more cash.' He puts the menu down. 'Enough of me. Let's choose and then I'd like to see the shots you've been taking today. I might pick up some ideas.'

There is so much I want to know. I bite my tongue to stop me flooding him with questions. 'I think I'll go with the steak. I don't usually eat meat or fish but if it's been kept well and is ethical, I'm happy.'

'Ah ha, a flexitarian. I'm with you all the way,' Finn says and puts down the menu. 'Two steaks it is. Unless you would like to share a starter? The portions here are huge.'

I find myself sharing hummus and pitta with a man I hardly know. There is something familiar about eating with someone. All those little dances of manners and taking turns are amplified, and yet at the same time conversation is easier as there is always the food to embroider with our comments and the inevitable discussion over who has the last portion. I let Finn, of course.

The steaks arrive. We both decline another drink. So far, he has never asked me about the attack. I wonder when it will come. Part of me wants to tell him I'm still scared of the woods and desperate to remember anything more to put that bastard away once and for all.

'I'm pleased you like your steak well done,' I whisper.

'Can't say I enjoy eating opposite someone who enjoys raw meat,' Finn says and laughs.

Any remaining awkwardness is gone. We tell each other about our families and childhood escapes. By the time we reach dessert (we both want chocolate brownies) we're onto our university life and first jobs. I know there is much left unsaid but I get a glimpse into the life of an animal crazy kid who kept a grass snake as a pet and, with his elder brother, spent hours building dens and dams in the woods and streams near his home, of helping feed the animals on Christmas Day to give his father and mother a rest before he and his brother were allowed to open their presents and the wrench of leaving to study finance in a city where his links with the natural world were the pigeons he fed in the park and the stray cat in the outhouse of his student bedsit. I want to ask why he didn't study something more in line with his interests. It seems too intrusive.

Only when we reach the coffee stage do we remember the photos. 'Do you want a look?' I say and hand over the camera.

'Are these the ones you just took?' he says as he scrolls through the images.

'Yes. That one of the guy in the middle was one of those perfect scenarios when it all falls into place at the right moment.'

'Why is it so clear and bright, like a decent day?' He tilts his head towards the window and a gunmetal grey, glowering sky.

'Settings,' I say.

'I remember you mentioning something about that earlier. Still seems like a complex idea.'

The waiter brings our coffee. Plain black for both of us. A bit of me is pleased we share another similar taste until a small voice reminds me it is only coffee. 'The best learning is doing,' I say. Do I sound too teacherlike?

'Better get myself on a photography course. Not that there will be many available.'

Before I have time to take stock and think, I have blurted out a response. 'I can show you the basics.'

Finn's face shows the amazement I hear in his voice. Isn't he used to people doing nice things for him? 'You'd do that? I mean, I promise I won't take up too much of your time. I'd like to make a start on some photos of animals, if that isn't too difficult.'

I shiver. 'As long as they aren't in the wild. I think it will be a long time before I have enough confidence to go out alone.'

He nods and takes a sip of his coffee. He cradles the cup in his hands. 'I suppose you'll only feel better when he's behind bars?' He puts the cup down and holds up both hands in supplication. 'Sorry. Me and my big mouth.'

He's right, of course. 'Not much chance of that. I'm the only witness, although I'm sure there are memories there somewhere. I just don't know where.'

'Nothing comes to mind?' A frown creases the skin between his eyes. Why is he concerned?

I shake my head. 'All I can remember is a black hat and a black face covering.' I pause. 'Not much to go on, is it?'

The crease lifts. 'No. Not a lot.' His tone changes. 'Back to business,' he says and rubs his hands together. 'What I really need is some help on photographing the whole set up so it's inviting for families. I reckon if I offer some cut price deals for a short time only, blame the pandemic, you know the argument, they'll start booking soon.'

'I'd invest in an adventure playground. Or at least a play area with logs. Like a forest school.'

'Tell me more,' Finn says. 'I'd really appreciate your advice.'

By the time we've finished coffee, we've arranged to meet at his farm next Saturday afternoon, unless any more restrictions are in place. I will bring all my equipment. Am I doing the right thing? Should we be mixing or can this be classed as a work-related meeting? Should I be meeting him at all? I've never trusted online dates. Is this any different? Once more I am my mother's child. She was a stickler for getting to know people properly before you even invited them for a cup of tea. This is 2020. I'm sure it won't hurt.

Chapter 13

She knows nothing. I want out.

Stick with it. Memory can come back. That will mean you are certain for a long stretch unless you can silence her.

I'm not a murderer.

Fool! There are more ways of ensuring silence. Money. Everyone has their price. Or love. How many times have you come across parents, children, spouses, even work colleagues when confronted with hard evidence say 'No. Not them?' Or go out of their way to create alibis, fake the truth, lie even.

I can't do that.

You may have to. One more drop and you could be free of us. The rest is your own problem.

The texting ends. Finn switches the pay as you go phone to silence, stows it at the back of the filing cabinet, pulls bales in front and closes the barn door.

Once back inside the house he pours a single malt and stands by the window to look out over the yard. A glimmer of moon shines through the hazy clouds, casting shadows of the outbuildings. If he did one more drop, he'd have enough cash to complete the renovations and the rest would keep him going for six months before the holiday lets kicked in. He could make a big thing of Easter. The damned virus will be conquered by then. People might be a bit scared of going abroad but a staycation with the family gathered would appeal.

Rachel? He had to be careful. What's the old advice? Keep your friends close and your enemies even closer? Six months, perhaps less, and the relationship can falter. By then he'd be certain she'd forgotten the image of him. He runs a hand over his eyes to blot out the memory. He hadn't wanted to hurt anyone. Why the hell did she have to be there? Why did she have to look up?

He picks up his proper phone. He needs to confirm arrangements to meet Rachel again. He'll ask a few more questions this time and if she is certain she can't remember anything, that will be the end of it. He'll do one more drop and let her down gently. He'll not ghost her. Perhaps he can invent an ex-girlfriend who comes back into his life. It does happen and it's not as if they move in the same circles. All this photography stuff will not be a priority once the farm is up and running and the holiday lets are bringing in a tidy cash sum.

Looking forward to Saturday. Must make sure the girls (sorry goats) are looking their best and Hettie the Highland cow has had a quick brush down. Can't do much about the sheep. They won't be looking cute until they produce the lambs.

He presses send. Done.

Chapter 14

Mark collects up the sheafs of paper. The maps, lists and images all point to one conclusion. There is a definite pattern to the sightings and that includes the timings of the tides. A cursory glance at the dates and times of the tides was enough. The boat or whatever it was, yacht or dinghy, big enough to carry a dozen people but small enough to be disguised as a fishing vessel or a rich man's plaything disgorges the cargo in a designated place. It is collected and dropped off somewhere else. The most likely place is the harbour where the canal joins the river. It's got good road access, there's enough craft but it's not overly popular as it's not upmarket enough for some. He's seen the marinas with restaurants, bars and shops with prices way out of his range. He could scout the place, and it would help if he had some back up, or at least some support.

He knocks on the door of the DCI. 'Ma'am, may I have a word?'

DCI Eve Fletcher, her head with its salt and pepper hair is bent over the desk. She speaks without looking up. 'What is it, Sergeant?'

He hesitates. Should he go in and sit down? He hovers in the doorway.

'For God's sake, man, come in if you want to but don't dither. If it's important sit your arse down.'

He sits in the metal backed chair in front of a desk strewn with papers, swamping the keyboards of two screens which act as a barrier between the boss and her minions. It was an office joke that the film all the children loved so much had been based on her attitude to her staff.

The chair squeaks. The face lifts. He stares into the cool grey eyes that never miss a clue.

'Well?'

'Remember the attack on the woman out taking photos?'

The DCI folds her arms over an ample bosom, encased in the usual ice white shirt and suit jacket. Today's offering is pale grey-blue, like the sea on a dull day. 'The one who reckons the countryside is crawling with wild animals when we know it's full of villains keen to escape the city and bring their crap down here? Yes?'

'I think there might be a link with other sightings and the people smuggling racket we know is taking place in Bristol, or rather was taking place.'

'Temporarily shelved but still of interest to the Bristol crew.' She taps a pencil against her teeth. 'Go on.'

Mark indicates the desk top. 'I've got some data I'd like to show you.'

In one swift move the DCI sweeps all her paperwork into a pile and deposits it on the floor by her feet. He only hopes he'll be out of the office when she is screaming for a lost file or a missing report. She is still of the old school; think in ink, spread the evidence before you and something will jump out. She was usually right. 'Get on with it.'

Mark places each piece of paper in the order he is going to use as his explanation. He opens up the map. The DCI takes one glance at the lines and highlighted areas. 'You've spotted a pattern, haven't you? Tell me about it.'

Mark moves round to her side of the desk and points out the links with the sightings, the distances, the tide times and his theory. 'The next thing would be to identify any craft which regularly go out and return within the space of high tides during the night. The harbour must have the information.'

The DCI smiles. 'Go and find it. You've got my permission to ask any questions you like.'

Mark walks out, head high.

'Someone's happy,' a voice calls.

Should he reply? If he's going to work here full time, he needs to join in the banter. 'I've got a possible lead on the people smugglers.'

'Where?' the voices chime in unison. Everyone wants an excuse to get out of the DCI's hair when cases are stalling.

'The docks,' he says and waits for the cat calls, advice, and general comments, helpful or not. They soon arrive.

'Bristol?'

'No, nothing there except a few pleasure boats and fancy restaurants. Same as Gloucester.'

'Can't even fish now. Portishead is an option.'

'Too big. Any unusual craft would have been spotted and reported.'

The voices die away. Mark takes his cue. 'Right and wrong. We might be looking at small pleasure craft but also a place no one bothers about any more.'

'Blake Point I reckon.' A Gloucestershire accent echoes through the room. 'We've always suspected there was a bit of illegal fishing, a few cartons of ciggies brought in at Christmas, small stuff. Never could get anything to stick. Like a bloody mafia they are down there. Enemies one minute and bosom friends the next and all hate us. Check out the domestics, same names been coming up for generations.'

Mark looks across to the speaker. Is it Todd? He's an old hand in the area. 'Yep. That's the hunch and the tip off.' Okay, so he is lying. No one wants to be outsmarted by a bit of obvious and very old-time detective work. At least Eve hadn't taken it on herself. Or handed it to one of his immediate superiors. This was one jaunt he was going to enjoy.

'Take Cassie with you,' a voice calls from the office. 'She needs the experience.'

The newest recruit to the team smiles and jumps up like a jack in the box. He'd been that keen once. 'Where is Blake Point?' She has the same colour skin as Ginny but her eyes and hair are darker.

'The end of the universe,' another voice calls from behind a screen. 'Don't say we haven't warned you.'

'Come on. We might get there with a few hours of daylight to spare,' Mark says as Cassie Turner grabs her jacket and checks her radio.

They saunter out of the building. Cassie climbs into the passenger seat and Mark switches on the engine. 'Are we onto something?' she says.

'You did some training in the big cities, didn't you? This is petty by some standards, but it might just be the tip of the iceberg and people are the same the world over. Where did you train?'

'Salford. My partner got a promotion down here. We stuck out a long-distance relationship for a year before I begged to be moved. It worked. Compassionate grounds, see. Family friendly policies and all that.'

Mark snorts. The policies are only as good as the paper they are printed on. When it comes to the crunch and a big operation is about to kick off, or now, when every few days another member of the team or whole teams are self-isolating, family-friendly means nothing. 'It'll be a doddle compared to inner city policing. We're still country bumpkins in many ways, despite what the media would have us believe.'

Cassie settles back in the seat. 'Let's go.'

Mark swings the car out of the car park and follows the road through the city, past the docks where many small pleasure cruisers are moored by the boating community. If he has no luck at Blake Point, perhaps he could try here? After all, playing at sea captains didn't mean you couldn't be a pirate or a smuggler from time to time.

He heads down the A38 towards Bristol, but turns off to the right before the nature reserve and follows the road for a further few minutes before turning left and driving parallel to the canal with the river beyond. Blake Point is announced with a sign welcoming careful drivers and adorned with images of yachts and sea birds. Another few hundred metres and he reaches what must be the village centre. An assortment of private housing and council owned bungalows for the elderly are scattered amongst some 1960s semi-detached family homes. Few have parking spaces. Most cars are on the road or in front of the buildings on a hastily constructed driveway. Another sign warns him the primary school is nearby. It is quiet, apart from a few excited shouts from children in the school involved in PE or some intricate game of their own creation. It is sited in what must be the original part of the village, near a post office and rows of terraced cottages built at a time when the workers in the docks would have lived within walking distance. There's one pub and a dilapidated building with a sign announcing it as a working men's club, like the ones his grandad frequented up north.

'It's a bit… a bit…' Cassie bites her lip as she looks around at the empty streets and closed front doors.

'Of a dump?'

'No. More sad… drained… as if the life's been sucked out.'

'The vampire village?' Mark says. 'It could catch on as a new mini-series.' He follows the road towards the harbour. 'It's like a lot of places. No work so you have to go to Bristol or Gloucester. People don't have the same sense of social commitment so no clubs, the church probably shares a vicar who is rushed off his feet, this just one of many places he manages. People get home and close the doors.'

'You sound passionate about it,' Cassie said.

'That's one thing about the recent lockdown. It meant people stayed local and got to know their neighbours better.'

'Yeah, and argued the toss.'

Mark slows to let a stray pheasant cross the road and disappear into the hedge. 'That doesn't mean people like each other any better,' he says.

Cassie gets out her notebook. 'What are we looking for?'

'We're keeping an open mind,' Mark says. 'We might pay a visit to anyone in charge, otherwise we're looking for small craft and a place further away from the main dock where a boat could pull alongside.'

'Not necessarily a proper wharf or a jetty?'

'Too obvious. Whoever does this is looking for a quick drop off, out of sight of prying eyes and nosy neighbours.'

Cassie nods. 'I get the picture.'

Mark parks the car. He taps his fingers on the steering wheel, speaking his thoughts out loud. 'It would be where it's easy to slip out for a little jaunt, pick up the cargo, possibly even from a bigger craft further out to sea. They come back, moor alongside the canal and wait till it's dark. Then slip along the canal tow path to a nearby waiting van.'

Cassie scans the deserted streets and the empty docks. 'If it's like this by day, what must it be like at night?'

'You go and have a quick walk along the tow path while I have a chat with the harbour master or whatever he is called.'

'Will do.' Cassie climbs out of the car and walks away from the car park towards the canal. It is easy to spot. A few narrow boats are moored. Smoke wreathes into the sky from a chimney on one.

Mark shivers. A fire on a boat? He shrugs. Rather them than him. He adjusts his hat and checks the time. Ten to one. Is there anyone here? An expanse of water, steel blue in the shifting cloudy sky, spreads out before him. A couple of white silos for grain storage are dwarfed by the skeletal grey of motionless cranes. A low-lying cargo boat is moored next to a red brick multi-storey building, like the ones around Gloucester dock. These had not yet been turned into desirable apartments with chrome and glass balconies and a variety of bars and restaurants on the ground floor. A sign states the port is not manned twenty-four seven and there is a phone number to call. He logs the number. It might come in handy, but he prefers a casual walk up and down. If someone stops him, all the better.

He steps onto the harbour side. It resembles the wharves along Bristol docks with concrete and metal bollards, tyres tied to protect the brickwork and the hulls of any craft that might moor up. The water slops at them. A few seagulls bob up and down on the surface. An oily sheen glitters in the shards of sunlight as they pierce the clouds. There is a brisk wind and the smell of salt, mud and rotting vegetation fills his nostrils. It is not unpleasant. His feet clatter on the concrete. He steps over a metal ring and continues towards the red brick buildings. One window is open. He walks slowly, absorbing sights and sounds, watching for anything that appears out of place, and rehearses in his mind the route any would be smuggler might take. A quick jaunt out to sea and you'd be within reach of a dinghy from a larger vessel, or could even moor close to a larger craft. From there, off load a dozen desperate and obedient refugees, hide them below deck and saunter back through the harbour to your safe space where a van is waiting and you're away.

'Can I help?' a voice calls as a door from the brick building swings open and a man in blue with a military-style, blue jumper steps out of the shadow. 'I don't reckon you want a trip round the bay to see the wrecks?'

'You're right. This is strictly business, not pleasure. It's a long time since I went on a boat trip.'

'We do a good Christmas one although this year…' He spreads out his hands before folding his arms over his rounded stomach. He looks fifty, although that could be the result of the lines on his face which suggests he has spent most of his youth outside. His hair though, is only tinged with grey at the temples.

Mark nods. He never shares any of his views on the current situation. Too political and too many often violently opposed views abound in the general public's thoughts. He'd already had enough dealing with the growing crowds of anti-vaxxers, deniers and lockdown breakers in the summer. 'Just a couple of questions if you've got a moment?'

'I'd invite you in, but I'm not sure if we are allowed and it's a good enough day to stand out here, isn't it?'

For a second Mark is certain this is a ploy to keep him out of the office. Why? He stops himself. He is not investigating a crime, merely speculation. 'Good idea. I spend too much time in an office as it is.'

The man gestures to a low wall by the water side. A new, blue electric Nissan Leaf is parked in a small bay with a white painted sign on the wall. Harbour Master. 'I'm Jason Bull. Harbour Master and at the moment Mr Do It All.'

'Sounds fun.' Mark seats himself on the wall at what he hopes is a socially distanced spacing and screws up his eyes against the sunshine breaking through the clouds. It's warm and he breathes in the air, tinged with salt and diesel.

'There are two of us but with all this shielding, self-isolating and furlough, it's me who takes up the slack.'

'Yeah?' Mark's instinct tells him here is a man who likes a chat and with the lockdown he's missed his interactions.

'Up to 2019 we had a good crew here. Now it's me and one other and he's only part-time.'

'Why the change?'

'EU, Brexit, you name it. People got scared, sat on their money, and moved a lot of business to the east coast.'

Mark nods. That would be a good reason for a bit of smuggling to bring in extra cash. 'What happens if I want to take a pleasure cruiser, say, from Bristol to Gloucester?'

Jason puffs out his chest. 'You have to contact Gloucester Harbour Trustees for permission to travel from here to the Severn Bridge crossings, and if you want to go upstream via the canals it's the Canal and River Trust. Pretty easy unless you need the bridges lifted but a simple pleasure cruiser, like the ones in Gloucester docks, can go in and out. It costs, mind, but with an annual license it works out pretty cheap for a decent day's boating.'

This is not sounding promising. Smugglers don't like paperwork. 'What if I wanted to deliver some, let's say, unusual goods?'

Jason slaps his thighs with one hand. 'I knew that's what you were here for. Never fails.' He pauses. 'Anyone would be daft to draw attention to themselves unless they were pretty certain they wouldn't be investigated.'

'What do you mean?'

'A fisherman who has been in and out for years on a few days a month wouldn't draw any attention. A keen boater with kids in tow over the summer holidays? No sweat. But a new craft, making a few journeys at odd times, and we'd want to know more about them.'

'What would you do?' Mark crosses his fingers that here is a man who liked a bit of flattery. 'If it was your chance to make a few quid?'

Jason's face clouds over. 'Either you are so much a part of the boating crowd no one would ever suspect. Or…' He pauses. 'You drop off between the bridge and here. Somewhere nice and secluded.'

'Are there such places?'

'Plenty, and most are known to the keen anglers. Or the elver fishermen. There aren't many licensed but we get a shedload of poachers in the season.'

'When's that?' Mark has never heard of fish poaching. Wasn't that salmon? He lets Jason continue.

'February to May. It was very quiet this year. No one dared get out and about once lockdown started and no chefs were buying. I reckon the herons ate more than the humans.'

Mark looks out across the still water of the basin. In the distance the lock gates are closed. It is all so tranquil. 'Is there anyone who might be able to tell me these best places? Just out of interest, mind?'

'Depends on what you want to catch. Upstream it's the usual coarse fishing with chub, carp, graylings and barbels around Stourbridge. Out in the open waters, it's cod, bass, turbot, whiting… depends on the month.'

'You sound as if you know plenty about it.'

'Love it. Sea fishing mainly. Can't spend enough time. Got me own cruiser too.' He stops. His face colours. Not much but there is a tinge of pink across the cheeks and a flush down one side of the neck. 'She's in dry dock. Won't get her repaired till next spring.' Is there a quaver in his voice?

'Can anyone go out?'

Jason has recovered his cheery chatter. 'Charter a boat and the owner will take you to a decent place. We had a spate a couple of years back with rich prats from London coming down for a stag weekend, hiring a boat and spending most of the weekend with their head over the side.'

'Good money?'

'For the owners, yes. Two grand a time for the weekend.' Jason shakes his head.

'I suppose you keep a record of the traffic up and down the river?'

Jason tilts back his head and laughs. 'Want to have a look? We've got nothing to hide on our side.'

'That would be good.'

Jason stands up and saunters back to his office. Mark follows at a distance and sanitises his hands with the bottle on Jason's desk. Jason taps away at a keyboard squashed between an open lunch box, a rusty tool kit and an in-tray with yellowing papers and dusty files waiting for attention.

'I'll print this out for you,' he says and disappears into a smaller inner office. Clattering from an old and very slow printer suggests Jason might be some time.

Mark scans the room. A white board with a to do list, a map of the river down to Bristol and the canal system to

Gloucester dominates one wall. Multi coloured Post-its decorate the surface. Most have dates and times with the name of a boat and occasionally a company. Angling Breaks was one. So too was Holidays Afloat. Snell's Fish was a wholesaler. Nothing much there.

Jason comes back into the room. He holds out a sheaf of papers. 'Here you are. Happy reading.'

Mark nods towards the whiteboards. 'Do you know all of these?'

Jason comes closer. Mark steps back. Weird how quickly it has become an automatic reaction. 'Most.' He points to a series of coloured Post-its. 'Yellow for trade. Blue for local holiday contacts, mostly small operators with a boat or two. Orange for national companies. Green for angling trips. Pink for individuals. Like this one here.'

Mark strains to read the spidery writing. 'Regulars?'

'Colonel B. J. White. Was coming here as a lad with his dad according to him. This one's something at GCHQ. *Don't ask me what I do or I'll have to kill you* sort of thing. Anyone I don't recognise I put a dot by their name. Just in case.'

'In case of what?'

Jason raises one eyebrow. 'In case they are a complete numpty and we end up having to rescue them.'

'Thanks for this,' Mark says as he leaves the office. The door slams behind him. Either he has overstayed his welcome or Jason is not as friendly as he pretends to be.

Chapter 15

'And why are you looking so happy?' Tashi is standing by the front entrance. The overcast and threatening sky does nothing to cheer up the pock marked grey concrete and peeling paint of the teaching blocks. At least it is dry under the front awning which pupils from Years 9 to 11 must use. She is on duty, checking everyone is wearing a mask, phones are stashed away and switched off and they are keeping to a safe distance. Some hope. She hasn't seen them all crowded round a phone, or if it's the younger boys, leaping on each other's backs, wrestling, pushing and shoving on their way home each day.

'I met up with Finn yesterday.'

'Oh ho? Do I spot a starriness in the eyes? A tendency to sigh and strike the love-torn breast.'

'You've been reading too much Victorian poetry,' I say.

'Y7 this is not your entrance,' she bellows at some girls who are still at the stage of awe and wonder at their new and very grown-up surroundings. They squeal and run off in the opposite direction, nearly banging into a group of Y10 — all long hair, brushed elegantly from their faces, skirts hitched up to their navels and as much make up as they can get away with. Was I ever as cool? My memories of school days are itchy jumpers, sweaty armpits and spots. A lot has happened in thirteen years. It feels longer.

'For your information, we met for lunch and talked. I'm helping him with the photography for his business venture. He's converting his outhouses and some of the barns to holiday lets.'

Tashi laughs. 'What a chat up line.'

I shrug. 'He's very nice. So far.'

'Well keep me informed. By the way, Y11 are self-isolating so you are online and will be needed to cover Y9 English. I think that's all, oh, and can you work all next week? We reckon we'll be more staff down.'

I nod. I like to feel of use. Perhaps I should get a full-time post. I like the hustle and bustle of school. 'See you later,' I say and go through the swing doors into the atrium. Here no money has been spared to create a good impression. It's more like an office block and an upmarket one at that. I head towards the administration suite, collect any post and head for the art block. Much as I miss the interaction with pupils online, today I need to rest my brain. After all these years, could I really have met someone special? Isn't that the dream?

I climb the stairs and walk along the glassed-in corridor. I can see down into the atrium below. It's quiet. Visitors are discouraged and where there would usually be hordes of people on a Monday morning, it's deserted except for the few pupils allowed in that way and staff. I unlock the door to Room 3, Creative Arts, Block 5. I pull up the blinds and for a moment, gaze at the estate and beyond that the distant hills, shimmering blue against the grey sky. For a moment I wonder what Finn is doing. I shake my head. I refuse to become a simpering female, and yet there is something special about feeling like this. I'm no longer twenty-eight, I'm seventeen and the whole world is at my feet with people to meet, places to explore and a future to dream. When did that change? I turn away from the view. That's enough introspection. I have a job to do and perhaps if a vacancy arises, I might be tempted. That means I'd better be the best. I set up the Zoom connection and check my lesson plans. Here goes.

I refuse to check my phone until break time. My stomach flutters as I pull it from my bag. There is nothing from Finn. My stomach sinks. Now I know I'm being stupid. We have the arrangements made for Saturday, isn't that enough? We've only known each other for a few days.

I bite back any disappointment and head for the staff room. I need coffee.

'How's things?' Jake smiles at me. He is dressed in what us ordinary members of staff call *desperate to be a leader* style; dark suit, crisp plain shirt, colourful tie and shiny shoes.

'Good,' I say. 'Do you want a coffee? I'm off to the canteen.' Since Covid, we no longer have a staff kettle or water heater. Coffee, tea and whatever else we want is served from the hatch in the staff area of the canteen. We can take it back to the staff room. For some reason I know Jake is going to ask me out and I don't know what I'm going to say.

'I'd like that.'

With all the staggered times, only Y11 and a few staff should be around. While Jake fetches the drinks, I find two chairs around a small low table. Usually, it would be piled with books. We have been told nothing must be left here or it will be removed and quarantined for seventy-two hours. That would not be a popular move with the kids or the pushier parents who like to find out if we mark their little darling's work diligently daily.

I don't have to wait long. 'There you go.' He places a paper cup in front of me and picks up his own. 'Cheers,' he says and is about to pick up the cup when he stops. 'How are you doing?' he says. 'If you want to tell me to keep my nose out of your business, that's fine, but my sister was mugged a couple of years ago when she came out of university late one evening and it was a while before she felt…' He hesitates. 'I suppose the only word to describe it is safe. She was always checking no one was walking behind her. Stuff like that.'

I nod. It's good to find someone who won't expect the usual breezy *fine* or *yeah, good thanks,* which it damn well isn't. For a moment I think of Finn. Would I tell him how I feel? Not that we've talked about what happened. I don't want to bring up the subject. For a moment I wonder why we haven't spoken about this. I focus on Jake. 'You're right. That's it exactly. I get spooked by things I wouldn't usually take any notice of.'

'If you ever need someone to give you a lift home, let me know. Or I can come over if you hear something or spot anyone behaving oddly.'

I am not used to people being kind. I suppose over the years I've pushed them away. Standing on your own two feet was expected in my family. Not that it was a family. Three people all intent on following their own lives is not the dream I have of family life.

'Thanks,' I say and I mean it. I change the subject. 'How's term going for you?'

He smiles. 'Kids either love maths or hate it. The kids who love it do their work, here or at home, and if they're good at the subject they can teach themselves. The ones who hate it will use any excuse to evade anything remotely like study.'

'It's the same in all subjects.'

'It's the kids in the middle I worry about. The ones who with a bit of extra support from me in lessons could shine.' He puts down the cup of coffee. 'Still, we've got to get on with it, haven't we?'

'That's all we can do.' I check my watch. I am due to cover Year Nine English in five minutes. The staff room is filling up with those about to start their break.

'Yes, I'm back on Zoom next lesson. Suppose we'd better get going.'

I stand up and take the paper cups and deposit them in the bin. Jake is waiting for me by the door. 'Thanks for the coffee,' he says.

'Thanks for the offer of help,' I say. I know he wants to say something else.

'How do you fancy a pizza later today? Nothing special. I'll book a table at the Italian in the High Street?'

For a moment I think of Finn. I dismiss the idea. We are not an item. We are not exclusive. We are not even boyfriend and girlfriend. What's stopping me? Nothing. 'That would be good.'

Jake's shoulders drop and he smiles. It's a sweet, crooked smile and I realise he's more attractive than I'd thought. There is something *apple pie and cream* about him, comforting, warming and… the word jumps into my brain before I can stop it. He is *safe.* I like the word. It's what I need.

We exchange numbers and he promises to text me. I am late for the start of Year 9's lesson and they are glaring at me mutinously. 'I know, sorry it's me and not your usual teacher,' I say and glance again at the lesson plan while they settle, and it fills me with horror. That's when I get an idea. Sod the plans. If kids need to write with power, horror is just what they need.

'Anyone ever seen *Dracula*,' I say. Some hands shoot into the air, others flap and eventually rise, even more just nod. 'Who has read the real story?' Hands drop. 'Today you are in for a treat,' I say and switch the board on. A few taps and on the screen is the opening passage. 'You are going to be the ones who are exploring when you find Dracula's tomb and have to report back.' I perch on the end of the front desk, electronic pencil at the ready. 'Any ideas what you might see, hear, smell, touch and feel?'

For a moment there is a pause before faces change, hands are in the air and waving at me. Today, at least, we can all enjoy something different and be scared by something imaginary, and far away from real life.

Chapter 16

Mark walks back to the car. Cassie is already waiting. 'Any luck with possible drop off points?'

'Plenty' she says. 'How do you fancy a quick stroll before we head back to the office?' By the smile on her face, she has spotted something.

'Go on, tell me what you've found.'

She shakes her head. 'I may be way off, but how many vans would you expect to drive along this tow path or stop here?'

They walk past a small collection of narrow boats. Some are inhabited, judging by the bikes left outside or a plume of smoke drifting upwards from a metal chimney, like the ones you expect to see on a fairy tale cottage with a tiny turret at the top. 'Where do these people park?'

'Most will leave their cars in the village. I asked the gentleman who was hanging out his washing earlier and he said this was deliberately kept clear of vehicles to maintain the peaceful nature of the environment.'

A sheep bleats. A crow caws. A dragonfly dances over the silky green water. With the man's shirts and towels flapping in the slight breeze, it could be a different century.

'Not that he said anyone took notice of it.'

Mark's antennae flick on. 'Really?'

'Yes. He reckons there's times when the place is like Piccadilly Circus. Does that mean it's busy?'

Mark smiles. 'Yeah. That's a phrase you don't hear very often now. So, it gets busy? With what is an interesting follow up question.'

'There's more,' Cassie says. 'This way.'

They round a gentle bend that lasts a good fifty metres. The dock and the canal boats are out of sight. In the hedge that separates the next field from the canal is a gate. It is padlocked. Who the hell would put a gate here and why? Mark walks towards the gate and climbs over. He surveys the field. Some dry-stone walls have been replaced by wire. A few small trees and the remnants of a hedge colonise the breaks. Someone has left out a set of small jumps, suitable for a pony. He turns back to Cassie. 'I've heard of a road to nowhere. Never a gate.'

'I reckon there must be another entrance or something. We'd need to follow the perimeter and it stretches a long way.' She shades her eyes against the weak sun.

Mark kicks at the grass beneath his feet. The recent damp weather has done little to soften the rock-hard earth after such a dry spring and summer. Not much chance of tracks. He bends down. The grass is still long. The warm autumn has not so far slowed the growth. 'Reckon any decent farmer would still have some animals grazing here.'

'Isn't it too cold?' Cassie says. 'I thought animals went in during the winter. Except sheep,' she adds.

Mark raises an eyebrow. 'Sheep?'

'Yeah, like the shepherds in the fields… Bethlehem and all that.'

He shakes his head. 'Please never apply for a truly rural force, will you? Stick with the cities.'

'I know. You all call me a townie. I am. This is the first time I've been so far south and west. I'm getting concrete and graffiti withdrawal symptoms.'

Mark kneels. 'Check this out.' He parts the grass. Beneath are ridges.

Cassie bends over. 'Is that what I'm thinking it is?'

'If you're thinking they're tyre tracks, you're spot on.' Mark straightens up. 'Where do you reckon they go?'

'I'd say straight across. Why waste time and energy going along the edges?'

'Unless you want to be shielded from prying eyes. There's plenty of cover from those trees and the odd bit of hedge and in the last few months, nobody's risked an evening drive to a nice little country pub since *eat out to help out*.'

'Want me to check?'

Mark nods. 'Go straight across and check out what's in the next field. Don't bother about going any further. Not today. I'll take a wander along the tow path.'

Cassie strides across the field. God, she has some energy. Mark clambers back over the gate. The earth along the tow path has plenty of dips and indentations but no true marks. It is bare of grass, like a goal mouth at the end of the season in a local division. That isn't an issue. There will be plenty of walkers and cyclists and as the old boy said it gets busy at times. That's when he spots something else. He crouches and rubs his finger over a greasy mark. He lifts it to his nose and sniffs. Oil. From an old engine? It's too far from the water to be from a canal boat unless someone had taken something to mend. That isn't likely. Could it be a quad bike or a cross-country motor bike? Over the first lockdown there had been plenty of incidents where riders, starved of their usual courses and stadium workouts, had pitched up on local hills and through woodland. He walks further along the canal tow path. It's certainly wide enough for a vehicle, providing you had a steady hand on the steering wheel. Could someone drive along here, pick up some cargo or people and reverse back? Surely there would be an easier way?

'Sir?' Cassie runs towards him and stops to gather her breath. 'There's a gap in the wall further away from the canal. It leads to a track. I presume it's part of a farm?'

'Could be,' Mark says. 'We've got plenty to go on here. Let's get back and write up all we've done. If there is a farm, we might need to pay a visit to the owner.'

They walk back in silence until they reach the first of the canal boats. A man is checking his washing. 'Saw you up there,' he says. 'That's where those damned kids mess around. Should be stopped. Joy riders I reckon or druggies.' He pulled a threadbare and very grey t shirt from the line slung across his boat.

'What have you seen?'

'Like I told the young lady, some nights there's voices, engines and God knows what else. I don't get involved. I keep myself to myself.'

'What sort of nights?' Mark knows the answer he wants.

'Nights when the tide's up.'

Perfect. 'Can you tell me a bit more?' he says.

'Sure. Come aboard and I'll fill you in.' He stands aside and points to a narrow plank covering the small gap between the bank and the boat. 'It's quite safe.' He disappears down a hatch.

'After you,' Mark says. 'Although usually I'd hope to be piped aboard.'

Cassie and Mark follow the man down a steep set of stairs to a wood-panelled living area. On both sides, windows let in light and are above the level of the water. It's strange to be so close. A wood burning stove warms the room. To one side is a TV. On the other are shelves crammed with books. They look like natural history. Red velvet cushioned seats are set into the wood panels below the windows and on a table is today's newspaper, opened at the crossword next to a pair of tortoiseshell rimmed glasses. They're like the ones his uncle had worn years ago. There's also a notebook and a mug full of different coloured pens. The man has his back to them and is filling a kettle at a sink in what must have been the kitchen. Until now, Mark had always wondered why narrow kitchens were called galley kitchens. Now he understands. Everything is within arm's reach with barely space to turn round yet it has a cooker, fridge, microwave and freezer as well as cupboards and a work surface on which is a loaf of bread and an open jar of marmalade with a knife stuck in it.

'Coffee? Tea?' The man turns. 'I'm Lewis Barnes.' He lifts a work hardened hand. 'I'd shake but…' He shrugs.

'I'm Sergeant Mulroney and this is Constable Parker,' Mark says. 'Coffee will be fine for me.'

'And me,' says Cassie. Mark notices her eyes working the small space, picking up as much information as they can. Not that Lewis is a suspect. Yet.

'It's black, freshly ground, with milk from the farmers' market and if you need sugar, there's honey from local bees.'

'You seem to like your food?' Mark says and takes a good look at the man, grinding beans, adding heaped spoonsful to a metal coffee pot and swirling the grounds around. He must be seventy, with long grey hair pulled into a ponytail which dangles down the back of his baggy and much darned green sweater. Brown cords and green Hunter boots complete the dress which is more aging hippie grunge than retired man of leisure, playing at boats.

'I like to eat and live decently, away from as many chemicals and additives as possible.'

He pours thick, black coffee into three small pottery mugs and places them on a tray with a jug of milk which he fetches from the fridge. A glimpse inside is all Mark needs. Here is a true foodie. Nestled between an earthenware container with eggs is a cheese wrapped in muslin, half a loaf, a container with some curry-coloured beans and shelves stacked with a rainbow of vegetables.

'Help yourselves,' he says. 'Sorry, there's no sanitiser. You can wash in the heads.'

'I'll risk it,' Mark says and takes one of the mugs and breathes in the aroma of chocolate, burnt oranges and a hint of toffee. With the amount of caffeine in here, he and Cassie wouldn't need a car, they could fly back to HQ.

Cassie pours thick, creamy milk into her cup and swishes the mug around. 'This smells good,' she says.

'Aye. Food should taste of food.' Lewis sits down. Grey-tinged eyebrows top bright blue eyes set in a lined face. 'Suppose you want to hear about the ruckus a few weeks ago?'

'What ruckus?' Cassie says and stops as Mark interrupts her.

'That's right.'

Lewis sits back. 'A right old to do it was… lights, a van and so much shouting. Now we've had kids partying here plenty of times, but they usually have a bit of music and you can hear a few of the girls giggling. Not this time.'

'Go on.' Mark drains the coffee mug.

'I peeked out of the window at the back there. A big white transit was parked in the field and the lights were off. Someone opens a door and the light goes on inside and that's when I see them… ten, fifteen, all barging to get on board.'

'Fifteen what?'

'Youngsters. Young lads.'

'How do you know they were young men?' Cassie says.

'Old men don't run and jump like they did. We plod.'

'What then?'

'The door slams, the van tears off and a little cruiser, like a weekend boat sets off upstream.'

'What's unusual about that?'

'Upstream? At night? Funny time for a boat trip. Now if they'd been going towards the sea, I could have understood. High tide was about to turn and they could have had a nice jaunt before holing up and waiting for clearance.'

Cassie glances at Mark. She has a question. He nods. 'What do you think was going on?'

Lewis spreads his hands on the table. 'Stands to reason. These lads didn't want to be found here. They had somewhere else to go and wherever it was, they didn't want to be seen.'

'Which evening was this?' Mark crosses his fingers.

'Last high tide. Couple of weeks back. Wednesday it was as I like the late film on *Talking Pictures*.'

Mark calculates in his head. Bingo. That must have been the evening that woman was attacked and it sounds like it could have been a similar van. Mark stands up. 'You've been very helpful. We may ask for a statement at some time in the future.'

'Anytime and if I see anything unusual… I know the drill.'

Mark places his card on the table. There is one other thing. It is a long shot. 'Do you happen to know who owns the land here?'

Lewis shakes his head. 'It did belong to an old gent who let it go to wrack and ruin. His son's in Dubai and has put it up for sale. The fields are rented to a local farmer for his sheep in the winter and a bloke in the village lets his daughter ride there from time to time.'

'Thanks once again. We'll see ourselves out.'

Once back on the tow path Cassie and Mark head back to the car. 'Are you thinking what I'm thinking?' he says.

'Too much of a coincidence he sees a van full of young men on the same night a woman is attacked by a man driving a van full of young men.'

'I'm interested in who owns that bit of land,' Mark says. 'It shouldn't take long to find out and we might get a further clue. If not, I reckon we could be in for a stake out when it's a full moon.'

They continue in silence. Once back at the car Cassie climbs inside. For a moment Mark remains where he is, surveying the water, the buildings, the aging cranes and rusty swing bridges. It all appears very peaceful. Or should that be too peaceful? The door of the harbour master's office is closed. A figure is watching from the window, standing well back so that Mark can just see the outline. Someone is very interested in what he and Cassie are doing and possibly when they are going. Part of him wants to wave. That'd put the wind up. He resists the temptation. Far better to let his watcher think he'd found nothing and would not come their way again. Mark smiles to himself. Wrong! He'll be back soon enough.

Chapter 17

Could this be classed as a date? I finish checking Year 11's portfolio, and try to switch off the nagging argument in my head by refocussing on the paperwork, ensuring names are correct and each mark is entered carefully. I'm pleased with what these poor young people have achieved, despite all the disruptions. Exam or no exam, at the end of the year there will be plenty of evidence for grading, and if a couple of the more reluctant artists got a move on and completed what they had promised at the beginning of term, they'd get decent enough grades too. If I want to apply for a permanent post, it will look very good on the CV.

My brain pings back to the forthcoming date. No. This is simply two work colleagues going out for a meal after a shitty day and an even shittier term. Moral support is needed by both of us.

Saturday isn't a date either. I'm meeting Finn to look over his project and suggest some images and if I can provide some of those images, what does it matter?

I close up the folder of paintings and sketches and stow them in Y 11's drawer. What next? Should I hang around here? Or go back home? If I go home, I'll be tempted to freshen up and change and that means I'll be treating the meal with Jake as something special. This is silly. I head down to the staff room. It's usually a good place to be after a hectic day, full of banter, small unofficial discussion groups and plenty of fresh coffee. Instead, it's empty and silent. Staff are not encouraged to hang around or socialise. Get in, teach, and get out is the new work pattern. I check my watch. The cleaners will be in any minute with windows wide open and every surface wet with sanitiser. Jake had texted to say he'd meet me outside the restaurant at half past five. Half an hour? My fingers stray to my phone. I pick it up and drop it back in my bag. I'm tired of social media.

I'll go and sit in my car. At least it's warmer than the school. It might only be autumn, but the wind off the estuary is like a blast from a freezer on over-drive and with all the available windows and doors open in the school, the cold permeates every room and corridor. At this rate I'll need to invest in some thermal knickers. I close the door behind me and negotiate my way down parts of the corridors which are supposedly cordoned off, with signs warning of slippery surfaces and the smell of disinfectant lingers. I head towards the main staircase and past empty display boards and bare classrooms. Usually by this week of the term they would be full of examples of good work to inspire the young children, tips to pass exams and notices to remind pupils of rules, regulations, and forthcoming events. There is nothing except remnants of coloured backing paper, dozens of staples embedded in the soft board and patches where sunlight has drained them of the original colour. It feels more like a prison than a school. I stick my head round the office doorway and swipe my name badge. *Rachel Thomas out* reads on the monitor.

Once in the fresh air I breathe deeply. For some reason I'm on edge. It happens from time to time. Flashbacks they're called. It can be anywhere. Even in the shower. I am there again. In the wood and fear grips me. Once I woke up sweating. Another time a strangled voice startled me. Mine. Sometimes I feel as if someone is watching me. They aren't. It feels like it. I glance behind me as I cross the school car park. It's still light, there are plenty of cars I recognise and yet I feel uneasy. I'm pleased to be inside my car and I lock the door.

I drive to the town centre. There are always plenty of people around at the end of the day. Parking is free after 3.00

pm. Somehow, I feel safer in a crowd. I turn down the steep slope and into the car park nestled by the church. The grey stone is glowing golden in the early evening sunlight. Shadows dapple the graveyard and huddles of school pupils cluster under the overhanging boughs of the yews. No social distancing there. I don't blame them. The squeals from the girls and the deeper laughter and shouts from the boys are comforting. In these first throes of adolescence, flirting is not a quiet pastime. At least hormones are telling their bodies that life is going on as usual.

I go to the car park by the police station and find a spot under a lamp post. The fake Cotswold brickwork and windows darkened by blinds remind me of a prison. The car park is nearly empty and as it is gone four o'clock I don't have to pay. I stop the car below the main entrance to the station. On the walls are painted the names of the senior people who can park closest. I know I'll feel safer there if it's getting dark when we leave the restaurant. I get out my phone. Ten past five. It will only take me a few minutes to get to the restaurant. Finn said the name of his farm was Wayside Farm. I type it in and add the name of the local newspaper. Any articles about it will come up, I'm sure.

I scroll through the list and there is an obituary. Must be for his father. I read it through. Just as Finn said, the farm has been in the family for years. His father was popular judging by the number of people who attended the service. The article ends with the simple statement that the farm on the common has been left to his youngest son, Finn, and some fields and outbuildings of the derelict Sandwell Farm have been left to a brother, Phillip, currently in Dubai. I wonder how he feels about that? I check the date. It was four years ago. I thought Finn had only moved here recently? Perhaps I'm wrong and he was commuting from London at weekends before the pandemic struck. I won't say anything for the moment.

The sun dips behind the hills and the world darkens. I shiver. I'm safe here, aren't I? I must be strong. There is nothing to be frightened of. I get out of the car, lock it and check if anyone is close by. The old gentleman with the shopping trolley and the mother with two young children in school uniform skipping and running by her side are not threatening. It's young, lone males I want to avoid. What a stupid thought, here I am going out to dinner with a lone male and meeting up with a different one at the weekend. Except that feels different somehow. Stranger danger is what we teach at school, except we know that most harm is done by members of the family or friends and neighbours. Do I know my attacker? Is there something I've missed? I glance around me. I'm being stupid again. I hurry past the coffee shops, with the outdoor seats still full. Nothing will happen in full view of witnesses, most of whom have their phones to hand. I'm safe here. I hurry round the corner by the restaurant. Jake is waiting outside. He breaks into a huge smile. Is it relief? Did he think I wouldn't turn up?

He's taken off his tie and is wearing a leather jacket. He doesn't usually wear that on duty. He's more a North Face or Regatta man.

'Hi,' I call out. For a moment we stand and stare at each other, not sure what to do.

'Shall we go in?' he says.

'Yes. Fine by me,' I say. I haven't realised how hungry I am and how much I plan to enjoy this evening. Who would have thought I'd have two different dates in one week?

Jake stands aside to let me go through the door. I sanitise my hands without thinking and am rubbing the goop into the skin when a visored waiter appears. He has the dark looks of an Italian. His accent is pure Newcastle. 'Jake, my mate. Over this way. I've put you in a booth next to the window. Can't have any of the clients from the school staring in and spotting you've got spaghetti dribbling down your mouth.'

I follow him to a leather seat and slide along a slightly damp surface. Sanitised, probably. The table top is damp too. A paper menu lies next to the cutlery, all wrapped in a white paper serviette. 'Andrew here understands the adolescent mentality. We were at school together until he gets the call to train as a chef and I went to spend all my time on maths and IT which I believed would allow me to play computer games all day,' Jake says.

'What a coincidence you both ended up here,' I say.

'We're both local boys.'

'Yes, pet. Moved here when I was fifteen but never lost the Geordie twang.' Andrew does a semi-pirouette to place a wine menu, another piece of paper, on the table. 'I'll bring you some water, bread and oil while you decide.'

'So, you're a local boy?' I glance round the room. All the tables have a reserved sign on them. The sienna-stained walls have swags of grapes and sheaves of wheat, interspersed with images of herbs, all painted so that they blend into the beige brown. It's like everyone's imagined perfect Tuscan Trattoria. I should be wearing a white dress and my bronzed arms, covered in chunky jewellery, rest on the table. I wish.

'Yes,' Jake says. 'I went to the boys' school and hated it. Got transferred to the local comprehensive and loved every minute. That's why I like teaching where we are. We've got all life there, not just the privileged few.'

'Were you one of the privileged few?'

'Dad was a vicar. Mum was the vicar's wife. Not privileged but on the right side, according to some people. If you know what I mean?'

Andrew sweeps back, and a plate of murky brown, balsamic vinegar, greeny-gold olive oil and pale ciabatta is placed before us with a carafe of water. 'Any ideas?'

'A few more minutes, but a beer would go down well for me,' Jake says. He raises his eyebrows towards me.

'A small glass of house red.'

'Coming up,' and Andrew is off again.

'We'd better check the menu or we'll be here all night,' I say and look down.

My mouth waters. I never realise how hungry I get at school until I'm faced with food or the prospect of food. As I read through the offerings, I wonder if I could find out more about the elusive Finn from Jake. After all, he grew up a local boy too. I wonder if their paths ever crossed.

Andrew is back with the drinks. As soon as they are on the table, he whips out a tablet and taps it. 'What can I get you?'

'I'll have spaghetti carbonara,' I say.

'And the pizza diabolo with a house salad,' Jake says.

'Coming up in fifteen,' Andrew says and taps the tablet. 'No, make that eighteen.'

Jake smiles at me and raises his eyebrows. 'I wish the kids at school were as time conscious as that.'

I nod and giggle. 'I'm afraid I'm a bit like them, always banging on about something as the bell goes and I realise I haven't told them what to do next.'

We share the bread and oils. He's good to talk to and more than eager to tell me about his life growing up locally. Always after he's asked me, of course. By the time we have finished the main course I feel ready to ask about Finn.

We are waiting for coffee. 'Did you ever come across a Finn Driscoll?'

'Finn?'

'Lives, or rather his father lived at Wayside Farm?'

Jake took a sip of his coffee. 'There was a Finn Driscoll who was part of the smart set. All polo players, parents were friends of the prince, chums with Harry and Wills, invited to all the fancy parties at the big houses in the area. I went to one at a place outside Tetbury. The marquees for the toilets were bigger than my garden at home.'

The restaurant is busier now. Every table is taken and the air is filled with the buzz of conversation and the chink of plates and glasses. There is no raucous laughter. No group is bigger than six and people are enjoying the chance to get out, not get off their face. 'One of the privileged ones?' I say.

Jake shakes his head. 'If I'm right, there was some scandal with his old man gambling and he almost lost the farms. I think they were up for sale at one time.'

'You are very well up to date.'

'Not me. My mum. She reads the local rag from cover to cover each week and is a member of so many groups whose main preoccupation is gossip and cake.'

''She sounds interesting.'

Jake looks at me from hooded eyes. 'She's quite a character. I'll ask her. What was the name again?'

'Finn Driscoll of Wayside Farm.'

'Got it. Now I reckon I should settle the bill and escort you back to your car.'

'That won't be necessary.' I scrabble in my bag for my cards. 'We can go 50/50.'

Jake shakes his head. 'My treat for someone I reckon is pretty brave to go through what you did and get back into the fiasco of school in such a short time.'

There is no point in arguing. He has already signalled to Andrew who is heading our way with the card machine. 'I'll sort out a decent tip,' I say and leave a ten-pound note tucked between our empty glasses. I make a note to invite Jake over for a meal at half term.

He walks me back to the car park. Although it is only half past seven the world is still, quiet, dark, and threatening. It was a good idea to park close to the police station. Lights from inside reassure me. As I unlock the car, Jake opens the door. I know he can't kiss me. I'm not certain I want him to. He's kind and in that moment, I accept he is not Finn.

'Will you do something for me?' he says.

For a moment I wonder what is coming. 'It depends.'

'Put my number on speed dial, and the police too.'

'Why?' What does he know? What does he suspect? My stomach clenches. My knees shake.

'I want you to know you can call me anytime if you feel anxious or if you want to talk or… anything. It's what friends are for, isn't it?'

'I promise I'll do it as soon as I get home.'

'Good, and thank you for a lovely evening. We must do it again.'

'I agree. That's what friends are for, isn't it?'

He grins at my repetition of his words.

As I drive away, he gives me a wave and I wave back. For the first time in weeks, I feel less alone.

Chapter 18

Mark opens the door of the incident room, or should that be open plan office which only comes to life when something big happens. It's quiet apart from the tapping of keyboards and an occasional voice as information is exchanged. Underneath, though, is an atmosphere of excitement, dread and despair which mix in a heady hormone cocktail and he loves every minute of it. Today he nods to his co-workers and superiors as he heads towards the small glass and wood panelled cubicle that the boss calls the office. He likes Eve Fletcher, or Miss Eve as she wants to be called. It's too familiar. Most still refer to her as *the boss* or *ma'am.* He prefers boss. Reminds him of the Bruce Springsteen songs his dad loves that were a constant companion on the long drives to a Scottish caravan site where they would tramp up and down hills for hours on end.

'Mark.' It is not a question. Despite the warmth of the tonality, this is a command.

'Yes, boss,' he says as he pokes his head round the doorframe. It is known the door is always open. A closed door means something is up or someone is about to get a roasting.

'Sit down.' Grey eyes in a face that is neither old nor young look at him without blinking. Today's blue jacket is hung over the back of the swivel chair. Why do women either dress in navy or black and with the crisp white shirt? They all look like penguins. Ginny always wears vibrant blues, yellows, greens and pinks, like a kid's painting of a rainbow. That's one of the reasons he'd been attracted to her. She had style and attitude. Still has. Can't put red, orange and purple together? Try me.

He pushes these thoughts from his head as he pulls up a folding blue metal seat and places it so that his back is to the door and the open office. 'Yes, ma'am?' He waits for the questions.

'What have you found out so far?' Eve leans back in the chair, tilted so that her chest juts out. Does she know they can all see the flimsy, lacy top and hints of even more lace on her bras?

'The dock area is worth keeping an eye on. Too many odd occurrences, if you know what I mean?'

'Go on.'

'It would be easy for a small cabin cruiser to travel up and down the river without attracting much attention. The Harbour Master practically told me how to smuggle and what he'd do.'

'Was he being helpful?'

That is why she is DCI and has passed over the likes of Todd. She has developed an instinct for spotting something most people would not notice or, if they did, ignore. 'That's what crossed my mind. He was too helpful. The old boy who lives on one of the houseboats reckons there's been some strange comings and goings along the canal bank. Lights, noise at night, that sort of thing.'

'Nothing that we could pin down?'

'No. It's just a hunch I had and I'm damned sure that hunch is right.'

Eve shuffles some papers on her desk and pushes a form towards Mark. 'Take a look at that.'

Mark scans the document. It's an application for Detective Sergeant. 'I didn't think we're recruiting?'

'We are. You've got all the right background. You've been on the courses and passed. We need a new member of the team. Brian's retiring and that means a shift round. The temporary acting-up post would be permanent within a few weeks.'

Mark notices his hand trembling. He places the document on the table. 'Do you think I'll get it?'

Eve smiles. 'I want you as a detective on my team, permanently. This smuggling incident could be the start or the end of something big and we don't want any other forces stealing our good work. Do we?'

'No. I mean. Yes. I'll do it now.' He is about to take the form from her when she replaces it under the mound of files on her desk.

'Online. You read about it on the weekly bulletin, didn't you?'

Mark nods and smiles. He knows the drill. 'Ma'am.'

He is about to stand up when Eve leans forward. 'I want you to continue to pry. Take a trip to the harbour once or twice a week. Go upstream. Downstream. Chat to the teens on their quads, the dog walkers, that woman who was attacked, even the people she must associate with who reckon we've a whole zoo of wild animals cavorting round on dark nights. I want a report every time you go out and an itinerary before you go out. We don't want to leave ourselves open to any criticism.'

'In case it all goes tits up? Sorry, ma'am,' Mark says and looks down. 'No offence meant.'

'No offence taken. I've heard and used worse.'

Mark senses the interview is over yet there is something else. It is a question he must have answered and if he appears a bit presumptuous, so what? 'Why do you want me on your team?'

Eve is not fazed. 'Good question. It's something I would have asked in your position. It's simple. You're imaginative, creative, you think outside the box. That's what we need. Fill that in online and you should get an answer by the end of the week.'

'That soon?'

'I said I wanted you. I get what I want.' Eve looks back at the screen. The interview is over now. Mark leaves the office, forcing the smile threatening to spread across his face into a grimace and a slight cough.

'Hope that ain't Covid,' a voice calls.

'Nope. Too much fresh air,' Mark says and sits down at a spare work station. He logs on.

'You won't be moaning about that soon. We've got a shedload of tipoffs about raves at Halloween. Reckon we'll all be coughing after breathing in the heady cannabis fumes and hippy crack.'

Mark looks at the form in his hand. No. Report first, while it is still fresh, and he makes a note to check if Jason Bull has a criminal record. He wants to call Ginny. This will mean more cash. Sod the report. He wants to find out exactly how much more.

It is six o'clock by the time Mark has finished the report and the online application, stopped at a supermarket and bought some sugar free colas for the kids and a bottle of Prosecco for him and Ginny to share. So what if it is mid-week? They deserve a celebration. The new post could net him a good few pounds extra depending on the grade.

He pulls into the space on the drive next to Ginny's small, silver Citroen and climbs out. He looks around at the houses, crammed into every available space. Two trees have been spared by the developers; one is a horse chestnut, the other a copper beech. It towers over the houses, a remnant from the old colonel's garden on which the estate has been built. The Lawns, as it was marketed, had made a big thing of the history and the setting, rural yet close to amenities. Ginny hadn't been taken in but at the time it was all they could afford. Mark takes a deep breath. The night air is cool but not cold. A faint whiff of manure floats from the nearby farm. Soon there will be the unmistakable smell of autumn. For a moment Mark is tempted to get out his poetry notebook as the moonlight filters through the clouds and lights up the chestnut tree. He walks across. The spiky shells of the precious conkers inside litter the ground. Some have been squashed on the road. The contents have been grabbed by the children. Can they still play conkers? Or has that been banned too? Like chase and tag? He kicks at a shell. It's still closed. He bends down and holds it, twisting along the mid line so it splits. One glossy, brown conker nestles in its silken shell. It seems a pity to disturb it. He stands up. A collection of words is forming in his head. A Haiku would work. No. He has things to do. People need his attention. One day he'll write more poems.

He turns back towards the houses. His mum and dad would have loved a place like this. They are a mix of two and three bedroomed semis with the occasional three bedroomed detached mixed in. All have a slight difference, whether it is a porch, the orientation of the garage or the mix of colours of brick and rendering to create an illusion of individuality. Mark stands outside one of the latter. Okay. So it's still owned by the mortgage company, but his name is on the deeds. Light spills from the top bedrooms. Are the children in bed already? Are they ill? No. They don't realise electricity costs. Not like his family growing up. When you went out of a room, you switched off the light and closed the door to keep out the draughts. What happened to old fashioned thinking like that?

The estate is fine for now but perhaps he and Ginny could aim for something a bit better. There was a new development planned for the other side of the M5 and the kids could still go to the same school. Perhaps they could check out the site at the weekend.

He pushes open the door. The smell of shepherd's pie wafts from the kitchen. 'You're in time, supper's about to be served,' Ginny calls. Two small bodies, or not so small bodies hurtle towards him and grab hold of an arm each.

'Whoa there, careful,' he says as he places the carrier bag on the floor and tucks a child under each arm.

'Mummy thought you'd be late but I said I knew you were coming home to read us a story,' Emily says.

'You will, please?' Andrew looks up at him from underneath a floppy fringe.

'Let your father get inside the house.' Ginny pokes her head round the door. She spots the carrier bag. 'Celebrating?'

Mark untangles himself. 'Yes,' he says. 'I'll tell you over supper. Let me get out of uniform and it's treats all round.'

'Treats, treats, let's hope it's sweets,' the twins chant as Mark bolts up the stairs. He strips off the uniform and pulls on an old sweat shirt and pants. When the appointment goes through, there'll be no more uniform. Trouble is that could cost. He'd worry about that later. He clatters down the stairs. It would be good to get a decent stair carpet. Except if they were moving, they could save the money for a new place. Mark sighs. He could spend that increase ten times over and still find excuses for more.

He goes into the small dining area off the kitchen and opens the carrier bag. Ginny is draining peas from a saucepan. She collects a glass container and pours them in. 'Hands,' she calls.

'Can't we use sanitiser?' Emily says and pouts.

'Soap and water are just as good. In the cloakroom. Now. And I'll check the soap, the towels, and your hands,' she says as she places the dish on a place mat with a scene of Stratford Upon Avon on it, a wedding present from a well-meaning, aged aunt. She bends down to open the oven door, flapping her hand against the escape of heat.

The four-place white painted table and chairs are already set for their meal, squeezed into the space the developers jokingly called the dining area. There is no tablecloth. Dents and scrapes in the top are evidence of its use as a battle ground for toys tanks and cars, a catwalk for Barbie and Ken and recently, a school desk.

'Do you need a hand?' Mark comes up behind Ginny and puts his arms round her. He nuzzles her neck.

'Heh, tiger, let's eat first,' she says and swats him with a red and white striped oven glove.

'Clean, Mummy?' Emily holds out her hands. Her latte coloured skin is still damp.

'Show your father.' Ginny reaches up to collect the plastic bottles of ketchup and brown sauce.

'Over here. Inspection required.' Mark salutes as Emily holds out her hands and turns them over. 'All spick and span. No extra duties for you. Stand down.'

'I'm sitting there.' Andrew hurtles into the kitchen. He pushed her out of the way. 'That's my seat.'

'What does it matter?' Ginny says.

Emily walks round the table and sits down in the seat opposite. 'It matters because when the TV is on, he can see the reflection so he can watch when we're supposed to be eating.'

'Snitch, you do too,' Andrew says and kicks at her.

'Heh. No more or you'll eat on the naughty step.' Mark wags a finger.

Andrew looks down. 'Get you later,' he whispers.

'No. You. Will. Not,' Mark says. Why did he sound like a Dalek?

'Come on, people. Settle down.' Ginny takes her place closest to the kitchen. 'Prayers first.'

Mark bows his head. He isn't a man of faith but it makes Ginny happy. A bit of him is grateful; without a knowledge of basic Christianity kids miss out on all the great stories, like David and Goliath. What a good lesson for kids today. You too can beat the big bully. Deep in his thoughts he misses the words Ginny says and joins in the amen late.

Ginny picks up a warm plate and spoons out peas. 'What's all this about a special occasion?'

'This is a very special occasion,' he says as he pours half a can of cola for the twins and peels away the foil from the cap of the wine bottle.

'What is it?' Emily wriggles on her seat.

'Food first, stories later.' Ginny places plates in front of each of them.

Mark holds up his glass. Ginny copies. The twins hold up their beakers of cola. 'You are looking at the soon to be Detective Sergeant Mark Mulroney.'

No one speaks. Ginny puts down her knife and fork slowly. It's like watching a replay. The twins take their cue from her and look from their father to their mother, each other and back again.

'Does that mean you get a gun and can shoot people?' Andrew's shrill treble breaks the silence.

'He can do that already, if he's been trained, can't you?' Emily says.

Funny how she remembers snatches of conversations he'd had ages ago with Ginny when she threatened to divorce him if he became a member of the firearms squad. It was no good arguing he was as likely to get stabbed as shot and there was more protection in a team. He was not about to be a lone shooter.

'I'm more in the line of investigations, finding clues, tracking things. Stuff like that.'

'Oh.' She is not impressed.

''Well, go on then, say something,' Mark says and takes a long drink. It's like fizzy lemonade. He wished he'd bought a decent red.

'I suppose that means instead of being on call, coming home late, missing meal times and spending more time on the job, you'll be working even longer hours and whenever there's a shout, you'll live in the darn place.' Ginny's voice is calm, cold and he has to admit, what she says has a ring of truth. He'd witnessed what happened when a murder took place or a suspected terrorist attack. They lived and breathed, ate, and slept the case until it was resolved.

'Yes, but only when there is a big shout. Most of the time I'll be investigating County Lines, fraud, and abuse. They don't need twenty-four seven, just meticulous trawling through evidence and following up leads.'

Ginny shakes her head. 'I thought we were getting a really good work life balance, the two of us,' she says and is about to direct a forkful of food to her mouth when she stops. She stands up and scrapes her food into the bin. She returns to the table. 'Eat,' she says. 'I've lost my appetite.'

The meal continues in silence, broken only by the twins asking question after question about being a detective. Would he have a badge? Would he drive a special car? Would he ever get to guard the Queen?

He answers as best he can to deflect the conversation back to school and friends, all the time aware of Ginny's pursed lips and folded arms.

It is only later when the children are cleaning their teeth that Ginny finally asks him the question he dreads. 'Why do you want this so much? We can make do, can't we? It isn't the money. It won't be very different.'

Mark is silent for a moment. He needs time to say what has always been in the back of his mind from the day he joined. He wants to make a difference. 'I suppose it's the next step,' he says. 'I want to do more.' How can he describe how he felt today; alive, asking questions, following his own hunches and leads.

Ginny walks over to him and holds out her glass for a refill. 'If it's really what you want, go ahead.' She wags a finger at him. 'Your poetry will suffer.'

'I can write poetry when I'm eighty. I can't be a detective then.' As soon as he speaks the words another realisation sweeps over him; there'd be time later. These were the years for his career and to make a difference.

Ginny lifts her glass in a toast. 'Well, Detective Sergeant Mulroney, we'd better try and get used to it, hadn't we?'

Chapter 19

Saturday morning is wet and wet in a farmyard, even one that's in conversion to an up-market glamping resort, means mud. With a few animals tramping around, that mud will be linked to something I prefer not to think about. Wildlife photography rarely means getting up that close to an animal. At least my old boots are clean and I'll not need full camouflage gear. Not for a farm. I pull out a pair of jeans, a cream Aran sweater and the warmest, thickest socks that are not half covered in darns. I check again. No holes either. Imagine blundering into Finn's home, leaving my outdoor gear in what would be the entrance to an immaculate farmhouse kitchen, all stone floors, handmade wooden units in pastel green or dove grey and a huge Aga with the obligatory dog basket and well trained and very sleepy pooch, only to reveal holes in the toes and heels of my socks. Despite being a farmer, he knows the Royal Family. Does that make him gentry? All those pre-Covid hours in dental waiting rooms reading *Country Life* have made an impression, after all.

I'll spend the morning working, pop to the market for lunch and be ready to arrive at two. I have the address. It isn't far. I pour my latest choice of coffee, Golden Valley local roast from the market and toast the last of the sourdough. Market made cherry jam and butter will complete the perfect breakfast. I take a tray and sit down at the small table in the window overlooking the street. That's when it hits me. I'd slept the night through and if there were nightmares, they hadn't woken me or come into my conscious mind. I take a deep breath. It feels so good. I don't expect it's over. Not yet. Every day that goes past without a disturbed night is welcome. I hope I'm beginning to heal. For a moment, I wonder if it's due to Finn. Or Jake? Or both? That would be Tashi's answer. Romance solves everything.

No. It's me. I feel stronger, more determined. Is it the thought of applying for a permanent post? That's when I realise what I want. To feel at home. To have roots and to be recognised. I don't want the anonymity of the city any more or even a large town. I want a local life.

I scan emails. Nothing that won't wait. It's time to check out any sightings. I haven't been onto the forum since… I shiver. Focus on the information. That's all.

I search for general information before checking specific sightings. Yes! Over the last ten days, there have been several and all have been logged onto a map of the area. The pattern is like an arc, including the woodlands I was searching. There's no decent footage though. Plenty of phone images in poor light. No wonder people are sceptical. I may still be the first. Should I check on my lapel camera? I know it came back with my clothes. It's still stuck in the cupboard where I'd shoved the bag. What if there is real footage of the cats? Except what if there is footage of him? I'm being stupid. The police have checked it all. I would have been asked to identify him, wouldn't I? I'll leave it for a bit longer.

I type in the IP address of the private site I want. The logo appears and I add my password. This is a site for people who are not sceptical and take a very scientific approach. The forum shows plenty of new activity all over the country and even in the outskirts of big cities. A post explains that a lot of wealthy people kept these animals as pets in the 60s and 70s and they escaped. They must be breeding as the poor old things would have gone to the pet shop in the sky by now. I scroll down the lists. Did lockdown in the spring and summer have an effect? With less traffic about they may have been bolder and with more people desperate to get out for their hour a day exercise, were we all more attuned to the natural world?

Should I give it all up? Perhaps if I get a decent job with decent pay, I can keep the fame and fortune for another day and concentrate on photos for the sake of it. That would be nice. I close down and check the time. Eleven. I need to shop, eat and be ready for my session with Finn. I'll grab a felafel at the market. For some reason I'm feeling hungry. Or is that nerves? I haven't been nervous about meeting a man in years. Not proper seventeen-year-old nerves. The *will he kiss me?* type which bring out a crop of the worst spots and make any anti-perspirant useless. Funny, I didn't feel as jittery as this with Jake.

****

At one-thirty I have cleaned my teeth twice, used mouthwash and am sucking peppermints. I didn't realise the felafel were quite so spicy. I am sitting in my car and double checking. Camera? Lenses? Tripod? Should I take the indoor lights and a backdrop or two? No. Except if it goes well, I could stage a couple of interiors. I leap out of the car, unlock the front door and race upstairs to collect a soft box and an umbrella light. That will be a start. If Finn wants me to have a go another day, I can be properly prepared.

I check the time. Am I late? I input the satnav. Twenty minutes. I should be on time. I pull out onto the street and check no one is hanging around. Part of me is still scared. But anyone would have made a move by now. I head down the hill, past the market and turn left to skirt the town. The satnav tells me to head towards Dursley. I hope it's right.

I take the next turning left and follow the steep, twisting, turning road through the trees. A few expensive houses cluster behind closed gates. I reach the top and follow the road across the heath. A few dogwalkers are braving the breeze and the mud.

At least it's stopped raining. I head along the ridgeway, following an old drover's road between harvested fields. Some are already chocolate brown after a recent ploughing. Dotted along the fields are clusters of trees. I imagine Finn's house will be set amongst trees like that. It will keep off the cold winds that blast this area. And there is the sign. Wayside Farm. I signal and turn along a track.

The smile that crosses my face as I see Finn waiting for me in the yard is so big, it might burst out of the car. He has on cords, a padded waistcoat and green wellies. For a moment, I have a picture of the archetypal landed gent. Except I know he is more than that. I pull up and get out to be bounced at by a collie cross.

'Not mine,' he says. 'I'm looking after him long term for the family who live over there.' He indicates a barrier of trees with a smoking chimney stack in the middle. It must be half a mile away at least. 'They have a new and very noisy baby.'

'What's his name?' I say and crouch down to be licked by a rough, pink tongue.

'Figaro Gypsy Master of Lions,' Finn says. 'Seriously.'

For a moment I say nothing. Laughter is bubbling up inside. I notice Finn is smiling too. 'So, when he goes AWOL, you'll be the one singing—'

'Figaro, Figaro.' Finn takes up the refrain. 'Yes. I know. So far it hasn't happened although I'm sure there will be a first time. Fortunately he also responds to the name Gyp.'

I giggle. The ice is broken. 'Where to first? I've got everything ready.'

'The goats and sheep,' Finn says. 'They're looking pretty respectable.'

He carries my bag and I follow between two metal barns. The round tops of the roofs are pockmarked with rust and holes. The gates at the front are held together with string and the paving underfoot is cracked and uneven. Finn must sense my thoughts.

'These are due for demolition, to be replaced by ones that will have a viewing area for the school parties,' he says.

'That will cost,' I say.

'Yep. All costed and if everything goes to plan, we can make a start in the spring.'

He sounds very determined. I suspect he has more money than he pretends. Wasn't he a city type till recently? 'Were your family always keen farmers?'

'My grandfather bought the land after the war. He and Dad were keen and even owned a second farm by the river.'

'What's happened to that?'

'Grandad died in 75. Dad took over. It was after Mum died in 2010, something happened to Dad's interest. He sold most of the fields. There's still a house and a few acres in the family but it's up for sale. Not that it'll fetch much. Arable land is dirt cheap.'

We round a corner. I'm not expecting the sight before me. A herd of different sheep are grazing on the remains of grass and some straw Finn must have put down. They look up expectantly when they hear our voices. 'They're amazing,' I exclaim and lift my camera. 'This will make a fabulous shot with them all clustered together.' I click away. 'What are they?'

'The ones with tight curly fleece are Merinos.'

'Like the wool?'

'Yep. The ones with the dreadlocks are Lincolns and the brown and white ones like teddy bears are Southdowns.'

'What about those with the weird horns?'

'They're Rambouillets, French Merinos. I hope we can get the fleeces worked by local spinners. In fact, at the back of the house there will be a series of workshops, available to rent by local craftspeople, and that includes spinners.'

'Can I get closer?' I'm not used to being so close to animals. Wildlife is much more distant.

'Yes. Don't worry if they nuzzle. They're hoping you've got some food.'

I clamber over the gate and take a step closer. The sheep are as interested in me as I am in them. I'm giggling, laughing, and talking to them in a stream of what I hope is sheep friendly language. I know Finn is leaning on the gate watching me. I take a few close ups of sheep faces and walk back. A punch to the back of the legs makes me fall forwards. I land on my knees, hands down in what can only be described as sheep poo and mud.

'Sorry,' Finn says. 'Shoo. Off you go, you lot,' he shouts. He jumps over the gate and helps me to my feet, supporting an elbow and arm, not holding my messy hands. 'They seem to like you.'

'I think I'd better clean up before we do any more,' I say and hold up my mud encrusted hands.

Finn takes my camera from my neck and opens the gate so I don't have to climb over.

'Gyp, over here, keep them in.' The dog crouches down as the sheep nose forwards. They have spotted the escape. Gyp stands and presses his nose close to the ground. He stalks the sheep and they back away.

'Clever dog,' I say.

''One of the best. I'd like to keep a couple to show the children how clever they can be. Would they like that?'

'Little ones, yes. But I reckon even some of my toughest, street wise lads would enjoy getting close. It would be a great art project.'

Finn leads the way to the back door of the house. 'This is the dog's bathroom,' he says as we enter a stone flagged room with a large wet area and a white ceramic butler's sink. Hanging from hooks around the walls are leads, collars and some blankets. A soap dish with a white towel is set on the draining board by the sink. 'You can clean up here and we can have a coffee and look at what we've got so far. The toilet is through the green door and I'll be in the lounge, that's along the passage there.'

I wash my hands and dry them before removing my boots and tiptoeing along the passage way. It is an old house. White washed walls are interspersed with black stained beams. Apart from the absence of horse brasses and prints of country scenes, I could be in a country pub. I walk through into what must be the lounge. A corner sofa dominates the room and curls round a low wooden table. A faded oriental style rug covers most of the floor. The rest is floorboard, proper boards, not fake veneers. Along one wall is a fireplace, like the ones you see in Tudor mansions. A log burner sits snugly inside. Light comes in through diamond lattice windows. The curtains are rich ruby velvet. Three small tables dotted around the exterior walls each hold a velvet tasselled lamp and the same tasselled shades half cover candle shaped wall lights. A TV is on a console in one corner and a laptop is connected to it. A small grandfather clock, or should that be grandmother clock, stands in the opposite corner. Its gentle tick is the only sound. With the right touches, it could grace *Home Beautiful.* Finn looks up from where he is squatting, pouring coffee.

'Black, wasn't it?'

'Yes. Well remembered.'

He glances up as if my words surprise him. 'I make a point of remembering such things.' He holds out a china cup and saucer, white with pink rosebuds painted on the outside and a thin gold rim along the edge of the cup and saucer. It must be vintage. 'My mother's choice of crockery.' He lifts up a saucer and peers underneath. 'Yes. Royal Doulton from the 70s I believe. It was a wedding present.'

'That's impressive.'

He places a cup and saucer in front of me. The surface is golden brown with froth and steam wreathes the air. 'Not really. It was placed in the cupboard with an invisible sign. Do not use unless the vicar or the Queen come for tea.'

'Did they?' I giggle.

'The vicar turned up when my mother died. My father didn't have the heart to use it.'

'I'm sorry.'

Finn shrugs. 'I was a late arrival so it was probably inevitable they would not live past my formative years. My brother's older than me so I grew up like an only child.'

There is still so much I want to know. I am reluctant to ask more questions. This is not an interview and might seem intrusive. Instead, I look round the room. 'This is a lovely place.'

Finn sits back on the couch. It creaks, like good leather always does. 'It will be when the new kitchen is installed, the heating replaced and the extension at the back completed.'

'You've got plenty of plans,' I say and sip the coffee. It is rich and rounded. I wonder if he grinds the beans fresh.

'Yes. Plenty. That's why I want to get the staycation side of the business up and running ASAP.'

'If cute animals bring in the punters, I reckon you've got your first million lined up.'

'I wish. Let's see those photos and you may be helping me on the right track.'

I take my camera and sit closer. 'Check out these,' I say and show him how to scroll through the images. For a second my fingers touch his. I snatch my hand away. He doesn't notice. I sit as still as I can and try to make myself small. I am aware of his breathing, his smell, woodsmoke, hay and something else. It's a smell I could curl up and die in. 'Well?' A stupid thing to say but I want to break the silence and I'm scared he'll hate them all.

'Brilliant. I love this one.' He shows me the image of the teddy bear like sheep peering into the lens. 'Can we do the alpacas next and perhaps the barn I've already converted.'

I sigh with relief. He likes them. I'm not useless after all.

****

It's early evening when we finish. The first stars are appearing in the sky. The cloud has gone and there's a smell of frost in the air. I have uploaded a dozen images onto Finn's laptop. The alpacas are divas and refuse to behave until they have extra food. The hens strut around my feet, their fluffy legs flapping like loose trousers. I use the umbrella lights for the chicks in the barn. It brings out their yellow down against mother hen's speckled brown. The goats are too inquisitive by far and Finn has to rescue me as one decides it wants to take a chunk out of my sweater. The converted barn is perfect; modern, airy and light with a safe place for children to play and outdoor seats for a family barbecue. The white and chrome bathroom and kitchen fit perfectly and the glass enclosed staircase creates a sense of endless space. If this is Finn's doing, he has talent.

I am stowing my gear in the back of the car. An owl hoots in the distant trees and a fox barks. It would be a good night for a hunt, if I had the courage. I shiver at the thought.

'Cold?' Finn asks. He is standing in a blaze of light from the open kitchen.

'No. Probably hungry.'

Finn slaps his hands together. 'Perfect. How about I phone for a curry and we share a pappadum or two. I think it's the least I can do.' He pauses. 'Unless you've got a prior engagement.'

I am about to refuse when I stop. 'No. Nothing planned except a ready meal and a glass of Shiraz.'

'I can run to a Cabernet Sauvignon or a beer? Goes well with curry?'

As he stands there, I feel a strange sensation running through me. Jesus, I've got fanny flutters. Yes. Nice as Jake is, I can't imagine him kissing me. I can't stop imagining what it would be like when Finn kisses me. I stop. What have I just thought? When, not if? 'Beer would be great,' I say and lock the car. I walk towards him. He is still smiling. I smile back. And if I don't get home tonight, what does it matter?

I stand by the wood burner, letting the warmth seep into my bones. In the kitchen I hear the sounds of a fridge opening and closing, the chink of glasses and the clatter as a bottle top is removed. Why can I hear everything so clearly, or am I super sensitive today?

Finn walks into the kitchen with two glasses of golden liquid. 'Buddings,' he says. 'Local, organic and ethical. That's how I want people to think of this place,' he says and wafts an arm round the room. ''The staycations I mean.'

I take a glass and together we move towards the sofa. I sit down and curl my legs underneath me, anything to quieten the pulse racing through my body and landing at my sex. 'I reckon you'll be close unless you want to take the whole eco thing further.'

Finn takes a sip of his beer and wipes away the small moustache of froth with the back of his hand. The low lights in the room are reflected in the glass. 'Such as?'

'Heat pumps, solar power, all that stuff and a display case to show how much electricity you are producing. When the punters arrive, there is a hamper full of local produce, the fridge is stocked with organic butter, cheese and milk and you use recyclable and earth friendly cleaning materials. Things like that.'

'Finn frowns for a second. 'You can get all this?'

'Yep. Try the Valleys project. They even have eco-friendly rubber gloves and what about that loo paper called Who Gives a Crap?'

For a moment there is silence. Finn raises one eyebrow. 'You're kidding?'

'No. Seriously. If you want it eco-friendly, someone somewhere will provide it for you.'

Finn nods. 'I like that idea.' He looks at me again over the glass and I want to go across and kiss him.

Chapter 20

Images of ships full of people, diving overboard, swimming out to a small island. The water level is rising. The grey-green, foam-flecked ocean changes to muddy brown, duck-weed covered rivers. Brick sides. Straight. Narrow. Bridges swing to and fro. Water rushes along and sweeps him off his feet. He's drowning. Cassie throws him a lifebuoy. Except it isn't Cassie. It's Ginny. But it isn't Ginny. It's that girl. Blood pours from her head. She's calling him. He can't make out what she's saying. A calendar with the full moon dates circled in red floats on top of the water as a small boat, people clinging to every free space, hanging from the sides, is coming closer. He can't get away. He kicks his legs, thrashes his arms around. He doesn't move. The cruiser is getting closer. Frightened eyes stare at him. He has to get out of the way.

****

Mark sits up in bed. Sweat beads his brow and upper lip. Not Covid, please? No. It's him. He's panting as if he's run after the twins. He rubs the back of a hand across his brow. The images fade. Except for one; the calendar and the dates of the full moon. That must mean something. He leans against the pillows. The room is bathed in the pearly grey light of predawn. His uniform is hanging, like a bat, from a coat hanger on the outside of the wardrobe. He can make out the pots and the jar of brushes on the small table Ginny uses for her makeup. Rain spatters on the window. What the hell is the time? Six-thirty? He closes his eyes.

It is no use. Sleep eludes him. He has to get up and check out what he has found out about full moons and tides. He glances at Ginny's sleeping form. He listens. No sound from the twins. He stretches. It's Saturday and no work for once. Not even a hint of overtime. He has the whole day ahead free. He slips the covers off and tiptoes to the door. He'll pop downstairs, check a few websites, make coffee and be back before Ginny wakes up.

He ignores the dressing gown Ginny's mother bought him last Christmas and pulls on an old sweatshirt over his t-shirt and jogging bottoms. He could never understand the expense of night clothes. It is another thing he and Ginny disagree on. She likes the children to have pyjamas themed with their bedroom. God knows how much it all costs.

Stopping outside first Andrew and then Emily's bedroom to check if they are still asleep reassures him. He'll have a few minutes to himself. In the kitchen, he pulls up the blinds. A greasy-grey, autumnal sky threatens rain all day. At least that might keep the joy riders away from the countryside. Too many people had got into the habit of popping out after lockdown ended and they couldn't go away. The countryside was their solution. The mess they left, not to mention the carved-up tracks in the woods and the crops battered by quad bikes meant extra work as the public complained. Each call had to be investigated for links to County Lines. Strange bike riders flagged concerns.

With the kettle on, he flips open his work laptop. Ignoring the emails, he types *full moon over the past six months.* He notes down the dates and opens the file he's created of dates and times of unusual activity reported by the public. The list is similar; not perfect. On one occasion the dates coincide. Most times it's a day or two out. Why?

He types a query; highest tide times over the past six months? A series of websites appear which seem to have the data he needs. He clicks on the first. Another list appears with information covering the next three months until Christmas. A tab at the top of the web page intrigues him. *Best tides over the past six months.* Another click and the screen fills with photos of board riders on the water. Some are in the daytime. Others are taken in dusk or at night. There is darkness apart from lights shining on the water from small head torches. The dates are close to sightings. There is also a list of places you can start and finish so someone could wait for you or pick you up and drop you off. Could any of these crazy individuals have seen something? A small launch is in the background of one of the pictures at night. That would be a good excuse. "We're back up." He could hear the justification. "We're making sure no one has an accident or gets into trouble. It happens." Accompanied with the shrug of the shoulders that shows the owner is merely being a good citizen for friends and family, no one would check, would they?

The laptop snaps shut. There's plenty more to investigate later. He's about to make the coffee when the door clicks open. 'Dad, can we play in the park today?' Emily climbs on his knee. 'You said you'd take us once the endemic was over.'

'It isn't over and yes, I will. Cattle Country suit you better if I can get tickets?'

'Cattle Country? Ace.'

He'll take the kids and Ginny. They'll have a day out. A proper day out. If they take a detour on the way back, he might just pass by some of the places mentioned. The chance of spotting a bore rider was slim but it would be good to identify these areas. Perhaps it would give him a clue as to possible drop off areas for other reasons.

'Be good, go back to your room till seven o'clock so I can treat your mum to coffee in bed. She deserves it.'

****

By midday the children are beside themselves with excitement. 'Can we stay the whole afternoon?'

'Not quite. Our slot is from two o'clock till three.'

Emily pulls a face as she clambers into the back of the car.

'No sulking.' Ginny frowns. She hates any signs of ingratitude.

She reminds me of my grandmother when I turned up my nose at meal times. "Think of all the starving children," she would say. It didn't make a lot of difference. I still hated liver and onions. Liver? Does anyone eat that nowadays? That would be a good theme for a bit of nostalgia. A real story poem, like a stream of consciousness.

'Dad? Dad?' A voice squeals in my ear.

'What?' Mark jumps.

'Your father is miles away, as usual,' Ginny says. There's a smile on her face. She touches his arm. 'Either a poem or a case? Which is it?'

'Neither,' Mark says and starts up the car.

'Liar.'

'Liar, liar, pants on fire.' Andrew claps his hands.

Mark ignores the words. 'Let's go. Cattle County here we come, but not before we have fish and chips and eat it on the harbour by the canal. It's a bit further on from Cattle Country and you will have digested it before you swing yourselves upside down or scare your mother and me half to death on the zip wire.'

The drive is suspiciously quiet. Usually the cries of 'Are we there yet?' and the moans that their precious tablets or games have been left behind drown out any music or the satnav. Mark doesn't need the satnav. He drives to the centre of Blake Point and stops near the fish and chip shop.

'What are we all having?'

'Burgers and one portion of chips for the kids and we can share a portion of fish and chips,' Ginny says. 'You know they always give us far too much.' She hates waste.

Mark climbs out of the car. A thin drizzle coats everything in a chilly mist. The sky is grey and the water in the harbour is as welcoming as a cold bath. A couple of kayaks bob around. Their bright orange colour and the vivid yellow of the helmets is the only relief amongst the grey, brown and sage green. Why does damp weather strip the world of colour? Mark waves to the woman serving. She holds up three fingers and mouths, 'Give me a couple of minutes.' The sign outside says one person only allowed in at a time and there is an elderly gentleman, resting both hands on a stick, waiting in front of the cabinet of hot food.

Mark glances back at Ginny. How does she manage to be so organised? There are plates, sheets of paper towels and bottles of ketchup and brown sauce balanced on the dashboard. She gives him the thumbs up sign. He waves back and points to his watch, holding up three fingers. She turns to say something to the children. He's a lucky man.

A bell clangs and the old gentleman opens the door. Mark jumps forward to hold it back.

'Much obliged,' he mutters before setting off down the street.

Mark steps into the warm, fetid air of the shop. The sweet smell of fried food mingles with the acid tingle of vinegar and the homely smell of the white paper. Didn't it use to be newsprint?

Mark reels off his order. 'Won't be two ticks while I warm up the buns,' she says and slaps two white burger buns on the griddle. Her white coat and jaunty Homburg style hat remind him of seaside trips as a kid.

'How's business?'

'Good,' the woman says. 'The lockdown meant as soon as the weather changed the trippers turned up in droves. Never had so many boats stop and buy food. Some days I was making twice what I usually do at the height of a normal season.'

Mark's antennae for anything unusual spring into action. 'All regulars?'

'Some. New people too and those that I like to call my new regulars. They come up on a good tide, moor up and set off upstream when it gets dark. Fishing, see?' There is a Welsh lilt to her voice Mark hadn't noticed before.

'I suppose they do the same on the way back?'

She shovels chips into two paper bags. There are enough to feed a family of ten, not four. 'No. I reckon they hole up somewhere and come back early the next day when I'm in my bed. Good money though. Sometimes I get orders for a dozen or more. Don't see how they can all fish crammed together on these small craft.' She removes the buns and adds the burgers, a slice of onion, lettuce, and tomato.

Mark has to ask one more question. 'I don't suppose you've noticed anything weird lately? Extra trips? Unusual goings on?'

The woman stops and tilts her head, eyeing him from under the brim of the hat. 'I knew when you came in you had an official look.'

'Just interested,' Mark says. He holds out his debit card.

'Interested my Aunt Fanny.' The woman taps at the card machine. There is a satisfying ping as it registers and the paper chugs out.

'Sorry. Just me being nosey.'

The woman holds out a plastic bag of food. 'You won't be the first or the last. Just mind who you ask. People round here have got their funny little ways. Enjoy the food.'

The conversation is over. Mark nods his thanks. He is deep in thought when he gets back to the car. 'Food's up, kids. Pity we must eat in here. There's a nice little seat over by the canal. We could have sat there, fed a few ducks.'

'Perhaps another time?' Ginny is smiling at him.

She must be pleased with his new post. Detective sounds better than policeman. Well, it does to Ginny's friends and family. Perhaps he'll be in their good books for once. It would be a change.

Cattle Country is the perfect antidote to a week spent in school for the kids. For him and Ginny it's time to enjoy watching as the twins climb, swing, slide and bounce as if they had been let out of prison. He and his mates had been the same. Give them a tree to climb or a place they could make a den and they'd be happy for hours. He and Ginny find a seat at a safe distance from the other families. All they need do is wave occasionally and promise to "Watch me" as Emily, Andrew or both climb higher or swing faster than they had done before. Ginny applauds as Mark winces, fearing broken bones, cracked skulls, possible disability, or death as the minutes tick past. How come he's the worrier? Ginny grew up in a large, boisterous family. Mark was an only and longed for child. Cosseted? Possibly.

He glazes his eyes so he cannot focus as Emily hangs upside down from a plastic bar and thinks about what he's detected so far. The harbour and the canal hold some clues. Someone knows more than they are letting on. Who should he question first? Cassie got on well with the old fellow on the canal boat. He'd enjoy another crack at the harbour master. Perhaps ask to see some logs of the boats passing through on the days there were sightings.

'I said I am pleased about the new job.' Ginny punches his arm.

'Sorry?'

'What is it this time? Money? Our children's future? How we're going to help Emily? It can't be a rhyming couplet that refuses to scan, you'd have a pen and paper out.'

'Sorry. I was miles away.'

She turns to face him. Her dark eyes flash. 'For once, can't we just be a family?'

Mark puts his arm round her and kisses the tip of her nose. 'Sorry. Again.'

She shrugs him away. 'Sorry is a word. Try *being* sorry for once and doing something different. Promise me, no emails, no phone calls, no working out scenarios, going through clues, thinking up what questions you can ask which person next?'

'I promise.'

Ginny sits back. 'Good. I've always said if there's an emergency, a crisis, a horrible murder, a riot, you must go and do what you're trained to do. I understand. The rest of the time, once work is over, I want you here, with me and our children, physically and mentally. Right?'

Mark shakes his head. 'You know me so well.' He holds up one hand. 'I promise. Scouts honour.'

'You were never a scout.'

'I was in the Beavers. That does count.'

Ginny leans her head on his shoulder. 'Thank you,' she says.

There is silence between them. It is a good silence. Warm, accepting and understanding. Mark watches Andrew at the top of the slide. It's not a slide. It's a sheer drop, isn't it? He closes his eyes. What exactly does he want to find out from the harbour master?

At eight o'clock that evening, two very tired children are asleep before Mark finishes the chapter. They'll have to wait and find out what happens to Mr Fox. He carries Emily to her bed, covers her and switches off the light. 'Good night, precious,' he whispers as he closes the door. He returns to tuck Andrew's sheet under him and straighten the Superman duvet. One hand clutches Ted Bear, in his very own Superman outfit. Funny how his children can appear so grown up one moment and like babies the next. He removes a thumb from Andrew's mouth. 'Good night, sleep tight, hope the bed bugs don't bite.'

He knows Andrew can't hear him. It doesn't matter. It's their secret joke. He leaves his door slightly ajar and goes down the stairs. Ginny is in the lounge and watching *Strictly Come Dancing*. He flops onto the seat beside her. 'Anyone interesting?'

She switches off the sound. 'Same old, same old,' she says. 'Can you find a decent film?' She hands him the remote and he accesses a streaming service.

'How about a gory crime?'

'Busman's holiday?' She raises one eyebrow at him.

'No rom-coms, no murder or torture or horror… reckon we might need to watch James Bond again.'

Ginny leans closer to him. 'James Bond it is. Oh, by the way, Mum's coming over tomorrow and she's bringing her new man for lunch.'

'Is that allowed?'

Ginny shrugs. 'I have no idea. I've lost track of all this stuff. Besides, no one is going to mind a small family Sunday lunch.'

Mark closes his eyes. He'd wanted some free time to spend on his poetry. All he needed was one hour. He could understand why men used to have a shed and his grandad kept pigeons when he lived in Bradford. Perhaps he could talk about that to Ginny. She complains she needs space. Well, if he babysits while she goes out with her girls or has a spa day, he can have a shed for his home office.

In bed that night, Mark goes over in his head all he knows so far. What are the links between the tides, the full moons and the sightings? Do any boats make the journey regularly and if so, who owns them? He'll talk to Cassie on Monday and mention what he found out to the boss. It might mean he'll have to make another trip to the harbour.

He turns over and close his eyes. A rhyming pattern, like one of Emily's skipping rhymes when she and her friends got the skipping bug and he and Ginny had spent a weekend turning a rope with the other end tied to the kitchen door handle. That would fit Cattle Country. What can he call it? It has to be nostalgic, reminding the reader of his or her own childhood games as they watch their own children, repeated through the years past and to come.

Chapter 21

There is a ring at the doorbell. Finn raises his eyebrows; 'Food is served.'

'I'll get some plates, shall I?' I call to his departing back.

'Please.'

I scramble to my feet and open the latched door to the kitchen. A steely grey light shows through the latticed windows in front of a deep earthen sink. 'Plates,' I mutter and open a few cupboards. That's the thing about a different kitchen. People have their own preferences. It's good to see Finn is a normal human being-packets of porridge and cornflakes jostle between pots of marmalade and marmite. I like a man who likes food but I don't think I could cope with someone too fussy.

I check below the sink. Yes. As I thought, cleaning materials. I gaze at the remainder of the stone-coloured units. They must be hand made. The handles are tempered steel, made to look old fashioned. It isn't a new kitchen; none of the fancy self-closing units and boiling water taps, but it is expensive and the black marble work surfaces have lost their sheen. Probably needs a good clean.

'Third unit from the sink for plates and cutlery to your right,' a voice calls from behind me. Finn places a brown paper carrier bag on the counter. A greasy mark colours one corner. The smell is wonderful.

I find two plates and cutlery for us both. The plates must be second best as they are heavier than the bone china. They look sturdy with black and gold rims. I reckon they still cost a bomb. The cutlery is from a distant era. A time of fish knives and forks, sugar tongs and pastry servers. The handles are richly embossed and heavy in my hand. Finn unloads the food. 'Does it need a bit of reheating?'

'Good idea. Poor guy got lost. We can have the pappadums and a beer first. It'll be like a proper restaurant.'

Finn finds a metal tray and places the containers on it, switches on the range style oven and pops the tray in the top. I feel redundant. 'Shall I pour the beer?'

'Glasses top right next to the fridge, beer in the fridge and the opener is under the counter top.'

I do as I'm told. I like feeling useful. I pour the beers slowly, titling the glass to one side. The head is perfect for a lager. Mum and Dad taught me well.

'You're a pro,' Finn says.

'My parents took advantage of the last financial crash to accept redundancy, sold up and have a bar in Spain. I used to help out during the holidays.'

'Not much of a holiday,' Finn says and places a pile of golden yellow pappadums on a white plate.

'I'm not one for lazing around. I'd rather explore a new place so I ignored the beach, took myself off walking for an hour or two inland every morning and arrived back in time to open up for the first pre-lunch drinkers of the day.'

'I think I'd be joining you,' Finn says. 'Right, you take the beers and I've got these.'

I kneel by the low table and put the beers on two glass coasters. They must be hand made. The glass is a mix of red, blue and purple swirls. Finn puts down the plate, adds another log onto the burner and sits opposite me. 'Cheers,' I say and lift up the glass.

'Cheers.' He offers me the pappadums and I break off a piece. 'Oh, forgetting my manners.' He leaps up and dives into the kitchen. I hear cupboards and a drawer opening and closing.

He reappears with two small plates, spoons and some kitchen towel.

'You think of everything,' I say.

Finn pauses. 'I'm not fussy but I don't like making do when with a bit of effort, things can be made a lot better.'

'I know what you mean,' I say. 'Why accept second best?'

'Exactly. Now unless you want to be left with second best bits of pappadum, dive in. I'm starving and won't be held responsible if I scoff the lot.'

'Scoff? I love that word. I haven't heard it since I was a kid.'

'Too many days spent reading comics I'm afraid. *Dennis the Menace, Minnie the Minx, The Bash Street Kids*…they all liked a good feed and they always scoffed the lot.'

Usually eating with someone new is embarrassing. Yes. We'd had a meal together last week, but eating in a restaurant is one thing and eating on a sofa, reaching forward to scoop up lime pickle and cucumber raita and transfer it to a plate without dropping it everywhere is something else altogether. This time with Finn, it is wonderful.

We've finished the food, stacked the dishwasher like an old married couple and are sitting in front of the wood burner. Gyp is snoring on the rug by Finn's feet. Ed Sheeran is playing through a laptop connected to some vintage style speakers. Outside the sky has cleared and the moon is shining through the window. For a moment, it feels like Christmas. I half expect snow to fall and carol singers to appear on the doorstep except singing isn't allowed, is it? I make a move. 'Thanks for a wonderful meal and some great company.'

'My pleasure. Those photos will make all the difference to the website. I can't thank you enough.' Finn eases the dog from off his feet and stands up.

I stand too. We remain where we are in an embarrassed silence. 'We must do this again,' I say. Why am I being so coy? I sound like a poor version of Jane Austen. Any minute I'll be having a touch of the vapours and moaning… Ooh Mr. Darcy.

'We will,' says Finn.

I'm pleased. 'I'll collect up my bags.'

For the next minute or two, we both busy ourselves. Finally, I am standing by Finn's front door. He shifts from one foot to the other. 'You know, there's an old saying, "It's an ill wind that blows nobody any good."'

'My gran used to say that to me.'

'It might sound awful but if that bloke hadn't hit you, we'd never have met, would we?'

I stop. 'How did you know it was a man?'

'It always is a man… when a woman gets attacked, I mean.'

'"The police aren't certain,' I say although I'm inclined to agree with Finn. That was not a woman's voice or a woman's shape.

'And you really have no idea?'

'No. None. Thanks again for the meal.' I stretch up and kiss him on the cheek. It could be friendly. I don't want it to be.

Finn places his hands on my shoulder and kisses me lightly on the lips. 'Good night,' he says.

I walk towards my car. He is standing in the light from the doorway. I open the boot and stow my gear away. I am about to get in when I stop. Hell, I'm a big girl, now. I can do what I want.

I lock the car and walk back to Finn. This time when I kiss him on the lips, he and I both know it isn't friendship we want. The kiss lasts forever. When I pull away, I bury my face in his chest. I'm still shocked by what I want. 'I don't suppose I could stay the night?' He can refuse and I'll go home. Except I know he won't.

'As long as you really want this? I can stop at any time. All you have to do is say no. I won't be angry.'

I put my arms round his neck. 'I want to stay.'

'Jeez.' Finn rests his head on my shoulder. 'I honestly didn't have this in mind when I invited you over,' he says.

'I know,' I whisper in his ear. 'Neither of us are teenagers. We're old enough to know what we want and take responsibility.'

Finn takes my hand and within seconds we are in his bedroom. It smells masculine. There is no need for any more talk. Clothes come off. Finn peels back the bedclothes and I dive inside the sheets. I shiver and pull him closer. His body is rounded, softer than I'd have expected for a farmer. We stop the kissing for a few seconds. 'Are you sure?' he says again.

'Of course.'

It isn't mind blowing sex, like the kids see on the porn sites they frequent. It is the way it should be, each listening to the other until the moment takes over and we both rush to the end in a torrent of kisses to collapse, breathless and sated.

****

I turn over, open my eyes and blink. Where the hell am I? The memory of what happened floods back. I made the right decision. Except where is Finn? I sit up in bed and listen. There is no sound. My clothes are neatly arranged on a wicker chair. Looks like a Lloyd Loom. My gran used to rave about those. The clothes weren't that tidy last night. I seem to remember half of them were off before we got upstairs. My trousers are folded and my jumper hangs from the back of the chair. My knickers? I leap out. A bra, socks and my knickers are under the trousers. It's all so neat. I feel a slob. The bedroom is cool. I shiver. I know where I am but where is Finn?

There is a whistle. It comes from outside. I creep close to the window and peer out from behind the curtain. Gyp is bounding around Finn as he heaves a bale of straw into a barrow and trundles it towards the barn. Of course. He's a farmer. Animals don't have a snooze button. I check the time. Seven o'clock? Is that all? I'm tempted to snuggle back in bed and hope he comes to find me. Not very supportive, is it? Instead, I pull on my pants and sweater and go downstairs. It's warm from the wood burner last night. I'm going to surprise him with coffee and whatever I can find in the fridge.

I'm in the middle of cracking eggs when I hear a voice outside the window. It's Finn's. I check. His back is towards me. He must be on the phone. Of course, I strain my ears to listen. So far everything has been too good to be true. I half expect a wife and six kids to turn up unannounced and we're done.

'No. I've told you. Nothing.'

There's a pause.

'Certain. Yes. I am sure. Now I'm keeping my side of the bargain, make sure you do too.'

He takes the phone away from his face and stares at the screen. He whistles to Gyp and heads off in the direction of the hens. I suppose they need letting out too.

I turn back to the counter and whisk the eggs. I empty the dishwasher and set two places at the counter. Bread is waiting to be toasted. A pot of local marmalade stands on a plate with a long-handled spoon I found in the cutlery drawer. If it was me at home, it'd be a knife. For some reason I want to make a good impression. With the kettle ready to boil and orange juice in two glasses, it looks presentable enough. I am about to open the back door and call when it opens.

'Heh, what's all this?' Finn is dressed as I'd imagine a farmer; muddy trousers, a battered waxed jacket and Hunters which he pulls off and leaves in the entrance.

'A little treat after last night,' I say and go across to him.

He puts his arms around me and I nestle against the cold of the jacket. 'That was a fabulous evening,' he says.

'I'm about to make some breakfast. I thought you'd be hungry.' Much as I'd like him to kiss me, I know where I want it to end and he's already probably done a morning's work.

He kisses me. I feel my insides melt. I'm like a teenager again. He breaks away. 'Perfect. I'll need to wash my hands. Animal fodder isn't a very pleasant hand lotion.' He grins and steps away. For a moment I wonder where his phone is. Still, probably in one of the interminable pockets these guys like to have.

By the time he gets back the toast is brown, the eggs are light and fluffy and the coffee pot is full. I sit at the counter top and indicate a second seat. 'Breakfast is served.'

'How did you know where I was?' Finn says and selects two pieces of toast which he butters thickly.

'For a moment I thought you'd done a runner except guys don't usually run from their own homes. Of course, I realised the animals needed looking after.'

'Correct. You'll make a farmer's wife yet.'

I am embarrassed. There is a whimpering at my feet. 'Sorry. Your master will get his food first,' I say. I glance at Finn. 'Dog food in the cloakroom?'

'Yes. Dry mix, two scoops and don't let him convince you he's starving and has never eaten before.'

Gyp follows me. He waits till I have placed the bowl on the floor before he lunges. There's a happy sound of chewing and slurping. If only everyone was as easy to please.

I return to the kitchen. I can't stop smiling. 'One happy pooch,' I say.

'Thank you.'

There is no more need for words. We eat, tidy away and are back in bed. It's late afternoon before I realise I have stuff to do before school starts. As Finn shows me to my car, I know this is special. I drive away. For the first time in years, I think I'm falling in love.

Chapter 22

Cassie is already at her desk when Mark arrives. 'Good weekend?' she says and looks up from the keyboard.

'Same old same old,' he says. 'It was good to get away from this.' He nods towards the notice board where a list of incidents worthy of interest has been scrawled in green marker pen.

'I reckon it was easier in full lockdown. No one went anywhere,' Cassie says.

Mark doesn't contradict her. Except he prefers a car theft or a shop break in to the domestics when he realised he and Ginny live a charmed life compared to many. 'What about you?'

'Yes. No.' She forces a smile before her face crumples into tears. 'Sorry.' She rummages in her bag for a ragged tissue.

Mark makes a mental note to ask the boss if they can't be provided with boxes of tissues. They need them. 'No need to apologise. Let me get you a coffee. I reckon you could do with one.'

By the time Mark returns with a flat white and a skinny latte for Cassie, she is more composed. He slides into the desk a metre from hers and leans forward. 'You don't have to say anything.' He stops. 'Sorry, force of habit.'

Cassie takes the drink and cradles it between both hands. Yes, the office is filling up around them. For some unknown reason, they are left alone. Do all police have a sixth sense when people need to be left alone? There is a clatter as a blind is drawn to close out the bright sunshine. The room dims. There is the low hum of chatter, the occasional scrape of a chair and much tapping. Unless something big takes place, this is the pattern.

'We had a row. Big one.' Cassie looks at him from under her perfectly arched eyebrows. Her uniform is always immaculate and somehow she manages to keep her nails long and shiny. One finger runs along her lip. 'It was silly, really.'

Mark nods. Let them speak in their own time. Allow stillness and silence to fill the space.

'Laura, that's my wife and me… well we want a family…'

So that's why her name has never been linked to any randy young buck. How come he didn't know? Did anyone? Cassie is always reluctant to tell people what goes on in her life. He'd thought it was shyness. 'Plenty of time. You're young. Ginny was thirty when the twins were born.'

She looks at him and lowers her voice. Not that it is needed. The noise level has increased and he's finding it difficult to hear. He tilts his head. 'That's the trouble. Laura is older than me. She's thirty-eight. Time is not on her side.'

'Ahh.'

'I'm not sure I'm ready. I've just started this job and it's great. I want to give it my all for a few years before…'

Mark feels a sense of déjà vu. Is this commonplace today? His grandparents didn't have the choice. You want sex, you're likely to create a new life. Now there are choices. 'If it's any use, I felt the same but when the twins came along, bingo. It felt right.'

'Laura is threatening to leave and I don't want to worry her family or our friends.'

There is no time for any more conversation. DCI Eve Fletcher strides into the main room. Everyone goes quiet.

'Right, everyone, there have been developments over the weekend. A witness has come forward.' The atmosphere between them is shattered as the boss plonks her bum on the desk by the board. 'It means we may have a lead on the people smuggling racket. Mark, Cassie, I want you to head down to Blake Point and check out the stories of what the locals were up to on the night of the attack on Rachel Thomas.'

'Any heads up on the new witness?' a voice calls.

'Yep. A surfer, or a bore rider as they call themselves, came forward to snitch on what he thought was an illegal party. Reckons he's seen a craft acting suspiciously when he was doing a late evening ride and the serious riders don't like anyone getting in their way.'

'Tosser.'

'Exactly.' Eve's tone of voice says it all. 'It seems they will surf at all hours of the day and night and expect the rescue services to be there when they fall in.'

'At least it might give us a lead,' Mark says.

Eve nods towards the *tosser* speaker. It's Todd. Mark remembers him now from the summer. 'Since you have such a low opinion of our surfer friends, you can go along to their open evening tonight. Take your cossie.' She gets off the table. 'Right. Back to it, people. Mark, can I have a word?'

It sounds like a question. It is not. Mark follows into her office. Eve has a copy of his job application in her hand. 'It's good, Mark. We should hear later this month. Till then, stick with the uniform and you are answering to me, right?'

'Thanks, ma'am.' He feels a surge of pride. Ginny's mum and sister should hear this too. Somehow throughout Sunday lunch they had managed to make him feel as if he wasn't quite good enough. Reminded him too much of school reports day.

'Good work, so far,' she says and turns away to the window to gaze into space.

Mark re-joins Cassie. 'Off to the seaside,' he says. 'You can take the old fella on the barge and check out the chip shop owner.'

'Does that mean we get a free sample?' All tears have gone. Cassie's eyes sparkle with the prospect of an investigation. Mark knows that feeling; which questions will release a torrent of information and which will make the recipient squirm and give something away?

'Don't bet on it.'

The moment for intimate life conversations has gone, yet on the drive to the harbour Cassie is quiet and Mark can see her biting her lip from time to time as she stares at the autumnal scenery. On one side of the motorway the hills are stained yellow, brown and russet. On the flat, fields of sheep graze between specimen oaks, towering above the dry-stone walls. Farmhouses and outbuildings in grey and white stone with black Dutch barns stuffed full of bales and rounds of black plastic covered hay are dotted in the landscape. On the other side, towards the river, the land is flatter. Stubbled fields where pheasants in their red and black finery strut are waiting for the plough. Wherever hordes of gulls flap and rise up before swooping to land again, that's where the plough will be.

Mark has already rehearsed the questions he wants to ask. He needs to check Cassie is doing the same. 'Got your questions ready for the old boy?'

'What? Sorry. Miles away.' Cassie turns her attention to the interior of the car. Mark would bet a dime to a dollar it's a wrench.

'Questions? Different tactics with different people?' He speaks slowly. Cassie stirs. She stretches her slim legs. Dancer's legs? Or runner's? He must ask. Or would that be creepy? 'I want to know more about the old boy in the canal boat. How long has he been there? Why there of all places? Who does he know? What has he seen, recently or earlier?'

'And the chip shop owner? Tell me more about her,' Cassie says.

'Good thinking. Don't waste time on questions when someone else has already got or might have the answers.' Mark signals and turns the car to the left. The roads are quieter but rural so he has to divide his attention between his answers and the road. 'She was cagey. Recognised I was something official but didn't say what and I didn't tell her. When I said I was being nosey, she said, "You won't be the first or the last. Just mind who you ask. People round here have got their funny little ways."'

Cassie makes a sound like a second-rate horror movie. 'Da da Daaa.'

'Exactly. Was she bluffing, bigging herself up or is something else going on?'

'What's your hunch?'

'The latter. She seemed too down to earth for dreams of fame and fortune, or at least a few likes on social media.'

Cassie leans forward. 'Is this the place where you take the kids?'

Mark slows. An errant pheasant struts across the road. 'Yes. They love it.'

She sits back in her seat. 'What's it like, having kids?'

'You'll never know till you have them and no one else can ever explain what it will be like for you.' He's out of his depth. Ginny should be here. She'd know what to say. He changes the subject. 'Right, anything you plan to ask Mr Lewis Barnes, our canal boat occupier?'

'Specifics. He's told us he's seen and heard stuff. So when? I've got a list of the dates there have been sightings. I'm going to ask about those dates.'

'And you think he'll remember? He hardly strikes me as being a Filofax type.'

Cassie laughs. 'That dates you. It's all online calendars, phones with built in reminders, like we have at work.'

'Even so.' Mark knows they all laugh at his lack of technical awareness. So what?

'He's either a twitcher or a birder. Either way, I bet he knows when he saw a lesser spotted what's his name for the first or last time each year, and it's recorded somewhere. It might jog his memory.'

'How do you know about the bird watching?'

'The books on his shelves were all about birds. I recognised a couple of the names on the spines and there was a very tattered copy of *Collins Guide to British Birds*.'

Damn. He's missed something so simple. 'I'm impressed. You'll be a detective yet.'

'I've got a good teacher.'

'Aw shucks.' Mark puts on a fake and very bad American accent. 'Getting me all embarrassed.'

'I mean it,' Cassie says and is silent.

No more is said till the car pulls up on the outskirts of the harbour. Mark checks his watch. 'Where do you plan to go first?'

''Too early for the chippie to start serving, if they open at lunchtime, so I reckon we call on Lewis Barnes.'

'You do that, I'll make my way over to the harbour office and catch up with you later.'

As Cassie walks off along the tow path, Mark is certain the curtains of the house opposite the harbour twitch. Except no one does the old net curtain trick anymore, do they? If people want to find out what's going on they stare and aren't backward in letting you know they're watching. It could be Neighbourhood Watch. Except as soon as they saw a uniform car, they'd be out and asking questions of their own.

Mark strides past the road barrier and crosses the narrow quayside to the Harbour building. He's about to knock on the door when it opens. Has he been spotted? Or has the curtain twitcher informed him?

'Yes?' The voice is surly.

'I've got a few more questions I'd like to ask.'

'You'd better come in.' The door is opened slightly wider. The light does little to illuminate the dark interior. 'I've got nothing more to tell you.' Jason Bull clears some piles of paper from the chair opposite his desk and sits down in the scratched Captain's chair behind it. Does he feel safer barricaded like this? Or is the physical barrier an anchor to a mental one?

'I'll be the judge of that,' Mark says and instantly regrets it. The man riles him and he knows it and there he is smirking because he's got the upper hand.

''Records,' Mark says and regains some of his composure. He gets out his tablet and taps it awake, praying he's remembered to charge it properly.

Jason spreads out his arms. 'Plenty here. What do you want to see?'

'I know there are several big tides, bores each month, I want to have a look at the craft logged to travel up river around the time of the bore.'

Do Jason's eyes narrow? Or did the lips twitch, before flattening into a straight line? Whatever happened was a tiny micro-movement, lasting less than a second. Mark prides himself on spotting such things. They always indicate a change of internal state, linked to a feeling. Annoyance? Anxiety? Or could it possibly be guilt?

He presses on. 'Let's say for three days before and during?' He doesn't mention the full moons. But he knows the dates off by heart for the last six months.

'Suits me.' Jason swivels the screen towards Mark. He taps at several keys and a table appears. He uses the cursor to point to the top line of each column. 'Dates, times, name of craft, reason for journey, return date if within 48 hours, contact name and phone number.'

'Can you print this off for me?'

'Not sure. Data and all that.' Jason raises one eyebrow.

'Don't give me that data protection lark. This is official police business and that takes precedent.' He hopes he won't be challenged. He's never paid a lot of attention on the training courses. If he is going to turn detective, he'd better do some homework.

'If it comes back to bite you on the bum, don't blame me.' Jason hits a key and stands up. A printer in the next room whirs into life. Jason disappears and reappears a few minutes later with a pile of paper. 'All the information is here. I suppose I could do a cut and paste but…' Jason's voice trails away as he hands it over.

There must be fifty sheets. Mark glances through them. There are no page numbers and the printer has not marked the grid lines. This is going to be a long job. 'Perfect,' he lies, hoping Jason isn't as good as himself at picking up the hollow voice which often hints at something not quite genuine.

'Good to be of help to the police. I wish you could be here on bore rider day too.'

'Why is that?'

'Too many kids reckon they can turn up and it's like a flow rider. We have to provide back up all the way along the river.'

'What sort of back up?'

All suspicion has gone. Jason is warming to his task. He counts on his hand. 'First Aid on the banks at intervals, St John's usually, traffic marshals to keep cars away from the water's edge and this year, social distancing. It's a nightmare. Plus, we have a whole crew on standby following the wave in case anyone gets into difficulties.'

'Who pays for this? Not your outfit?'

Jason shakes his head. 'There are a lot of rich people out there who'll do anything if little Edwin or Edwina wants to have a go. Plus, some of the pro surfers have their own backup team. This sort of thing is good on their Instagram accounts. The pros follow all the procedures. The amateurs don't.'

'Are you saying that some of the people who turn up will not be on this list?'

'Probably half,' Jason says. The smirk reappears. 'Some pros will go out at night if there's a chance of a big swell.'

Mark taps the sheaf of papers. 'This is the best list you've got?'

Jason nods. 'Course over lockdown, we were all supposed to be at home. Most people obeyed.' He places a hand on his heart. 'There could be others that slipped through.'

Mark is being fobbed off. This is a blind alley. He'd bet a pound to a penny Jason knows every craft that went up and down more than once and probably has a list of those he only saw once. 'It must get difficult having to be out here at all times of the night and day. You must have to travel a fair bit?'

'No. I live over there.' He jerks his head towards a small development of two bedroomed cottages close to the harbour. 'Comes with the job,' he says and scratches his head. 'If you've finished, I need to get on. A shipment of barley is due to be unloaded today and I'll be zoning off the road for the lorries to arrive.'

'I'll be back if there's anything else I need,' Mark says.

'I thought you would. My door is always open.'

Except when it's shut. Mark stops by the door. 'You've been very helpful.' For a moment their eyes meet. Both know the other is playing a game and both know neither of them can prove it.

Jason moves first. He collects his Hi-Viz jacket from a hook on the back wall cupboard. 'Any time,' he says.

Mark retreats to his car. Cassie is not back yet. It'll give him time to look through the printout's blur of names, dates, times, and numbers. He'll need a ruler and a highlighter for this. He smiles. The smile transforms into a grin. This is what he loves most.

His phone rings. 'Cassie?'

'Can you come and join us, Mark? I think you should hear this from Mr Barnes, himself. I won't say anything else.'

'Be with you in five,' Mark says and places the papers in the glove compartment before climbing out of the car and locking the door. He's about to set off along the tow path when he spots Jason looking his way. For a moment Mark is tempted to wave. He doesn't. Jason is still watching him as he walks towards the canal boats. A lorry draws up at the harbour and Jason is obscured. The hiss of hydraulic brakes sounds through the still air. A red Renault curtain sider has turned up. The driver springs down, a clipboard in his hand. Wouldn't barley need to be transported in closed containers, like they did for flour? He shrugs and makes a mental note to find out more later.

Cassie and Lewis Barnes are seated at the small table along one side of the barge. The surface is covered with notebooks and bird books. Cassie was right. Lewis Barnes knows his birds. He is wearing brown overalls, liberally spattered with mud and grease stains. His nails are black. It looks like oil.

'Constable said you wanted to see me?' Mark sits down in a wooden chair. It creaks and wobbles. He makes a mental note to sit as still as possible and plants both feet on the floor. 'Do I need to take notes?' He glances at Cassie.

'I've taken them, but you might want to make your own.' She looks at him and bites her lip. She's nervous, poor kid.

'Sorry, Lewis.' Mark fishes his tablet from his pocket and opens it up. 'Carry on.'

'Yes. As soon as she mentioned lights and unexpected noises and unusual craft, I knew what she meant. There's a bit of a pattern. Before or around a full moon we usually get a load of surfers, waiting for the decent tide. During the day that is…'

'And at other times?' He looks across at Cassie. Where is this going?

'That's it. No one surfs at night along these stretches. Too dangerous. Except for a couple of pro riders and they start further up. The thing is, there's often a little boat, like a cabin cruiser, passing through.'

'Can you be more specific about dates?' Hadn't Jason said bore riders went out at night if there was a good swell?

Lewis slaps his hand on the table top. 'Certainly can. Geese,' he says.

'Geese?'

'Yes. Wild geese. Travelling south for the winter. Some of them stay on the mudflats or at the reserve along the coast.'

'I'm still not certain how…' Mark begins.

'I'm a birder, not a twitcher and I like my water birds… gulls, ducks, waders, and especially geese.'

''Go on.' Mark spots Cassie watching him.

Lewis opens a notebook. Loose pages flutter out. 'Now, where is it?' He flicks through the notebook again and prods a finger at a page. 'Here it is. The arrival of the first white-fronted geese… usually around early October. This year it was late September.' He displays the note made in perfect cursive handwriting and in an ink pen.

First white fronted geese. Ten. Afternoon 29 September, 2020. Approx 4.30pm. heading West.

'I was so pleased I stayed up late that night, checking through if this was a record and it was. Climate change? Eh?'

Mark nods. Lewis is in full flow. He'll let him carry on.

'Never before have they arrived so early. That was the night I heard and saw the cabin cruiser. It was about eleven, the swing bridge opened for it and it passed through. I stayed below deck and it chugged past. That was another thing.'

'Another thing?'

'Yes. It was struggling. As if the engine was stalling or it was heavily loaded.'

'Did you get a look at who was driving?' Mark says and corrects himself. 'I mean who was at the helm?'

'Skippering,' Lewis interrupts.

Mark holds up a hand in apology. 'Okay, skippering?'

Lewis shakes his head. 'I did get the name of the craft. *Lady Luck* she was called and she was low, either shipping water or over loaded. Like I said, some of these part-time fishermen pile up the insides with fancy seats, a bar…' Lewis' voice shows his contempt for such niceties.

'Anything else?'

'I mentioned it to Jason the next day. He said there was nothing to worry about. A bloke got delayed and should have gone through earlier in the day. I reckoned he was hiding something.'

Mark's mind is flicking over the possibilities. 'Could it have been a fisherman or a group of surfers?'

Lewis looks straight at Mark. 'The bore riders came two days after. They know exactly when the tide will be the best height. Fishermen usually have their tackle and bait piled up on the roof or along the side of the craft.'

Mark smiles and closes up the tablet. 'Lewis, you've been very helpful.'

'Any time. Now I'd better get back to working on the old engine myself,' he says as Mark and Cassie negotiate their way through the barge to the exit and scramble up the ladder.

'Trouble?' Mark stands in front of the engine.

'Not something I can't mend. Not that I'm going far but it's good to have it ready in case.'

'In case of what?' Mark's ears note the language.

Lewis shrugs. 'There are some people who'd like to get rid of me.' He indicates the other barges.

'Surely, they can't do that? You and all these other people live here.'

Lewis laughs. 'Most of those belong to weekend trippers or for holiday lets. They bring in more cash,' he says. He takes out an old spanner and wipes it on an oil-stained rag. 'Recreation brings in more money than old sea dogs like me.' He smiles at his own joke.

'How much more?'

'See that boat there… *Nancy Girl*?' He indicates a painted barge.

'Nice place.'

'A grand a week in high summer. My rent's only two grand a year. Stands to reason, get rid of my berth and you could put in two barges. You're looking at thirty grand a year minimum.'

'I see. Thanks for the information and good luck with the engine.'

'Oh, it'll keep me occupied for a while. She's got a few years left in her.'

****

Mark and Cassie walk back along the tow path. 'You did well,' he says.

'I never feel I know what to ask.' She sounds embarrassed. 'Sometimes I reckon I'm just winging it.'

'Aren't we all?' Mark says. 'Aren't we all?'

Chapter 23

'Well, what happened to you at the weekend?' Tashi leans closer. I edge away. If we don't stick to the rules, how can we expect the teenagers to conform?

'I don't know what you mean.' I huff and puff to prove my innocence.

She sees straight through the façade. 'You've met someone, are about to meet someone or have won the lottery, and as I know you never do the lottery, it must be one of the other reasons.' Tashi taps a finger, with a pearly pink and perfectly manicured nail, on the top of the desk where I'm trying to reconnect with Planet School. Why is it systems that worked perfectly on Friday have developed more bugs than the handles on a toilet door by Monday?

I wipe a stray wisp of hair behind my ears and look up at her. If I am ever half as well-groomed as Tashi I'll be eternally grateful. Her red suit and pale cream blouse suit her colouring. I wonder if a farmer's wife needs to be as well groomed. I stop the silly thoughts and drag myself back to the present. 'Yes, I had a wonderful weekend with Finn.'

'Oh.' Her lips purse slightly. 'Is that wise?'

'I've met him three times. It isn't as if I was out on a drunken pull at the local cattle market… sorry, club.'

'If he's a farmer as you say he'll know all about cattle markets.' There is a faint shiver across Tashi's shoulders. She does not approve.

'Actually, he is a farmer and I've been to his place. It's a bit run down but it is a farm.'

'He could still be a maniac hiding behind the veneer of the Young Farmers Club.'

'I don't think he's that young.' I realise we'd never mentioned our age. It didn't matter.

'Even worse, he could have a wife and ten kids, or two wives and twenty kids hidden away.'

I shake my head. 'There's no evidence of a secret life. His house, or rather the family home, is perfectly respectable with more photos of dogs and horses than people.'

'Ah ha. He's a social outcast,' Tashi says with a note of triumph.

'Now you're being silly.'

I know she wants to touch my arm, give me a reassuring hug. It is against the rules though. 'I'm worried,' she says.

'What about?'

'You?' A bell shrills in the corridor. We have very little time before the hordes descend and I still haven't got the IT system up and running. 'We're all worried about you. After the attack, we thought you'd need some time to adjust.'

I smile. 'Thanks, Tashi. If the truth is known, being with Finn is the best thing that's happened to me for years. It's the perfect medicine.'

'I shall still worry until we have all met him, checked his credentials and Mamaji has given her verdict.' She is teasing but I know she's also serious.

'I promise we'll have a drink or a coffee outside somewhere. I don't want to frighten the poor guy off.'

'Next week?'

Next week might be too soon for Tashi's scrutiny. I'm not sure how Finn would react. 'How about the week after?'

'Deal.' She claps her hands together as *concerned friend* is replaced by *stern teacher*. 'Year 9, queue up with social distancing, masks on and phones off,' she calls. The bustle and burble from the corridor stop.

'It will be fine,' I say and tap at the screen again. Why isn't this working?

'Oh, and IT are doing an upgrade. The system will reboot in ten minutes. You'll be fine then.'

She flounces away. I know she means well but I'm certain there is nothing to worry about with Finn. Although I must ask him how old he is. I reckon he's late thirties. He might have some baggage. My stomach knots. Please let him be Mr Ordinary.

'Okay Year 9, come in and go straight to the places I assigned you last week. Hand sanitiser is by the door.' I raise my voice above the general chatter. Tonight, I'll ask Finn a bit more about his past. His birthday would be a good starting point.

'Good weekend, Miss?' A question like that from a hormonal teenage boy needs no answer. Whatever I reply will be twisted. 'Today we will be revising the delights of the apostrophe. With your work partner, come up with a list of rules that would help a younger pupil understand. You have five minutes.' That will keep them quiet.

****

Why is that by the time break on a Monday morning arrives, I feel the weekend never existed. I am on duty in the hall. A queue of young people snakes around the interior and along the corridor. They'll be lucky to get served. 'Unless you are desperate for a drink or something to eat, please go outside and get some fresh air.' No one moves. Is it because I'm just a temporary teacher?

Jake, in navy suit and crisp white shirt, arrives at my elbow. I'd forgotten I was rostered on dinner duty with him. 'You heard what the teacher said, and I have it on authority that Reuben Collins, Zak Neeson and Stephen Connolly were here at breakfast club and ate the counter clean. Give the rest a chance.' There is the familiar sound of teenage grumbling, part whine and part groan. The queue shortens by four or five. The others glare and stay where they are.

'You make excellent backup. I need it,' I say.

'Yeah.' He rubs an ink-stained hand through his hair which springs back. 'That'll change when you are here permanently,' he says and claps a hand over his mouth. 'Sorry. There was some departmental gossip about new permanent posts and plenty of people reckoned you should be first in line.'

'I'm flattered I have made a good impression.' It's true. Staff room gossip is heavy on criticism and low on praise.

'My Y9 tutor group were devastated when you were off. They moaned all the time.'

'I bet they moaned when I came back and they had to catch up.'

Jake nodded and laughed. 'True.'

There is silence. Should I ask him if he had a good weekend? It seems intrusive. It's what everyone does though, isn't it? What if he asks me? I succumb to social pressure. 'Did you have a good weekend?'

'I wonder what a good weekend is now? There used to be a choice of things to do. Even if you didn't feel like doing anything, it felt good to have the choices.'

I nod. 'I'd love a gig or a play. There's something about a live event. I know you can buy these big screens and surround sound but even a cinema trip is special.'

'And you don't upset the neighbours.'

I laugh. Jake relaxes. 'That's another thing. Have you noticed how everyone has gone so quiet? It's as if we're frightened to make a sound in case we kill someone with our breath.'

'I reckon when this is all over, we'll find out that you have to be very close for a very long time to infect another.'

I feel my skin warm. I must be blushing. The thought of Finn and me did that. I hope Jake doesn't notice. He might think it's his presence. The bell rings. 'Time to get back,' I say. 'Double English with Year 8 followed by art A level.'

'How about a meal later this week? This time I'll cook. I think we're allowed to meet up.'

How do I refuse? I'd have to provide an excuse. Except it isn't as if we are an item. We're just two colleagues, aren't we? 'I'd like that.'

Jake's grin splits his face. What am I getting myself into? 'I'll text you,' he says and is overheard by a couple of girls I recognise from his tutor group and my English group.

'We heard that, sir,' the brunette says. Julie. That's her name. She's got potential if she applies herself. Too interested in romance and her ability to attract any male within five miles.

'Good, Julie, because Ms Thomas and I will soon be discussing potential grades and agreeing, I hope, that you could be straight As.'

I notice her face change from surly to amazement. Got her interested and it's true. 'Really?'

'Yes. Especially if you get the next pieces of homework in on time and can offer some of your ideas in class,' I say as I waft past. I hope I'm making a dignified exit. As I pass Jake I wink and he raises one eyebrow. We understand each other.

'Absolutely, Ms Thomas. The same could be said for Alicia and Tamsin. Don't waste these opportunities.'

We leave the girls. I am sure they'll be telling everyone what they saw and making us into an old couple before the evening is out. I hope Jake doesn't have the same idea.

The rest of the afternoon passes in a blur of my good humour, and I know why. It's Finn. Friendship is all right. Nothing is as electrifying as the prospect of a new relationship.

I am on the sofa surrounded by Y8's attempts at descriptive writing. As the text we are studying is *Dracula*, I am not surprised we have zombies, headless corpses, and more vampires than on a Halloween night of trick and treating. Most students like to focus on the blood and gore moments. Only a few identify the subtleties of a decent build up. I am engrossed in one of the latter when my phone rings. It's Finn. So he's old school and likes a chat, rather than a conversation in messages.

'Hi. How are you?' Am I sounding breathless?

'Good. I was on my way to the shops and wondered if you wanted anything? I can pop it over. Might save you some time.'

I check my watch. It's gone eight. 'You keep weird hours, don't you?'

The laugh from the other end of the phone melts my stomach. 'I prefer to shop when the animals are all settled. There's too much to do during the day and now it's getting darker, the hours of light are precious.'

'Sorry. I didn't think.'

'You weren't brought up a farmer's daughter. So, anything I can get?'

There's nothing I need except I don't want to say no. I want to see him. 'A bottle of wine and some company would suit me as I never drink alone midweek.' I'm lying. Why do I want to impress him?

'Red or white?'

'Red would be good. It's a cold night.'

'Red wine coming up. Where do you live?'

I tell him my address. 'You can park next to my car. There's space if you don't mind bumping over the kerb.'

'I'll be with you in twenty minutes,' Finn says and the phone goes dead.

Twenty minutes? I check round the flat. It's tidy enough and cleanish. I pile up Y8s books and place them on the table next to my bag. I smooth the throw over the sofa, plump up the cushions and find an old air freshener from the kitchen. A quick squirt will have to do. Toilet? Is it clean? I chuck some bleach down the loo and swish it round with the brush. It smells too strong. I flush. That's better. Clean towel? I can't have him using mine. I pull one from the airing cupboard. It's fairly new and soft. That will do. I've never been one of those people who drape drying pants over radiators so no embarrassment there.

I go back to my small lounge and switch off the main light. Instead, I use the two small ones and light the three pillar candles on the hearth. It creates a cosy glow. I fetch two glasses and polish them on a clean tea towel. Should I change? I am in an old pair of jeans and an oversized purple sweatshirt. Except what else would I wear at home? This isn't like an old film where the women changed when their men folk arrived home after a hard day's work. I stand in the centre of the rug. The candles flicker, the light dances off the glass photo frames and reflect in the silent TV. Music? No. Too cheesy. Except I don't like the silence. Probably because I can hear my heart pounding as I wait for the doorbell to ring.

I plump up some cushions. No. I squash them with my hand and place them at random along the back of the velvet covered sofa. Too much like a makeover programme. I pile them up at one end. That's better. Looks more like the before image. I'm wandering, running a finger over imaginary dust on the bookshelves, straightening the photos on the wall and picking at non-existent crumbs on the plain beige carpet. At least the sofa covers the threadbare bits.

This is ridiculous. I slump down on the sofa. At least that'll mess up the place. I stretch out my legs and catch sight of my old slippers. They were once leopard spot ballet slippers. Now they resemble a moth-eaten tiger. Even the spots have splodges of red from the tomato sauce I spilt on them, not to mention endless blobs of turmeric. Why the hell do I even wear such shapeless things? They've been washed so many times the shape has stretched. I peer at them. Is the sole coming away? I take them off and shove them under the sofa. I must buy some decent ones.

The bell rings. It startles me. I jump up. Perhaps padding around in socks is acceptable. I'd take them off except I'll end up with freezing cold feet and I'm not sure if my toenails need a repaint. Still, he's already seen me naked so I can't have put him off. The bell rings again. 'Coming,' I call out.

I open the front door. It's the first time I haven't peered through the frosted glass to check it's not my attacker. It feels good. I open the door. Finn is standing on the front step, a bunch of flowers in one hand, a bottle in the other and at his feet a carrier full of packets and plastic containers. 'Thought we might like a few dips,' he says.

My face breaks into an ear-to-ear grin and I can't change it. I must look like the Cheshire Cat from *Alice in Wonderland.* 'Come on in,' I say and step aside.

'Thank Christ. It's freezing outside. I reckon we'll get a hard winter.' He thrusts the flowers at me. 'A little treat.'

They are supermarket. I recognise they come from the most expensive range and bury my nose in a mix of roses, carnations, and pompom peonies, swathed in slithery cellophane paper. 'They're gorgeous,' I say.

He closes the door behind him. 'Any locks needed? Chains?'

For a moment I wonder what he's talking about. 'No, nothing special,' I say. 'I reckon whoever attacked me is on the other side of the planet by now.'

'Still no idea who it might be?' He doesn't move. There is a light frown and a crease has appeared over the bridge of his nose.

'No idea,' I say.

'Because if there was, you know you can tell me in confidence, don't you?'

'Thanks. I've got links with the police and a liaison officer in case that happens.'

'Oh.'

Why is he so interested? He must have read my mind. 'Because if you need new locks, window catches or an alarm system I'd be happy to help out, and if you ever feel you do remember anything about your attacker, you can come and stay with me till he's caught.'

'I appreciate that, thanks.' I walk into the lounge. I want this conversation to end. Finn follows. 'I'll put these in water if you can open the wine.' I stop. 'Sorry, I need to take your coat, show you where the loo is don't I?' I am jabbering. What must he think?

'I reckon I can find a place for my jacket and the toilet is either upstairs or past the kitchen. Right?'

I turn and face him. 'Sorry.' I feel my cheeks go red.

Finn puts the bag on the floor, the bottle on the table and crosses towards me. He takes the flowers and places them on the table. 'Forgot the most important thing,' he says and kisses me briefly. 'It's good to see you again.'

I kiss him back. I don't want him to stop. I am about to suggest we go upstairs when he breaks away. He picks up the flowers and hands them to me. 'You sort these and I'll arrange our late-night picnic.' He plants a kiss on the tip of my nose.

I head into the kitchen area. I select a vase from under the sink and run the tap. From the lounge I can hear the rustle of bags. 'Do you need any plates?' I call out.

'No. We'll be fine,' Finn replies.

I place the flowers in the water. I know I should cut off the stems and probably add the sachet of plant food. I stop. Yes. That will give me a bit of time. I feel flustered and strangely hot, despite the chill air.

It doesn't take me longer than a couple of minutes and by the time I go back into the lounge, Finn is seated on my sofa. Spread out on the low coffee table are dips, crisps, nuts and bite sized sausage rolls with two glasses of red wine.

'These are so lovely,' I say and place the vase on the table next to the TV. I doubt we'll be watching anything.

'I reckoned you might need cheering up after school. I keep reading about how hard it is, kids getting positive results, self-isolating, teachers having to change plans. Sheep are much easier to deal with.'

I sink onto the sofa next to him. I don't care if I'm snuggled close. It's where I want to be. 'It's a nuisance but we're getting used to it,' I lie. I don't want to appear a misery.

He picks up two glasses of wine and hands one to me. 'You haven't really answered my question.'

'Oh, about recognising… that person,' I say and cradle the stem of the glass between my hands.

'Yes. No dreams? Nightmares? Flashbacks? They could give you a decent clue. The police might get a lead, you never know.'

Why is he so interested? Or is he simply concerned? I shake my head. 'I can truthfully say if that person walked past me in the street, I would have no idea. Besides, as I said, I reckon he's miles away by now.'

Finn nods. 'Good. I mean… not reliving the incident.'

'I reckon I was in the wrong place at the wrong time and I need to get over it and move on.' I stop. I know what I want to say. 'You've helped enormously.' There. Done. He can run away if he likes. It's true.

He holds out his glass and looks at me across the rim. 'That's one of the nicest things anyone has ever told me,' he says. 'To us and the future. The past is forgotten.'

I clink my glass against his. 'To us and the future,' I say. I like the sound of that phrase.

Chapter 24

Mark takes the call at eight thirty am. 'Yes, ma'am?' It must be trouble. She'd never call otherwise.

'Get down to the harbour. Suspected accidental death. The locals reported strange activities along the tow path last night. Heard a few noises and wake up this morning to find a boat upside down in the water.'

'Any idea what sort of boat?' Was this the cabin cruiser he'd been after?

'Canal barge. Lived in but no sign of the owner. Divers are on their way. Take Cassie with you.'

The line goes dead. Mark can imagine the boss sitting back, wondering how the hell she'd find enough manpower for this and the countless other things. He corrects himself. Manpower? Better not use that in front of Ginny. He finishes dressing, slings his jacket over his shoulder and runs a hand over his chin. Damn. He needs a shave. He pulls open the drawer and runs the heads over the darker areas as he stares at his face in the mirror. All last night had been spent studying the printouts. There was definitely a pattern, and he was particularly interested in a small craft called *Lady Luck*. She was toing and froing around the time of the tides and full moons. He hadn't tracked her down to a fishing or leisure company so it must be a private individual. Pity he couldn't phone up for number plate recognition. Did they have the same thing for boats? Or should that be maritime craft? He runs a hand over his chin again. Better.

'Sorry, love,' he calls to Ginny as she sits supervising the kids' breakfast routines, sipping a mug of coffee from the new and very expensive machine she'd ordered. What was wrong with instant? Or a decent filter?

'What for?' Her lips turn down at the corners. Her eyes flash under the purple blue of her eyeshadow. It's like a bruise and matches her sweater.

'The boss wants me to investigate a suspicious sinking of a boat.'

Ginny raises one eyebrow. 'That needs you?'

'Will there be a dead body?' Andrew looks up from his plate of cornflakes.

'Gross.' Emily wags a finger at him.

'And blood?' Andrew is not to be deterred.

'No.' Mark squats between the two children. 'This is to see if your old dad, soon to be Detective Sergeant Dad, can set up a crime cordon. If it was anything gory, the big team of Detective Inspectors would be there.'

'Will you be an inspector?' Emily said.

'One day,' Mark says and stands up. His legs creak. He should go to the gym more often.

'When will you be home tonight?' Ginny is not amused.

What does she expect? He's a policeman, not a nine to five call centre sales executive… at least he's still working. Like teachers, nurses and undertakers, some work goes on forever. That would be a good subject for a poem. He kisses Ginny on the forehead. 'I'll be back for supper. Promise, and I'm in charge of bedtime so you can put your feet up and you two…' He lowers his head and stares at the children. 'You two had better be on your best behaviour or someone gets dunked in the bath.'

Andrew grins. 'You wish,' he says.

Emily tosses back her curls. 'I want to have a shower. On my own,' she says. 'So I can use my new strawberry foam gel. No one at school has a bath with their brother anymore.'

'You can have a shower and do your hair in our bathroom,' Ginny says.

Mark shrugs and looks over at Ginny. 'What for?'

'Tell you later,' she mouths.

Mark smiles. Emily is growing up. That's the reason. 'See you tonight,' he calls and goes out the kitchen door.

Cassie is waiting for him outside her house. He's offered to pick her up each morning as they are rostered together for the next few weeks at least. He draws up in front of an old style three storey Victorian semi. The front garden has been gravelled and a battered SUV and an electric run around stand side by side. Paint flakes from the sash windows and the guttering is split and hanging loose in parts. It must take a shedload of cash to heat and maintain. He glances up. Yes. The roof has a few cracked tiles.

'Good morning.' Cassie slides into the seat next to him. Her dark hair is tucked in a neat bun behind her neck. A few wisps frame her face. She smiles. She could be an artist's muse with that colouring. 'Something wrong?'

'Sorry. No. just admiring your house. Late Victorian?'

'House? Ruin more like and it takes a ruinous amount to repair.' Her voice is sharp. 'That's why we need two salaries.'

Mark remembers the conversation from the other day. 'How are things?'

'Frosty,' Cassie says. 'Very frosty. So I am extremely glad to be taken away from the field of combat.'

Mark changes the subject. 'What have you been told about the incident?'

Cassie removes her tablet and swipes through the screens. 'I think it might be one of the canal boats we saw last week. I reckon some kids have got in, messed around and not realised what they'd done. Remember Lewis said some of the boats were used as holiday lets?'

'Yeah, and no one is holidaying at the moment, right?' Mark says.

'Right.'

'Presumably it hasn't sunk completely?'

'No. The cabin top can be seen.'

'I wonder if the little devils have holed it.'

'Holed it?' Cassie turns and frowns.

'Yeah. Stuck a hammer in the side below the water line. It'd take a while but it'd sink and if they were up to no good, the water would cover any traces.'

There is silence as Mark takes the road over the M5 and heads south along the A38, driving between fields where a tractor is ploughing and the sky is filled with gulls. They swoop into the air before settling on a newly turned patch, the dark brown of the ruts of earth contrasting with the dirty yellow of wheat stalks, cut long ago in the dusty days of a hot, late summer. The image would be perfect for a seasonal poem. He turns his attention back to Cassie. Should he ask her how she is? Or would that appear creepy? She'd practically bared her soul to him. What the hell? He had a duty of care. 'How are you feeling about things at home?' Is that vague enough?

Cassie shrugs. 'We're still on non-speaking, speaking terms, if you know what that is?'

Mark nods. 'I know what it is for Ginny and me. We answer any question in monosyllables and any conversation is limited to practical matters.'

Cassie turns away. Mark glances at her in the wing mirror on the passenger side. No tears. Is that a good sign? 'Exactly. We are talking about everything except the one thing we should be talking about.'

More riddles? No. He recognises that. Avoidance tactics. Been there. Done that. 'Awkward, isn't it?'

'Yes, and it won't get any easier as we have guests this weekend.'

Mark scratches behind one ear with his hand. 'Is that allowed?'

'We are in a care bubble with her mum and dad who are in their late eighties. We won't go anywhere with crowds but they could do with a change of scenery.'

'Do they know what's going on between you two?'

'Oh yes. And they've probably been judge and jury already.'

Mark lets out a sigh. 'It's tough when family take sides.'

'They always have done,' Cassie says. 'I am a disappointment to them.'

'You? How? Decent job, good prospects, you don't seem like the wild partygoing type to me.'

'It's not that. I'm female. They are old school. They would have preferred me to be a red-blooded male with a career and sperm to provide the grandchildren.'

Mark shifts uneasily in the car seat. The wheel wobbles slightly. 'Sorry.'

'Not your fault. They're a different generation. Laura said her mother didn't believe there were such things as lesbians until she was a married woman and they repealed the homosexuality act in 67.'

Mark whistles between his teeth. 'We've come a long way. Not far enough.'

'No. Definitely not far enough.'

The car stops in front of the harbour. A small crowd has gathered. The local community support officer and a constable Mark vaguely recognises from a training course on policing modern Britain have taped off the tow path and are keeping people well away from the scene. A diver is padding towards the canal where the roof of a barge pokes out of the water.

'That's Lewis' houseboat,' Cassie says.

Mark glances at the crowd. 'Anyone seen Lewis Barnes?' he calls out.

There is a murmur of no and a few shakes of the head. 'His bike's there,' a voice answers.

'He hasn't got a car,' Cassie says to Mark.

'Get in there, now,' Mark yells at the diver who steps off the tow path and sinks into the water. 'We'll need back up. Call HQ. Tell them we might be looking at more than a sunken boat.'

Cassie turns away and speaks into her phone.

'Cordon off the whole tow path and the gate that leads to the fields,' Mark shouts to the PCSO. 'Constable, check when and if anyone here saw Lewis Barnes this morning.' With any luck he's gone off birdwatching somewhere and this was a bit of vandalism by some bored kids.

There is muttering from the small group of people who move backwards as asked and huddle together, watching what is happening. One of the women looks familiar. She has a white overall under a red puffa jacket. Could she be a nurse? Or a dentist? Or do they all wear colours. Cooks sometimes wear white. That's it. She's Mrs Chip Lady.

The surface of the water moves as the diver surfaces and paddles towards Mark. Mark kneels down on the tow path. The diver removes his face mask. 'There's a body down there. I can't get to it. We'll need to lift the whole boat out of the water.'

'Gender? Age?'

'Male, about seventy. Green sweater. Brown trousers. Long grey hair.'

'Can you rescue him?'

The diver shakes his head. 'He doesn't need rescuing. I know a drowned man when I see one.'

He's interrupted by a siren as a fire tender and rescue vehicle arrive. Mark walks forward and explains the situation. The rescue team spring into well-rehearsed action. The diver had already radioed his findings and with Cassie contacting HQ, the situation will soon be taken out of Mark's hands. So far it still resembles an accident or perhaps even a suicide. Except Lewis never struck him as a man about to end his life. An accident? Again, unlikely unless he was drugged or drunk when the boat sank.

****

Half an hour later the duty doctor is kneeling over the body. 'Well?' Mark says.

'I've ruled out suicide and an accident. I'll know a bit more when I cut him open.'

Mark winces. He's still squeamish about death. 'Time and cause?'

'Time? Body's been in the water at least ten hours. That puts the time of death at midnight or before.'

'Likely cause?' Mark leans closer to the body. Lewis is spread out on his back, arms by his side. He could have been asleep except for the pallor of his skin and the flesh which is bloated and puffy, as if water has seeped into every pore.

'Not drowning.' The expert tilts Lewis' head. A gash at the base of the skull still leaks blood and God knows what else. 'Someone hit him and there are marks around his wrists.'

Sure enough, a red weal where a rope or some sort of binding has held the wrists together circles the flesh. This is murder. 'What are those spots on his feet?' Mark points to the soles of Lewis' bare feet. Small red circles, like blisters, can be seen amongst the grime and hard skin.

'Not sure. It might be a coincidence. A lot of people go barefoot on a boat. Keeps the wood in good condition.'

'Not Lewis,' Mark says. 'He wore Hunters. Even inside.'

'I'll know more when I've got him back to the morgue.' The doctor is matter of fact.

Mark raises one eyebrow. 'You mean you'll be able to tell me what he had for supper? It's pretty clear this is a murder, not just a horrible accident waiting to happen.'

The doctor shakes his head. 'There might be drugs in his system, if he put up a fight… you know the sort of stuff.'

'Mark nods. 'Yes. And if it is murder, who did it and why?' He is saying his thoughts out loud.

'I'll leave that to you,' the doctor says and walks away whistling.

Mark is aware of Cassie's breathless voice. 'No one saw anything.' She stops. 'That's Lewis.'

'Yes. Possible, no, certain murder unless forensics turn up something unusual.'

She shakes her head. 'Poor old guy. He liked a quiet life. Said he wanted to get away from the rat race which is why he came here.'

Mark's ears pricked up. 'A quiet life? What do we know about him?'

'Shall I carry on questioning that lot?' She tilts her head in the direction of the small crowd who are still craning their necks to see what is going on. Mrs Chip Lady has gone.

'Yes. Find out who knew him, if anyone, and more importantly, did they notice anything unusual last night? We'll start house to house once I've cleared it with the boss.'

He watches as the rescue service winches the boat completely out of the canal. They let it rest on some struts borrowed from the harbour. Water gushes from the hole and from a number of other gaps. Not much chance of decent prints or forensic evidence. This means back to investigations in the old style. Gather as much information as you can about the victim, identify possible suspects, find motives, check alibis. He scans the crowd. Cassie is listening as some old dear in a red coat is pointing at the canal and the harbour. He can't make out the words but from the tone and the body language, something has rattled her. Out of the corner of his eye he spots the door of the harbour master's office open. A face peers out before it is slammed shut. He'll check Jason's alibi. Just as a precaution, of course.

He speaks into the phone on his lapel. 'Ma'am. A body has been found. I've secured the area and set Cassie on some preliminary enquiries. The rescue services have lifted the boat and forensics are ready to remove the body.'

The reply is not what he expected. He is to wait until she and her team have arrived. They will decide who and what to investigate. For the moment he is to keep the area secure.

He ends the call. What is the point of asking him to take the initiative and then change their mind? He's on guard duty, like a soldier outside Buckingham Palace.

Chapter 25

She knows nothing. I'm certain. I want out, remember. You agreed. One more pickup and I'm free to go.

Finn hits send before wrapping the phone in a waterproof bag and placing it in the bottom drawer of the filing cabinet. With the cabinet facing the barn wall and a bale of hay or two surrounding it, prying eyes, not that he was expecting anyone, would never spot anything. It had been a good hiding place for his stash of dope when he was a bored teenager. He couldn't be too careful though.

He must end this. He'd checked his bank accounts yesterday. There is enough to start on the refurbishments and if he is focussed and finds a few bargains, two of the holiday lets will be ready by spring. Staycations are going to be the holiday of choice for a few years to come, he'd bet a pound to a penny. For the first time in years, he feels positive and that has as much to do with the prospect of paying off the farm debts and keeping it in the family as it does with a certain Rachel Thomas. He likes her. Could it be more? He whistles to Gyp and sets off towards the farmhouse. Time will tell.

Chapter 26

The open plan office has been set up like an incident room. The wall facing the windows is stripped of its usual assortment of posters and notices, and images of the current crime scene with a photo of the victim have been fixed to the shiny surface. Already questions in red and possible links via black arrows pepper the spaces. The boss is standing by the board. She looks up as Mark comes in.

'My office in five?'

Mark nods, makes his way to a free desk and logs on. He scrolls through the junk. Not even a message from the Chief Constable. Must be slipping. A murder is usually a signal for some hand wringing and requests to make a supreme effort to catch the culprit. Mark logs off. Pity the Chief Constable doesn't have the same attitude to domestic violence or aggravated burglary. Why can't the top people understand this level of behaviour often leads to worse? Have they forgotten everything they learnt on patrol? Mark checks his watch. He'd be there in four and a half minutes.

'Ma'am. you wanted to see me?' He stands at the entrance, shifting from one foot to the other like a small boy outside the head teacher's study. The room has its familiar lived in appearance; coffee cups strewn over desk surfaces, empty sandwich boxes stuffed in the bin, assorted coats hanging over spare chairs and different shoes and boots on newspaper in front of the table on which a large laser colour printer is spewing out sheets.

'Yes. Come in and close the door.' She collects up the sheets and switches off the machine.

He does as he is told. This is serious. Without waiting for him to speak she launches her first question. 'Do you think this is linked to our people smugglers?' She places the papers in a brown manila file and sits down opposite him, hands clasped in front of her.

She has him there. 'I have no evidence, but something doesn't quite add up.'

'Good. Same feeling here. The trouble is the Chief Constable is on my back, desperate to clear up this murder before it affects the tourist trade. Not that anyone will be going anywhere if infections don't decrease.' She sniffs.

For a moment Mark has forgotten about the pandemic. He's forgotten Ginny's birthday so many times it's a joke between them. Once he's involved in a case, that is it. He might as well be on a different planet. 'I've got a few lines of enquiries and Lewis Barnes had been very helpful.'

Eve raises one eyebrow. 'What sort of helpful?'

'No names,' Mark explains. 'Just his observations on top of a shed load of data to sift through.'

'Sift.' She spits out the word. 'From now on, you report only to me. Use Cassie. There is a link but I'm damned if I have any idea what it might be and we're short staffed. All hands on the murder inquiry. You know how it is.'

'I've got the data from the harbour of small craft going up and down around the time of the sightings. I need to check if there are any patterns, same names recurring, same people booking the craft. That sort of thing.'

She leans back in her chair. The buttons of her white shirt strain across a broad chest. 'So, a regular visitor takes a craft, loads it up and disgorges the cargo upstream?'

Mark smiles. 'That's where I'm at.'

There's a sudden movement. She flicks a switch and picks up a phone. 'Traffic? Can you let DS Mulroney have access to all

CCTV along the M5 on whatever dates he selects?' She listens for a moment before putting the phone down. 'Just a hunch there might be a common number plate on a van at the same time.'

'Thank you. That's excellent. There is one thing, I'm not a DS.'

'You are now,' Eve says. 'Welcome to the team, Detective Sergeant Mulroney. Welcome to my team.' She nods towards him. 'And that uniform can go.'

It is no good. A smile breaks across Mark's face. He wants to look serious. He is investigating a possible murder linked with people trafficking, isn't he? He stands up and opens the door. Should he say anything? 'Thank you, ma'am,' he manages to stammer out.

'No need for thanks. You'll make a good detective.' Eve's face softens. 'You've got the right blend of intelligence and intuition.' The face changes. 'Now, go and do your stuff and if you want to celebrate tonight, make sure you're sober tomorrow morning.'

He is about to leave when her voice stops him. 'I still can't believe that woman's camera picked up absolutely nothing about her attacker. I thought these badger-hugging types had the latest spec on everything technical. Could our team clarify the images?'

Mark turns slowly. Does she know? Does she suspect? If it ever came out, he'd be under investigation by standards. Goodbye promotion. Hallo traffic control and school visits. 'There was nothing, ma'am.'

'It was just a thought. Pity.' She bends her head over the desk. The interview is over.

The catcalls and whistles greet him. 'Detective Sergeant now? Part of the A team?' There are other calls which he ignores. Bastard features as a common theme. Is it light hearted or is there an edge?

'Take no notice of that lot. We need some more brains round here, like me.' The man Mark thinks is called Todd stands up and comes across and holds out a hand. 'D I Todd Jarrett. Welcome on board.'

Mark takes the proffered hand. It's firm and Todd's lithe figure suggests a lot of time spent in the gym. Perhaps Mark could do the same? Detective work involves a lot more sitting down than people think. 'Thanks,' Mark says. 'I know I'm in good company and can learn from you lot.' Is that the right tone? Respectful with a hint of banter?

'What's she got you on today?' Todd continues.

'To trawl through CCTV on the M5. Anyone like to change places?' He looks around and grins.

'Welcome to our world,' a voice calls from behind a screen.

Mark makes his way back to the empty desk where he'd logged on earlier. Sure enough, an email confirming his promotion and a request to update his warrant and ID is sitting in the inbox. He should have been pleased. He is. Except for one thing. That damned video. Should he contact Rachel and ask to check her camera one more time? Pretend he's searching for something else? Checking on timescales? Except she'd wonder what he'd done with the original, wouldn't she? Unless he could sit with her and get her understanding on the action, frame by frame? It might be worth thinking about.

Cassie slips into the seat beside him. 'Well done, Detective Sarge,' she says. 'Anything you want me to do?'

'Yes. There're some CCTV images to download. We're searching for white transit vans on screens around the time the sightings took place.'

'Same make? Same number plate, right?'

'Yes. And there's another thing.'

'What?'

'If these drop-offs are around the harbour at Blake Point, the CCTVs on the bridges between junction seven and junction eight might be of particular interest.'

He doesn't wait for her response; trawling through CCTV was the least exciting part of any information gathering. Someone must do it and that someone is usually a junior member of the team. Mark has his own work and the niggling feeling that he ought to chase up that sodding video footage. Except what could he say? "Sorry I stuffed up. Can I have another look?" What if Rachel was one of these anti-police crew? That would look good plastered over social media; *attempts to find attacker of lone female hampered by police IT cockups.*

There's enough bad press as it is, and after the summer everyone is super touchy about negative reports, whether justified or not. He sits down at the desk and opens the file of printouts he collected from Jason. DS or not, he'll remain old school; technology can let you down. This was going to be done the old-fashioned way, with pen, pencil, ruler and highlighter. A cup of coffee arrives. He looks up.

'Thought we might both need a shot of caffeine,' Cassie says and smiles. 'It could be a long session.'

Mark spreads out the sheets of data on the boats travelling through the locks and the harbour en route to Gloucester in date order. He double checks against the times of the high tides, full moons and the sightings of the transit vans. He starts with February. As he expects, prior to lockdown, the late winter had been a bumper time for pleasure craft, especially around February 14th which was obvious and March 21st. Why that date? He checks the calendar. Mothering Sunday, of course. Treat Mum to a day out with lunch. Were they allowed? His mind, during and after the first lockdown, had become a blur of similar days, punctuated by terrifying news reports and increasingly anxious people. No. A trip on a private craft was still allowed, the *Stay at Home* message was not yet in force. March, wasn't it?

He selects the first print-out for February and scans his eye down the list of craft. He discounts fishing trips with named leisure companies. Too obvious. He also ignores the private trips hired by big companies. They were part of the hospitality scene for those who were being courted to invest or buy. No. It's the smaller craft he's interested in most of all. He highlights them; *Lady Luck*, *Big Brenda*, *Seize the Day*, *Princess Pam*, *Cost a lot*, *Big Spender* and the rest. Twenty in all.

He repeats the process. By the time he reaches April, one name stands out – *Lady Luck*. Whoever owns her has taken a trip every month. Interesting that there hadn't been sightings every month. Perhaps a few had been missed. He continues and bingo, *Lady Luck* has been on the water every month. Hadn't Lewis mentioned a craft called *Lady Luck*?

Mark leans back in his chair. The afternoon sun slants through the slats of the blinds, showing the motes of dust peppering the air. The room hums with activity. Quiet voices exchange ideas or information. Hushed voices speak over the phone. Printers whirr and the tap tap of fingers on keyboards fills any spaces. The room is warm. Someone has opened a window. A faint breeze clatters the blind. The ragged song of a territorial robin percolates through the air. He glances towards the boss's office. She's on the phone and gesticulating. Someone's getting an ear bashing.

On the incident board, Lewis Barnes' face stares out next to an image of his feet with the red marks and a question. *Torture or abuse?* Why would anyone want to kill an old man like him? Unless he knew something or knew too much? He hadn't made any complaints to the police about unusual activity, had he? Or had he made his concerns known to the harbour master?

Mark goes back to his computer and checks for incident numbers around the date *Lady Luck* was on the water. There is nothing. Why would there be unless something specific had happened. Lewis was not a trouble maker, snitching on his neighbours at any slight. Calling 101 or Crime Stoppers might be more in his line.

He checks his access to local 101 calls and Crime Stoppers. There is the usual litany of grievances and misunderstandings, late night parties, noisy teens outside takeaways and plenty of concerns over violations of lockdown. Lewis Barnes had made two calls to Crime Stoppers. One in March and one in May. It was described as antisocial activity in the harbour and canal area. He scans the reports and the conclusion.

Persons unknown had created a disturbance along the Severn Canal at Blake Point. No further action was taken.

Mark checks against the dates of *Lady Luck* and retrieves his notes of the time spent with Lewis Barnes. Bingo. On all occasions, the cruiser had travelled through the locks earlier in the day before the disturbances had taken place. This would fit. Get through the lock and moor up before disgorging the clientele into their transport. If there was a good tide, it could be passed off as back up to the people riding the waves or if it was a full moon, it might be ideal for fishing.

Someone knows who owns *Lady Luck* and why she made these journeys. Mark returns to the printouts. Didn't Jason say that reasons for journeys were logged? He checks against the details of *Lady Luck*. All it says is recreation. He calls the phone number. Out of use. He doubts if it had ever been in use. Something is wrong. He needs to pay another call on Jason Carter. This time he'll have his new warrant card and if he has to, he'll take the place apart to find the details of who owns *Lady Luck* and how they can be contacted.

'Sarge, there's something I want you to see.' Cassie leans over and whispers in Mark's ear. 'I think I've found the van.'

He slews his chair to face her screen. 'Go on, surprise me.' He rubs his hands together and sits back.

'Check this clip here.' She points to a grainy image of a white transit van. 'We can see the number plate.' She enlarges the image and the system clarifies the letters and digits. 'This is the same van coming from Bristol an hour earlier. It's spotted later as it travels north along the M5 before it turns off towards Quedgeley. That's when it's noticed by a member of the public who contacts us about a group of men emerging from a van along the Moreton to Hares Ditch Lane.' Cassie smiles. Mark recognises that smile; it's the satisfaction of a breakthrough.

'Any more?'

'Jeez, Sarge, that took me the best part of two hours.'

'Looks as if it could be a long night.' Mark smirks. By the way Cassie is reacting, she'll be there all night and all day and all week if needed.

'I'm onto it.' Cassie returns to her chair and disappears behind the screen. Mark contacts the vehicle data base. Damn. A hire company. If they were legit, they'd have records. Even if the van was different every time, there might be a common name or common starting place. He calls the company and waits while he is informed his call was important and they would get to him as soon as possible.

'Able Cars and Vans.' The voice startles him.

'Detective Sergeant Mulroney. I need to find out the name of a driver who hired a van from you in July this year.'

There is a long whistle. 'You'll be lucky. We took over in late August. There were no proper records. Invoices? You must be joking. How the hell they made any money is beyond me.' There is a chuckle at the end of the phone. 'I reckon you lot should investigate the place. Money under the counter, that sort of stuff.'

'So no names?'

'One thing they did have was CCTV.'

'Still working?'

'We changed the system to a modern one and dumped the old lot in the storage shed. It'll still be there.'

'I'll be down later.'

'Certainly. Hope we can be of service.' The phone goes dead.

Mark's previous cheerfulness has evaporated. More CCTV to watch. Unless Cassie comes up with some positive information from the other sightings which would give him a name and a possible lead? He rubs his hands together. He loves his work.

Chapter 27

I want to tell everyone how good it feels to be with Finn. I'm scared. They'll think I'm getting in too deep, too soon. Perhaps I am. I don't care. The mist over the hills is clearing in the grey light of a cloudy, October day. The leaves on the trees have turned to golden brown on the hillsides. The trees in the car park are festooned with berries which make excellent weapons when aimed at a sensitive spot. Who on earth in their right mind thought any fruiting tree was a sensible choice for a school? I would have had the place full of monkey puzzle trees. No one can climb up them. They hurt when you try and break off a branch, they don't lose leaves so no mushy mess underfoot which every child brings into the school and no fruits or seeds. Perfect. Was it only two weeks to half term? I might need to walk if the weather turns icy next month.

I slow down and park. Jake is on duty. He waves. Oh, please don't come across and speak. It's not that I don't want to talk to him. I want to remain in my Finn bubble. The broad smile on his face as he crosses the car park should have been a warning.

'Rachel, good morning. Looking forward to half term?'

'Yes.' I busy myself collecting books and my laptop bag from the boot.

'How do you fancy a day out at the weekend? I want to go down to Weston, you know, walk along the beach, fish and chips, end of season sort of thing? It would be fun if you could come along.'

'Can I check?' I stall. What the hell can I say? An outright refusal might seem weird as we had been getting closer. Yet if there was a chance with Finn, I know what I'd prefer. Okay, a braver woman would come clean. Except there is still something holding me back. It all feels too good to be true with Finn. I am waiting for the crash and I suppose part of me wants someone around when it all happens. 'A friend might be coming up to Bristol for an interview on Friday and I said I'd be around.'

"Might be?'

'Yes. References were taken up but so far she's heard nothing. I'll text her today and get back to you?'

'Perfect,' Jake says. His cheeks have flushed pink and there is a faint redness on his neck above the white collar. He's keen on me. I feel even more of a bitch. He likes me and I'm not being fair. I decide then and there I'll check with Finn and if I haven't heard by the end of the day, I'll agree to Saturday with Jake.

I wait till lunchtime and escape into the art room which doubles as my base and form room for Y9T who, I hope, are keeping a social distance as they flirt and fight their way through early adolescence. Honestly, if I ever need another job, I should offer my services as an agony aunt for some online teen blog. I text Finn. I am fed up with being a patsy, waiting for a man to get in contact. If he is one of those love 'em and leave 'em types, I'd be the one leaving. Pronto.

Attempt one.

Hi Finn

Hope you are OK this morning. Really enjoyed your company. Just wondering if you have any plans for the coming weekend as I've got the chance for a quick visit to Weston with work colleagues

I delete that. Too boring. Makes me sound like a workaholic with no friends outside school. What the hell can I write that doesn't sound needy or desperate? Or worse, pushy?

I am about to give up when a text bounces in. Alleluia!

Hi Rachel,

Any plans for the weekend? If not, I'd love to take you to the arboretum. The trees are fabulous and perhaps I might pick your brains about camera angles.

I'm a liar.

I want to see you again.

Finn

PS The stuff about the trees still holds true but that's the least of my reasons!

I smile. Why didn't he call? Most men would have spent hours talking and setting up a date. Not Finn. I like that. It feels more equal. I text back.

Funny. I was in the middle of texting you about the weekend. I'd love that as long as I cook in the evening and we share a large bottle of wine. You're welcome to stay the night too.

My finger hovers over the *send* button. Do I sound needy? Or desperate? We'd spent two nights together. I was pretty sure that counted as a proper relationship and not a friend with benefits hook-up. What if he is using me for sex? No, he wouldn't bother about planning to go somewhere. I press send. What the hell.

I'm instantly filled with regret. I'll be glancing at my phone every minute waiting for a reply. To distract myself before the next lesson I go onto the Black Beast of Gloucestershire website. I haven't bothered since the attack. I shiver. The memory still makes me sick. I'd expected to be more frightened, you know, scared to go out, jumping at every sound. I'm on edge but I'm trying to convince myself it was a very random attack. I was in the wrong place at the wrong time. It happens. At least it hadn't made me scared of going out in the evenings. Except I wouldn't be wandering the woods alone for a few more months. If ever.

A breeze from the open windows rustles the pile of art work on the desk at the back. I pull my jacket round my shoulders. If we have this level of ventilation in the middle of winter, I'll need special Arctic wear. I wonder if the head would let us wear ski clothes? The website loads. I scan the information on offer. Suspected sightings near Newent and above Cheltenham. Nothing local. Someone has posted the newspaper report about me. I check the message board. Plenty of commiserations. I post an update to say I'm fine but wouldn't be going out for a while unless anyone had a shared hide where a group of us could do a night watch. There was one message that intrigued me.

I reckon there are plenty of others who are on the lookout for these creatures. I'm sure I saw an outside broadcast van parked up in the track off the beacon circular walk. The darkened windows were a giveaway although I wouldn't have chosen a white van. Too visible. Should have taken the number but we've had lampers around here too recently and there's no way I want to get mixed up with them.

Badger 99

I re-read the message. The van I'd seen had been white. Was it the same one? No, white vans are commonplace and the people on these websites know what they're talking about. If Badger reckons it was a film crew, they're probably right. Still, it might be worthwhile alerting Mark to this. If it was lampers, he might be able to pass the information onto the rural crime squad. We all dreaded bumping into them. They're violent and scary. Well, if you find watching and betting on dogs ripping wild animals to pieces you must be some sort of sicko.

The message from Finn comes in as the bell sounds and Year 12 art A level saunter in. 'Your files are at the back. The desks have been sanitised and all the equipment for the next module is set out. You need sketching boards, cartridge paper and a set of B pencils.'

I scroll to the texts.

Great. 2 pm on Saturday? I'll pick you up. We'll probably need wellies or walking boots. The tracks are sodden. Let's hope for a bit of sunshine. Do you mind if I bring an overnight bag? I hate rushing off unshaven! I do have to be back for nine am. The animals like regular food times.

I smile.

Perfect. See you then. If you need a chat, you know where I am.

Part of me wants to see him before Saturday. Part of me is quite relieved. Things are happening fast. Too fast? I don't know. I do know I'll have to speak to Jake. I really can't carry on meeting him unless it is accepted it is on a friend only basis and I'm pretty certain that's not what Jake wants. It is better to be honest.

'Okay Year 12. Let's be honest, unless there is a big improvement in the amount of homework and private study, I can guarantee you will not get the grades you want and could achieve with a little more application.'

Silence. My words have struck home. Let's hope the effect lasts.

It is nearly five by the time I have cleared away, set up the lessons for the following day and prepared the materials I need. I like to have everything ready to go in case there are any last minute glitches in IT and I have to get by using video or even audio alone without sharing screens. I am heading down the stairs, stepping over the scrubbed patches and avoiding the damp handrails when I spot Jake emerging from the corridor leading to the staff room. Has he been waiting for me? Impossible. I am getting paranoid.

'Hey, Rachel,' he calls out. 'Good day?'

'So so,' I say. My stomach sinks. I have to tell him. 'Sorry for not getting back to you earlier.'

'No worries,' he says. Why do some guys sound like an Aussie soap? 'I expect you were busy.'

'It's not that.' Whatever I say I'll probably sound like a bitch. I shouldn't have gone out with him, except aren't women allowed male friends? The teens seem to cope okay.

'I suspect you are going to say you respect my friendship and that's how you want it to stay?'

How does he know? 'Yes. There isn't anyone else but there could be. If you see what I mean.'

'Someone you would like to get to know better?'

'Yes. I'm sorry.' God that sounds lame.

'No need to be. That's what we do, isn't it? Meet someone as a friend and sometimes it changes, sometimes it doesn't?'

I look at him standing in the dusk of the late afternoon, the glare of the strip lights putting half of his face in shadow. It would have made a great portrait. 'I'm sorry,' I say again.

'We're colleagues and mates, right?'

'Right. That hasn't changed.'

'Good. So, when you're ready and if the other person doesn't mind, from time to time we might go out and join the other staff for a meal or a drink, as mates, right?'

'As work colleagues,' I correct him. Friends still sounds too intimate.

'As work colleagues, of course,' Jake says.

We're in an empty corridor. Neither is making a move. There is nothing more to be said. 'Right. Better check for any snail mail.' I scurry into the staff room. It is empty apart from Tashi sitting on one of the blue padded seats, a cup of coffee resting in one hand. The other is splayed along the back rest. She pats the seat next to her.

'Are we allowed? Social distancing and all that?'

'Who cares?' she says. 'How goes it with Jake?'

I slump on the seat. 'Jake?'

She shrugs. 'He wanted to know if he should ask you out. Were you involved with anyone? I said no but I suspected there might be someone.'

'That's why he didn't seem surprised.'

'You could do worse. He's a decent man and we know more about him than this Finn fellow.'

'You don't trust him, do you?' I look into her brown eyes. She seems worried. The lines around them are deeper than usual.

'No. I don't. Do you?'

'Of course,' I say. And I do. Or I think I do.

Chapter 28

Mark calls Ginny. 'What now?' No mistaking her feelings; he's in trouble and it's going to get worse.

'Sorry. Something serious has come up. I'll be home at about seven.'

That means I do the tea, bath, and story time. Again.'

He can imagine her standing in the kitchen, by the sink, her head turned away so the twins, if they were there wouldn't hear too much. He suspects Andrew has ears like a bat. Emily's are more selective.

'Can't be helped. Murder is always top priority.' He still hasn't told Ginny he is covering the possible people trafficking too.

'We need to talk.' Her voice drops. 'Emily's teacher….' He can hear her feet clipping over the floor and a door is closed. She must be in the hall.

'What about Emily's teacher?'

'She realises Emily needs help, but the school can't afford it.' There is a sniff. 'They can spend enough on fancy new logos.'

'What does she suggest?'

'That's it. She doesn't. There are diagnostic tests they can do for things like short-term memory issues. When I asked her how long it might take, she says it could be eighteen months. I went on Mumsnet and they suggest testing for dyslexia if any child exhibits certain behaviours or characteristics.' There's a pause. 'The description is pure Emily. I've checked online and there are plenty of centres near here. The one in Swindon has excellent reviews and there's another in Cheltenham, or we could try Bristol.'

'Whoa. What's all this about? Are you telling me she is dyslexic?'

'Like I said, Emily's behaviour ticks all the boxes.' There is urgency in her voice.

'As soon as I'm back, I promise we'll go over this. What's the cost?' Mark holds his breath and hopes it's all part of a charity.

'About five hundred for the assessment and then there might be additional teaching. I reckon that could be thirty or forty pounds a session.'

Mark stifles the gasp ready to escape. He takes a deep breath. 'Jeez. That could be thousands.'

'Isn't your daughter worth it?'

'Of course but the school should—'

'Ginny interrupts him. 'Should, should, should and you should have a work life balance which you don't and probably never will have.' She ends the call.

Mark stares at the phone as if Ginny will say something more. He wants reassurance. Dyslexic? Isn't that when you can't read words properly? Word blindness? Does that mean she'll never learn to read properly? Images of his daughter in some dead-end job, paid a pittance and all because she needed more help at school and didn't get it. Not on his life. He must get her the help she needs. He puts the car into drive and heads towards Able Cars and Vans. He'd check the damned CCTV and be back as soon as he could. He and Ginny would work something out.

The afternoon traffic has eased. The school run is almost over. A few coaches trundle along, half full, seats taped over and the kids peering out with masks covering their faces. Would Emily be bullied if she struggled? He remembered kids in his class and how they had been tormented by their peers. Kids are cruel. He flips the sun visor to shade his eyes from the low-level light and turns along the dual carriageway towards the industrial area by the canal on the outskirts of the city. Car showrooms jostle next to breakers yards, wood stores, and a warehouse selling second-hand office furniture and building supplies. A sandwich bar and a chippy serve the workers at lunchtime and a newsagent is squeezed into the remaining space. Everywhere needs a coat of paint with broken or faded signs announcing the best bargains of the day. Just driving through is depressing enough.

The sign for Able Cars and Vans is the brightest piece of neon in the area with a star and the name emblazoned on a tail-like arrow. Mark turns left and passes between a pair of green painted gates, wide open but topped with barbed wire and a series of dagger-shaped points, like the fencing surrounding the frontage where a number of small vans, camper vans and larger white transits stand side by side. Mark stops the car and gets out. Now he knows what the sheriff feels like when he rides into town in the old films he'd watched with his dad. He's certain he's being watched. He slams the car door shut, pulls on a mask and places his cap on his head. He hates the thought of wearing ordinary clothes; he feels safer, invincible in the uniform. The security cameras are trained on the gates and the entrance to the office, next to a roller door that must be the workshop.

The door opens. 'Saw you come in.' A cheery face in a red bobble hat and grease-stained blue overalls holds the door back. 'You must be the bloke who phoned earlier?'

Mark nods. 'That's right, Detective Sergeant Mulroney.'

'I've set up the old PC with the video footage. It's pretty easy to scroll through once you get the right file.'

Mark walks into the office. It isn't what he is expecting. A blue and black patterned carpet covers the floor of a room as big as the boss's office at HQ. A pale wooden desk with a black leather seat is in front of a series of rusty and very dented, four drawer filing cabinets. Three more black leather seats and a two-seater sofa surround a small coffee table and a water cooler takes up one corner. Two screens on the wall show images of the front gates and the car park. A young man in black jeans and a black and white check shirt is sifting through one of the filing cabinet drawers. 'I wouldn't be surprised to find mice in here. Or judging by the dates on these files, dinosaurs would be more like it.' He turns. 'Sorry. Thought you were…' he glances from Mark to the bobble hat man.

'This is Detective Sergeant Mulroney to see the CCTV we inherited.'

'Rather you than me. I've set up the PC in the back room. Everything is on memory sticks so take your pick. The only thing is the system did have date and time automatically included at the bottom of the screen, so the first image gives you the start date.'

'Sorry. You are?'

Bobble hat speaks. 'I'm Dan, the owner, and this is my partner, Seb.'

Seb holds up one hand and does a slight wave. 'Pleased to be able to help.'

Mark is intrigued. 'You haven't been in business long?'

Dan takes off his bobble hat and scratches the streaks of bleached hair. 'Started in July. We did a shed load of work in the summer. People preferred to hire their own vans rather than trust hotels.' He claps a hand over his face. 'Sorry. I should have a mask, shouldn't I? Except as we're partners, we don't bother when there's just the two of us. We're our own bubble.'

Mark nods. 'If I'm in a room on my own, I can't see any problems.'

'We are all Covid secure,' Seb says and points to the hand sanitisers dotted around and the extractor fan which whirrs in the background.

Funny Mark hadn't noticed it before. 'I'll need to take the memory stick with me.'

Seb looks disappointed. 'Ooh, I thought we'd have police protection for a while.'

'Trouble?'

'People are desperate,' Seb says. 'They'll try to take anything.'

'Can I ask you a few questions while I'm here?'

'Fire away.' Dan pulls out a small blue plastic, fold up seat and sits next to Seb. He points to the sofa.

Mark sits down and gets out his tablet. 'What sort of people hire vans? Anyone unusual?'

Seb answers. 'That's the thing. We took over a business that relied on small vans, local traders who needed one in an emergency, ordinary people moving house or shifting furniture. That sort of thing.'

'It wasn't good business,' Dan says. 'Why wait till people have a problem.'

Seb takes over. 'Exactly. So, we bought a few camper vans and advertised them as perfect for family camping holidays. There are four seats at the front and shed loads of space for all the stuff. It's working. We've got bookings for half term, for Christmas and next year is filling up nicely.'

Mark taps away. 'There must have been repeats before.'

'Not many.'

Mark's heart is sinking. He'd imagined he'd find a pattern. 'Do you know where they take the vans?'

'We do a mileage check before and after. A lot of the vans are used locally over a weekend.' Seb leans forward and taps at his screen.

'I presume that will change with people going on holidays,' Mark says.

'Probably, but we'll worry about that later.' He runs a hand through his hair and scratches his chin. 'Here it is.' Seb swivels the screen to face Mark. There is a spreadsheet with each van's registration number, the date it was hired and the number of miles completed, plus a separate column with symbols and letters.

'What's this for?' Mark says and points to the last column.

Dan raises his eyebrows. 'That is his code. I have no idea how it works.'

Seb leans back in his chair. 'It tells me the state of the vehicle when it arrives back, the smell inside, the rubbish, how much fuel they have replaced, stuff like that.'

'I thought people had to bring it back in a decent condition.'

Seb's eyes roll heavenwards. 'Oh pleeease. We've had it all; used condoms, dirty nappies, sand and mud, wet seats, vomit and the deposit hardly covers the cost of decent valeting.'

Mark's antennae pick up. Damp seats? Sand? 'Any long-term hires or recurrent names?'

Seb taps a pencil on dazzling white teeth that ought to have belonged to celebs and influencers. 'None except the plumber along the road who hires a van when he trials new staff and possibly the fishermen of ye old England.' He smiles in the direction of Dan.

'Twice a white people carrier has come back with wet seats and sand everywhere.'

Mark makes a note on his tablet. 'Name?'

Seb reaches back and places some white paper in a printer. 'I'll let you have the file of our contacts. Probably against some box ticker's rules except as this is a police enquiry, I don't suppose it matters.' He looks up. Is that fear?

'If the police want it, they get it,' Mark says.

'Thank God. The last thing we want is trouble with data protection,' Seb says and hands Mark several sheets of paper. He glances through them. There is plenty to read.

'I'll collect the memory sticks and be off,' Mark says. 'But if you do notice anything suspicious, give me a call.' He reaches into his pocket and pulls out a card. It is the first time he's handed one over with his new grade and if he places it on the desk with a more than usual theatrical flourish, so what?

'Will do.' Seb takes the card, glances at it, and sticks it into the top drawer of the desk.

'I'll come out and lock the gate behind you,' Dan says.

'Is that necessary? Are you expecting trouble?'

Dan walks beside Mark at the required two metre distance. 'The old boy we bought the gaffe from reckoned he was broken into on several occasions, the vans were used and dumped in the countryside. He reckoned it was kids joyriding but how did they get home?'

'That hasn't happened to you?'

'Not yet. We did find the wires cut through one Sunday morning, but they must have seen the CCTV and gone to find an easier target.'

'Thanks for this.' Mark flaps the envelope in one hand.

'Hope it's of use.' Dan waits as Mark drives the car out through the gate before closing it and locking it with a large padlock.

He heads back to HQ. There's plenty to go on. All he needs is one image or a name to link the harbour and the smuggling and he is certain one of those cabin cruisers was involved.

****

HQ is buzzing; murders are rare in this part of the world. Mark escapes into the small cubicle he's commandeered as his workplace. He gets a coffee from the machine, switches his phone to vibrate and plugs in the memory stick. It scans for a few seconds before images of the garage appear with dates and times. He double checks. Which dates is he interested in? He scans the list of the tides, full moons and the sightings and selects the first he's highlighted; April 5th 2018. This is going to take a long time.

He's got to May 2020 when Cassie swivels towards him on her chair. 'Got a sighting of a van in August which travelled from Gloucester to Bristol, disappeared and reappeared doing the reverse journey.'

'Registration number?'

Cassie shoves a piece of paper towards him. 'Not new but not so decrepit it'll get stopped by the traffic crew.'

'Right. Let's check against the data from the van hire.' Mark spreads out the sheets. Sure enough, the van had been registered and in use until August. He can imagine Seb wanting something a bit more upmarket. He'll call them later to check where it went. He looks at the name on the hire form. Charlie Blake, three days hire, paid in cash, van returned on time. Not much to go on. There is a contact phone number.

'Cassie, can you call this number? Find out if it still belongs to Mr Charlie Blake.'

Cassie disappears behind the screen again. Mark continues to scroll through the images. A lot is black space with the occasional outlines and bright, gleaming eyes of urban foxes as they nose around the bins and squeeze beneath the fences and if he isn't mistaken, in the gaps in the fences. 'Phone is a pay as you go or was. It's either out of juice, credit or has been discarded. Shall I get onto the phone company?'

'Yes. Find out the calls that were made, who and where and when in early August if you can.'

He turns his attention back to the screen and skims through the night images. He rechecks the hiring details. No times. The date is clear. The van was returned on 5th August. He speeds up the images. Time is flying past as hours shrink to minutes and minutes to seconds. Mark's hands go clammy. It's always like this when he believes he's on the verge of a discovery. His stomach twists and he's breathing fast. He slows down the images as he reaches 8 am on the morning of the 5th. There are Seb and Dan opening and locking the gate behind them. This must have been soon after they took over.

Is that it? A white van slows and stops by the locked gates. The time on the video registers 9:25. That figures. Get it back by 9:30 am to avoid another day's hire. Someone clambers out of the driver's seat and stands, back turned, and speaks into a small intercom. It's no longer there. Another of Seb and Dan's improvements. Except it wasn't controlled from inside. The gate is padlocked. Someone would have to come out and open it. The man shifts from one foot to the other before stepping away from the intercom and as he does, Mark gets a clear view of the face of Mr Charlie Blake. Except he knows him by another name. Peering from underneath the hoodie top is Jason Carter, the harbour master.

Bingo. Mark slaps one hand on the desk. It's time to pay another visit to Mr Jason Carter There are a few questions he needs to ask. Of course, it could be a huge coincidence. Perhaps Jason was shifting stuff for his old mum or gran. No. You did that in daylight. Getting off on a family holiday? Ginny's friends liked setting off and driving all night to arrive at the campsite early. They'd feed the kids and shove them in sleeping bags in the back of the car. The kids would wake bright and early but there'd never be any of the 'Are we there yet?' or the perpetual squabbling. Everyone would spend time on the beach, check in and collapse all together after burger and chips at seven pm. He'd suggested it to Ginny but she didn't like driving at night so that was the end of that idea. No. Jason doesn't look the family type. There is something odd going on unless he is a keen fisherman?

Mark shakes his head. Too many questions need an answer. He checks the time. What if Jason is also connected to the boat? That would give plenty of ammunition for a thorough check on him, his finances, his background and anything else he could dredge up. He leans round the corner of the cubicle where Cassie is working.

'Sarge?'

'Have you managed to find anything out about *Lady Luck*?'

Cassie picks up a piece of paper. 'Owned by an offshore company that specialises in holidays, trips out, corporate events, stuff like that. Currently furloughed.'

'This furlough deal… does it mean they can't trade?'

'Not sure. I thought it was for companies whose livelihoods had been cut by the pandemic and the requirements for social distancing. I was talking to Steve of Fraud and he reckons a number of businesses are still up and running and creaming off government cash.'

'Thanks. Anything else?'

'It might be a coincidence.' She taps a pencil on her teeth.

'I like coincidences. Tell me more.'

'*Lady Luck* was owned by a local man until he was made bankrupt in 2013. The boat was bought by Marine Logistics, based in the Bahamas but they have an office in Portishead.'

'Thanks, Cassie. Keep trawling through.'

'Will do, Sarge.'

Mark needs to pay another call to Jason. Perhaps Bristol might have something on this company. He is owed a few favours after an insider tip on a Bristol County Lines gang who turned up on his patch a few months ago. He was able to give names, addresses and colours of hoodies of the lads and lasses they tried to recruit. That was worth the dirt on a boat, wasn't it?

Chapter 29

I promised one more drop and that is it.

Finn waits. The message is brief.

We will tell you when and where. The exact location of the van will be revealed later. It could be soon with little warning. Please check in regularly. No one likes being let down. Then we decide.

Finn runs a hand through his hair. Why the hell did he get involved? He knows why. Approached by a bloke who wanted to rent the field next to the canal for his daughter's pony, the talk had turned to cash flow, or lack of it. That had led to a phone call to another to another. Would he have any clout or was he simply a messenger? Strange how he'd disappeared and the pony had never turned up either. Nor had the rent. Still, the drops he'd done so far had netted one hundred grand and this final one meant another ten thousand quid in the account he'd set up. He called it money from sale of animals and transferred it from the farm account monthly, as if he was in employment, to his main bank account. Enough to get set up here and nobody kept a check on animal sales, unless it was for food or breeding purposes.

There's another ping from the phone.

What about the girl?

He is certain of the answer. Rachel is no threat and for that he'd thank God if they believe him and leave him alone. It's another reason he wants to get out. He hasn't felt so good for years and he reckons he could have a future with her, if she's interested. He types.

Clear. She knows nothing.

He waits for a minute. No more texts. The conversation is over. He stows the phone in the plastic bag and in its secret place. He would have to check it regularly though. What was his excuse? A sick animal? Yes. As good an excuse as any. He closes the barn door and looks up at the house. It's nearly over.

****

Finn is coming out of the barn. Yes, I suppose I'm breaking some lockdown rule except we aren't in lockdown anymore, are we? I can always claim Finn is in my support bubble. I wave as he walks across the yard and I make the sign for a drink. He gives me a thumbs up and taps his watch, holding up five fingers. I know he has more animals to check. I fill the kettle and switch it on. I know where everything is now. Not like the first time I'd been here. He must have thought I was incredibly inquisitive or dim. I hope it was the former.

I check WhatsApp as I wait for the kettle to boil. Why have I been so coy about Finn? Usually, I'd tell the uni girls. We still keep in touch even though we are scattered to the four corners of the planet. Am I scared? Or superstitious? If I tell someone and let slip how happy I am, will it all come crashing down? What the hell. I type and press send. It's a simple message stating I've met a new man and so far, I haven't discovered he's married already, a murderer or on the run. That will keep them informed and intrigued. I switch to Facebook and add a few likes. It's not time to change my status. That's asking for a kick back.

The latch on the kitchen door clicks. I jump up. 'Sorry, I got carried away with stuff.' I wave my phone.

'Social media… the death of decent letter writing and the curse of the age for romance and privacy,' Finn says and grins.

'Since when did you write letters?' I say and place my arms on his shoulders.

'I'll have you know I was always dutiful about my thank you letters at Christmas. Father was a stickler. We had to have them finished on Christmas afternoon or no cake and crackers.'

'You must have had a very hard childhood,' I say and kiss him on the lips.

'I'm making up for it now,' he says. The next kiss takes us to the sofa. We just about make it to the bedroom.

It's midday when I wake. I must have dozed off. Finn is nowhere to be seen and his side of the bed is cold. He hasn't just gone for a pee or to make coffee. I stretch and hear the back door click. Animals? I thought farmers fed and watered them every night and morning and that was it. I know puppies are needy until they grow up but chickens? Goats? The metal gate scrapes. He must be heading into the empty barn. It's the only one that has such an elaborate entrance with gates and fences. Finn says it's for lambing. There aren't lambs now, are there? Finn says they stay out all winter and he will bring the pregnant ewes closer to the farm in February and March.

I pull on a fleece and trousers and head downstairs. I know he keeps a store of bales in there as well as some odd bits of equipment. I want to help. I may not know one end of a cow from the other but I can do something, can't I?

My feet slide into a spare pair of wellies by the back door and I slip outside. The smell of autumn, smoke, damp earth and rotten fruit fills my nostrils. Should I make some noise? Sing? My rubber soled feet make no sound on the paving stones. Someone is talking. A vet? There are no cars or vans and Finn would have said something. The voice is serious, deep and whispered. I can tell by the tone whoever is speaking is rattled. I creep closer. A few words are clear.

'No. Last one. Agreed?'

There is silence.

It is Finn's voice I can hear. 'Last one. I'm out. Get it? Out.'

There is silence again, followed by some scrabbling sounds like something being pulled across a floor followed by the clang of metal, like a filing cabinet. I run back to the house and pretend to lean over the top of the stable door. Just in time. Finn appears from the dark interior of the barn. He seems surprised to see me.

'Ready for some lunch?' I say as brightly as I can. Where is his phone? In a pocket?

'Why don't we head down to the market and pick up some food? I need to freshen up a bit but it's open till this afternoon and the crowds will have gone.'

'Good idea. I'll let you go first. I reckon you might need it after scrabbling around in the barn.'

'What?' Finn's jaw drops. His eyes narrow. For a second, he looks uncomfortable. 'Oh yes. The barn. Just double checking the stock. I thought I'd ordered… not to worry.' He pauses. 'Tell you what, you jump in the shower first and I'll just double check.'

It doesn't sound convincing. I am used to dealing with kids who will bend the truth to save their skins if necessary. I can usually distinguish those who are telling the truth and those who want you to think they are. 'Will do.' I close the top of the door and bolt it onto the lower section. Through the bevelled glass pane in the centre, I can see Finn watching the door. I move away. Still no sign of his phone.

I remove my boots and cross the cold stone floor. On the kitchen table is Finn's phone. I pick it up. Does he have two phones? Why? I know some businessmen have a number. Even the head has two, but most ordinary people can't keep track of one. Unless they have something to hide. The kids a few years ago were always banging on about BB Messenger and how it was used by gangs. I can't see Finn as a gang member. Why does he need a second phone? I am tempted to take his phone to him and say, "You might need this," but it might appear as if I'm prying. No. I'm sure it's nothing.

I run upstairs and switch on the shower in the bathroom. It takes a while to warm up. As I undress, I wonder if I haven't been too trusting. Tashi would say that's my weakness and I should be more ruthless. No. I'm being silly. That's all it is. Except I would like to find out about that other phone, if there is one. Or could I have imagined it?

Finn comes into the bathroom as I am in the shower. 'Any luck?' I call.

'What?'

The sound of the water must be muffling my voice. 'The stock. You said something about the stock?'

'Yeah. There might be a bit of trouble with one of the goats. I'll check again later.'

I switch off the shower and step out as Finn hands me a warm towel. He didn't mention animals, did he? 'Stock? I thought you were talking about equipment, not animals.'

'No, animals.' He pauses. 'We'll have to make a farmer's wife of you yet.' He is fazed again, I'm sure but as he wraps the towel around me and I get closer, all I can think about is sex. Jeez, I'm worse than a teenage boy.

I break away. 'Perhaps you can tell me more over lunch?'

'Perfect.' He strips off and I step aside to let him in the shower.

I go into the bedroom and sit on the small blue velvet chair. This is such a female room with its blue patterned curtains and the tie backs. Guys don't bother, do they? Perhaps this was his father's taste. He might have had a female friend. Or has Finn not told me everything about his past relationships? Was one more important than the others? I dry myself before dressing. Am I being paranoid? I push aside my doubts. I am with a wonderful man, yet something still makes me feel slightly uneasy. I'm really tempted to find out if he does have a second phone. Tashi would ask him and demand he showed her proof. I like to think I am more subtle.

There will be time.

We are sitting in the organic café, sipping coffee, and savouring home-made carrot cake with creamy frosting. I couldn't wait for lunch. I'm starving, as usual. Piled around us are the fruits of our shopping; fresh sourdough, cheeses, homemade chutney with gingham checked covers held in place with thick twine and tomatoes still on the vine, red like jewels, nestling against the sharp green of a fresh lettuce. I'd insisted on paying. I cradle the cup between two hands, watching the continual stream of people as they flow up and down the narrow streets. There's always a buzz about Saturdays in this small town. The locals all greet each other, the kids run around and in between the visitors who walk and gaze open mouthed at the stalls and small shops selling everything from olives to an ebike.

Barbours and pastel cashmere scarves slung round shoulders under cascades of wavy hair announce a mummy with money from one of the villages, multi coloured trousers and bobble hats adorn those who prefer a more hippy, alternative vibe. All blend somehow. Occasionally I spot the familiar face of a member of staff, a parent or child. Interestingly, the teens emerge later when most people have gone home. I suppose they prefer to keep some distance away from family, needing space to grow and become their own person.

Finn is unusually quiet. His face is taut; small frown lines furrow his brow and his lips turn down at the corners. 'Penny for them?'

'What?' He jerks his attention back to me. 'Sorry.'

'You seem a bit distracted. Is something wrong?' Part of me is certain he'll be reassuring and this is not going to turn into one of those *I think we need to talk,* talks which is man speak for *I'm dumping you.* Unless the recent bedroom activity which was extended and passionate was to say goodbye? No. I've experienced those before and after he's got his breath back, all the guy wants to do is to get out of the place, not go shopping for lunch.

Finn puts down his cup and looks at me. The grey green sweater brings out the hazel flecks in his eyes. Like a cat's eyes.

For a moment I feel a pang of regret. I've missed the search for the beasts. I was so certain I'd identified a favourite hunting spot. 'Sorry. I've got a few business worries,' he says.

'Such as?' So that was it. Was this about to become a sob story? Is he after my hard-earned cash? No. If he'd wanted a sugar mama, he should have gone on a cruise and found a rich widow or divorcee. No. Finn isn't like that.

He takes a deep breath, glances at the outside before turning his attention back to me. 'A business deal I was involved with is coming to its end and it's always a bit tricky, you know.'

I don't but I guess he is describing buying and selling and finding the correct moment when the market is up or down or whatever it should be and you jump in and make a kill. 'Tell me more.'

He shrugs. 'That's all there is, really. I'm just waiting for the right time and it will all be over.' His shoulders sink and he exhales. 'That's what I want now, a simpler life, sorting the farm and being with you.'

'Me?' This is heaven to my ears.

'Yes. We get on so well, you're shit hot in bed and I fancy you like hell. I reckon we've got a chance to make this work long term.' He looks away and I can tell he's blushing.

I can't resist teasing him. 'Which is more important?' I place my hands around his clasped ones.

He looks at me and grins. The playful Finn is back. 'Sex now, of course, but as I become increasingly decrepit in my old age, I'm sure that will take a back seat. How are you at Scrabble?'

I giggle. 'Who says I'm going to stay around that long?'

'My old age is closer than you think,' Finn says and winks before his voice softens. 'I'm serious. I reckon we could go the course. If you want to try that is.'

'What do you mean?' I am half expecting him to say we should become exclusive, boy and girlfriend, the sort of things you see on Love Island.

'Let's make it official we are an item.'

'How do we do that?'

'We become Finn and Rachel instead of Finn plus one or Rachel plus one.'

'I can do that. Anything else?'

'Yes.' This time he takes my hands in his and squeezes them. 'I'd like to get you a friendship ring, not an engagement ring, a friendship ring. I want it to be a sign we're serious about exploring where this can go, and it tells everyone else to back off. We're taken.'

'I don't know what to say,' I manage to stammer out.

'Say yes and we'll head off to a delightful jeweller's shop where I can find you a vintage ring that says, "This is my girl." He lets go of my hands and beats his chest like they did in the Tarzan films from my childhood.

I punch him. 'Shhh,' I say and glance round the café. No one is taking any notice. We are just two people, enjoying being together.

'What do you say?'

'I think it is a great idea. Finn and Rachel? Rachel and Finn? That sounds better.'

Finn stands up. 'Come on then.'

That is why I am the owner of a small gold band set with amethyst, garnet, citrine and opal. It appears they were called promise rings and were all the fashion in 19th century England. Just wait till I tell Tashi.

Chapter 30

'I said I'm sorry. The murder of this poor old bloke has shaken everyone.' Mark expects an explosion or at least a few swear words. Instead, there is silence. How long does it last? It feels like minutes.

'I see.' Ginny's voice is flat.

'You know what it's like.'

'Yes. I do know. And there's something else I know. You put the death of a stranger above the welfare of your family.'

Ginny's words cut to his heart. 'No, that's unfair. This is work—'

'And work takes precedence over everything else. Do you realise the day I've had, and to cap it all, Mrs Cook, Emily's class teacher, comes out onto the playground in front of all the mothers and asks for a private word.'

'So?' What's the problem? Teachers need to speak with parents and carers, don't they?' What was she supposed to use? Semaphore? Smoke signals? ESP? The words remain unsaid.

'So? So?' Ginny shrieks. 'It's the humiliation. Everyone will think there's something wrong or that Emily's a bad girl.'

'She never gets into trouble. You know how much the kids snitch on each other. No one has a bad word to say about her.' He can hear snuffling at the end of the phone. He wants to be there with Ginny, to fold her in his arms and tell her it'll be all right. Could he leave the interview with Jason till tomorrow? Better not. People he wanted to investigate had a habit of disappearing. Did they have ESP? 'What happened?'

'Huh?'

'Tell me what Mrs Cook said, a quick heads up will do.' He crosses his fingers on the steering wheel and looks out at the flat expanse of wetland before the river. He'd deliberately taken a back route so he could pull over and respond to Ginny's text. The sun shines through the clouds and casts shadows from the trees over the road.

'She's certain Emily shows signs of being dyslexic and the school can't have her assessed for at least eighteen months. There's a waiting list apparently, and it's got worse since the pandemic started and they missed all those months in the spring and summer.' The words tumble out.

'What happens if they discover she *is* dyslexic?'

'She gets some extra help. By that time, she'll be nearly ten. Most of her primary years will have gone. She can't go to secondary school not being able to read and write.' Ginny's voice rarely trembles like this.

'It won't come to that.' Mark pulls a face. His dad had trouble with reading and so did his brother. Is it hereditary? Is it his fault?

'I searched again online when I got back.' Ginny speaks faster, as if she's come alive.

'And?'

'Like I told you, there are plenty of centres locally. I called one of them and they said she could have an assessment for five hundred and fifty pounds next week. They'd do a full report we could take back to school with their recommendations and if the school didn't have the facilities or the expertise, the centre would find a suitable tutor.' She is panting by the time she gets to the end of the speech. Has it been rehearsed?

'That's… useful.' He wants to say, "What a of lot of money for something the school should fix," but he discovered years ago that so much about getting a decent education was dependent on cash.

'Can we at least think about it?' Ginny's voice is calm. He'd expected more anger or wheedling.

'Tell you what, I'll finish up here and get back as soon as I can. We'll talk once the kids are in bed. You can show me these centres and what they do and how long they think it might take to get her up to speed.' Five fifty plus a few lessons can't break the bank… the kids' swimming lessons over the summer didn't cost that much.

'They reckon two half hour sessions a week, plus at home practice on a daily basis for eighteen months.' Ginny takes a deep breath. 'The sessions cost fifty pounds each.'

Mark swallows hard. A hundred pounds a week is four hundred pounds a month for eighteen months, and with the assessment he's looking at a bill of over seven grand. They can probably manage if Ginny takes on more hours. 'Let's talk properly tonight. We'll work something out. Better go. Love you. Tell the children Daddy's sorry but he has to earn their daily bread.'

'I will, and Mark… thanks for listening. Love you.' The phone goes dead.

Mark puts the car into drive and it slides away. Daily bread? He hasn't used that for years, not since school prayers. Our Father and all that. Was it the thought of Emily struggling at school that brought back the memories? He'd been lazy but had sailed through everything, not like his cousin, Sid. Still, Sid had the last laugh. He'd become a plumber and was now installing jacuzzis for the rich and famous in their rustic hideaways. He employed ten others and drove a Porsche. Except Mark didn't want Emily to go through the bullying Sid had suffered, even after he'd threatened to punch hell out of whoever made fun of him. Were girls nicer? Perhaps Sid would lend him the money? No Sid would give it to him. He was too generous.

Mark turns right and follows the road to the harbour. A few kids play on bikes. They stop as he goes past, staring before one sets off and heads down a small pathway. Someone doesn't like the idea of a policeman turning up unannounced. Who might that be?

He stops in the car park by the entrance to the docks, adjusts his cap and walks towards the harbour master's office. The door opens before he is within ten metres. Someone has been watching, or he's been tipped off.

Jason speaks first. 'Any more news about poor old Lewis?' He shakes his head. 'Terrible business. The local people are convinced it's not someone from round here. We all know each other, see? Like family we are. We look after each other.'

'There's no news yet,' Mark says. 'I've got a few questions I'd like to ask you, and we can do it here or HQ. Your choice.'

Jason's face blanches. The bluster has gone. 'I've got nothing to hide. Better come in, away from prying eyes.' He nods towards Mark's car. Mark turns. The kid on the bike is circling slowly. He stares at Mark, or is it Jason, for a few seconds before he rides away.

'Friend of yours?' Mark says as he crosses the path and stops in front of Jason's office.

'Him? He's a nosey little toe rag. Always on the watch for something to pinch and sell.' Jason folds his arms and stands, legs apart. Why doesn't Jason wear a uniform? Or is that coastguards? His navy cargo pants and white t-shirt are splattered with paint and grease. Perhaps with lockdown, there'd been maintenance work building up. He was hardly going to welcome the Queen.

'What sort of things does he pinch?' A bar of chocolate is not worth the paperwork but perhaps he was County Lines.

'Anything. You must have come across him before?'

'This place is a haven compared to most. A few domestics and anti-social behaviour are the only crimes on the book. Until recently.'

'Yeah. Poor old fella. Still, that kid's a nuisance, hanging round the village at all times of the day and night. A few of our patrons come down here with top of the range cars. They don't want to find a scratch down the body work.'

Here was a lead. Youths that hang around at night know what's going on. He might have seen a lot over the past few months. 'What's his name?'

'Tyler Matthews. His mum helps at the chippie. Lives at number five Briar Close.'

Mark makes a note to call round on the kid later. 'I don't suppose I can come in? I do have a few questions to ask.'

Jason remains where he is. 'I'm a busy man.'

'It won't take long.'

Jason stands aside and lets the door swing open. The office is as dark and cluttered as Mark remembers it. Jason clears a pile of ropes from a chair and points. Mark sits down and gets out his notebook. He's going old style today.

'Don't start by asking me where I was on that night the old boy copped it, I've given my statement. So has everyone else round here,' Jason says and sits down behind the desk.

'We've got those. My enquiries are about another business.'

Jason leans forward. 'What?' The flat tone is at odds with the furrowing of his brow. It doesn't last long. 'Anything to be of help?' The tone is wheedling, like Emily when she wants more pocket money. Jason spreads his hands and rests them on the desk. Is he as relaxed as he wants to appear?

'Vans,' Mark says and waits for a reaction. There is none.

'Plenty round here from time to time. What sort?'

'White transits hired from Able Cars and Vans on …' Mark reels off the date.

Jason shrugs. 'Sorry. News to me. Can't help you.'

'I think you can,' Mark says. He gets out his tablet and taps the screen before twisting it so Jason can see it. 'Is this you?' The image clearly shows Jason speaking into the intercom at Able Cars and Vans. 'There are several others. If it's not you, the resemblance is striking, don't you think?'

Jason sits back and folds his arms over his chest. He glances round, teeth biting at his top lip. 'Okay.' He holds up his hands. 'I admit I do a fish run for a mate from time to time.'

'Fish?' This is a wind up.

'Fish. Elvers to be precise. The chefs in London can't get enough. Trouble is, they're on licence to a small group of people. My mate isn't one of them.'

'I'd call that poaching.'

Jason shakes his head. 'No. We get them in the sea. That's open to everyone, isn't it? Or why do all these rich blokes spend a fortune to bob up and down for hours?'

'You tell me.'

Jason scratches his head. Is he stalling for time? 'We do the same for a bit of sea bream, a few others in season. As it's all fresh, hand caught and reaches the kitchens in record time, the animal or fish huggers can stuff their faces and call it ethical.'

'You get paid for this?'

'I take a cut. Made a few grand last year and it's legal. You could come out with us one day, catch a few and sell them on.'

Mark focuses on Jason's face. It is a good trick. Take your time, wait, and stare. Most bleat a bit more information and some even confess. Jason fidgets in the seat. 'Like I said. It's fishing and selling what we catch and if there's a law against that, I'm giving up membership of the human race.'

Mark pauses. Is it stealing? If not, there must be plenty of Health and Safety rules Jason and his mates are breaking, if it's the truth. There is another line of questioning he could take. 'You make some cash, eh? Tax free?'

'I pay enough to the tax man and his mates,' Jason says. He leans closer and his voice drops to a whisper. 'On a good day, we can pull conger eels, shark, and rays. Twenty kilos is a decent weight and there are plenty who will pay for that sort of fish. Not just chefs.'

'Can you make a living?'

'Plenty do,' Jason says. His voice returns to its normal volume. 'You should come out with us. A trip every month and you'd have your holiday fund sorted in no time.' Jason is a cool character.

'The van you hired was used for transporting fish?'

'Yep.' There is no trace of fear. Either Jason is telling the truth or he is a master of deception.

'I'd need to have names and addresses of these establishments.'

This time there is a reaction. A faint shadow passes over Jason's face. 'Listen, if I could tell you I would, but a satnav postcode is as much as you get. There's usually a bloke waiting at a car park or down a side alley. He hands over the cash, I hand over the fish.'

'If by any chance a name or an address or part of a postcode comes back to you, I'd be grateful if you can let me know.' Mark stands up.

Jason jumps and opens the door. 'Of course. Anything to help. Don't forget, that offer of a share of the catch if you want to come out and fish with us. You'd be very welcome. You could make five grand a year.'

Mark draws in a breath of fresh air as he walks back to the car. Has he been offered a bribe or is this a genuine way he could earn a bit of spare cash? Others did work on the side. Why not him? Fishing is a hobby and if by chance you caught something others prized, is that a crime? That's the trouble, it probably is a crime. He'll ignore Jason's offer and pay a call on Tyler Matthews before he heads home.

Tyler Matthews' house is not as Mark expected. From the description of the lad and his behaviour, he should have been parking along the road of 1950s and 60s council houses that were either sold to the owners in Maggie Thatcher's day, a thing his father never forgave, owned by Housing Associations or in the hands of private lets who cared little about social justice and more about the cash lining their pockets. Briar Close is a small development of four and five bedroomed houses and his mother works in a chippie? His dad must be loaded. Or they have found a very lucrative way of supplementing their income.

He drives into the cul de sac and parks on the road. Number five is on a corner plot and smaller than the others. He walks up the paved driveway and past a small, silver Citroen. The double garage door is open and a blue BMW is parked inside amongst a trail bike, three off road cycles and a number of vintage models Mark remembers from his youth. Someone likes their bikes. He knocks on the door.

'Yeah?' A voice speaks from behind the door. Is there an intercom? Mark looks around. Yes. The place is bristling with surveillance of every kind. What the hell for?

'DS Mark Mulroney here. I need to have a word with Tyler if he's around.'

The door opens. 'What's the little shit done now?' The man who opened the door is small, thin and his fingers sport tattoos with the word DAD clearly visible between heavy gold rings. A thick gold chain hangs round his scrawny neck. An England cricket polo shirt and grey joggers complete the outfit.

'Can I come in?'

The man stands aside and Mark steps into a white hallway with a pale wooden floor and a huge glass and chrome mirror attached to one wall. A small girl in a pink dress peers round a door. Behind her is an open plan kitchen, or family room, as Ginny is fond of describing the latest trends she notices in her friends' homes.

'Who is it, Daddy?' The child speaks in a lisping voice.

'Nothing sweetheart, you go and play. Daddy will be back soon.' The door closes. 'Well?'

'Is Tyler around?'

'No. Haven't seen him since yesterday when he got sent home, suspended from school again,' the man says. 'I'm Tyler's stepdad, Dave Hawkins.'

'I only want to ask him a few questions.'

'What about?' The tone is belligerent.

'In case he spotted anything unusual these past few weeks.'

'What sort of things?' The words shoot out like a machine gun.

'Anything.' Mark fishes into his pocket and hands over a card. 'When he or his mum get back, tell him I want a word. Unless his mum's around?'

'At the chippie. Extra shift. If anyone's seen anything suspicious it'd be her. Ask her.'

'I have and will,' Mark says. 'Thanks for your time.'

The man opens the door and Mark steps outside. 'Daddy, has Tyler been a bad boy again?' a small voice chirrups.

'Nothing for you to worry about, princess. If he's been naughty, you know what Daddy will do, don't you?'

There is a giggle. 'The naughty step.'

The door slams behind Mark and the chain is put on.

Mark gets back into his car. Where would a kid like Tyler hang around on an evening in a village? There is no parade of shops. His mum works at the chippie. The pubs wouldn't want him or any mates cluttering up the place. Strange Jason didn't mention a gang of lads. Is Tyler a lone wolf?

Mark starts the car and pauses. Should he call Ginny and say he's on his way home? What if he's delayed? No. She might worry if he was late, like his mum used to when he and his mates stayed out at the local recreation ground. Mark slaps the steering wheel. Where could a kid hang around and find a place to sit down? The recreation ground. Or were they called playgrounds today? Even if it was fenced off and designed for younger kids, he'd spent a fair amount of time there when he was a lad with his mates until they got chased away by someone who knew his mum and dad. So where is the recreation ground here?

Mark drives slowly along the High Street in the dusky light of early evening. A few bats flit around in the gloom and the last red streaks of the sunset are smeared over the sky. He'd bet the owls are already hooting in any nearby woods and the foxes are setting out. Perhaps he could try a sonnet about early evening, the end of the day and the excitement of the start of the night? It would be good to work on something like that for a change. He stops at the crossroads and checks the local map on the satnav. There's a playing field at the back of the church. He won't need directions. The spire stands high above the roof tops as it has done for years, calling the peasants to worship and conform to the elite. It would be a good place for kids to hang out; no one would visit a church this late, even if they did on a Sunday which he doubts. He has a few questions he wants to ask Tyler, when he finds him.

Chapter 31

'I know it's soon. I know it's quick. It feels right.' I am shifting from one foot to the other before Tashi's fierce stare. The sounds of the school diminish as lessons begin and everyone is shepherded to their classrooms. I have one free lesson. Trust Tashi to be in the office when I collect the keys to the art block's main teaching room. It will be my form room from now until the end of the academic year if I want it. I do. I want to belong to a school, to a class as their *Miss* and yes, I want to be someone's partner, girlfriend, exclusive, significant other, whatever is the key phrase of the moment.

Tashi tips her head in the direction of the quadrangle. We are getting used to holding information swaps in the freezing cold, rather than in an office. There are some things you want to say and not necessarily record so online is out. I follow the tailored, navy suit, cherry red fleece, and red ankle boots. 'Come on, Rachel, tell me what's happened.' There is a smile flickering at the corners of her crimson tipped mouth.

'Finn and I are an item,' I say, reverting to the jargon we used as teenagers.

'I thought you might last out longer after the last disastrous incursion into Love Island.'

'This is different.'

She tilts her head to one side and her hair flops onto the suit collar. 'I think I remember you saying that at the time too.'

'We get on so well.'

Tashi shakes her head. I half expect a wagged finger. 'As long as he doesn't break your heart or he'll have me, the children and Mamaji to deal with and that is not a pretty sight.'

I giggle. 'I'll warn him.' I feel my throat constricting and my eyes are prickling. Am I that hormonal? 'Tashi, thanks for everything,' I manage to squeak.

'If it weren't for protocol and the thought of a thousand teenage eyes watching our every move, I would give you a big hug and tell you to take care and follow your heart, which you will do anyway.'

I nod. I'm certain this time it'll work out.

She is about to return to the office block when she stops. 'Oh, and congratulations.'

'What for?'

'If you check your internal email, there's a request for you to attend an interview for Head of Art and Design as from January 1st. It's a full time, permanent contract and you're the only candidate.' She turns on her heels and leaves me staring after her, mouth open and knees beginning to shake. I want to call out, ask her how this has happened. Except I know how. When you find a decent member of staff, you move heaven and earth, no, you'd move the universe, to keep them. My classes are well attended, there are never any discipline issues and they are all making good progress. I hope it's also because I fit well with the ethos of the school; no one wants a maverick in the staff room. I skip back to the main block and up to the room which will be my base. I check the emails and there it is. I will need to bring evidence of pupil progress, a set of lesson plans for a term's work and an individual lesson plan, amended in the light of previous achievements. Nothing I can't do standing on my head and blindfolded. It is for two weeks' time. I type my acceptance.

Once it's sent, I wander round the room. The light is perfect up here. The art work we can do will be fabulous. I can move the furniture around over the holidays so that the natural light shines over the pupils' heads onto the tables and desks. The grey metal lockers will be placed as a divider to cover the stock and store area and there'll be a wall for information and huge reminders of what needs to be handed in and when. I twist round. On the other two walls I'll have children's work, mounted. I'll show them how to present their work and we'll change themes and colours with one display space showing a fine art poster, a painting of the month for discussion, educating and broadening their artistic knowledge. We'll start with Banksy. I hug myself. I'll call Finn. Except he's probably with the animals or repairing the fences or was he making a start on the new conversion? I'll text him.

Guess what? I have an interview for a FT and permanent post in the school as from the start of the new term. It means this place will be my home. Tell you more when we speak next.

Xxx

The bell rings. Is that the end of my free period? Year 10 will be here any minute. Poor kids missed so much preparation for this year, they are floundering. I plan to end the lesson early and have a Q and A to check they know what is expected and when. I'll repeat the process at the start of every term with every class. It might reassure them and if I upload the advice on the portal, their parents can see it. It hits me. I am, or will soon be, a proper Head of Department. That means I will have the two newest teachers and three-part timers reporting to me. Perhaps I need to invest in a couple of suits?

'Ere miss, when do we do life drawing, nudes and all that?' Alfie slides into the room ahead of everyone else. How he manages to get here so early amazes me, unless he has bunked off the previous lesson. His tie is half way round his neck, his mask has fangs painted on it and his arms poke out from the sleeves of his blazer.

'Sorry, Alfie, if you've chosen art as an option because of the nudes, you will be very disappointed. It was worth a try, though.'

He grins as he takes off the mask and I smile back. At the moment there is no place or no time I would rather be than here and now.

Finn does not return my text. It's the end of the day and I go home, alone. Why hasn't he returned my message? Should I text again? Or call? I don't want to come across as needy. What's the current term for showing you are interested? Crack on? Graft? Yes, that's it. Should I crack on and graft? The language repels me, except there is nothing to stop me texting again.

Hi

Hope you've had a good day. I'm at home in case you need to catch up.

That's not bad, is it?

I spend the rest of the evening amending lesson plans, marking course work and wondering about the interview. What questions will they ask, or will it be one of those when you have to prove your competencies? I go through the list of classes from this school and my previous post and check my pupil progress log. All very satisfactory.

I'm in the middle of crunching data to show that I have a good hit rate of passes when my phone goes. It's Finn. 'Sorry I missed your texts. I've been repairing fences and the damn phone died on me.'

It's dark outside. How can he mend fences in the dark. 'You're working late,' I say.

'If I went by daylight, I'd work twenty hours in the summer and seven in the winter. The old Land Rover has arc lamps which keep even the birds awake. I've had a robin singing in my ear since six o' clock.'

I check the time. It's gone eight. 'Have you just got in?'

'Yep. Stuck the phone in the charger and there were your messages. Sorry.'

'No. I understand. It's a very different work from mine.'

Finn laughs. 'What is it they say? Never work with kids or animals? I reckon we both have our fair share of awkward sods to deal with. At least they aren't as aromatic as me at the moment.' There is the sound of a large sniff. 'Yes, sheep dung, wood preserver and the grassy aroma of mud and flattened grass.'

'I'd take that over Y8 male sweaty socks and bodies with an overlay of whatever deodorant spray they have pinched from the local shop.'

'Talking about getting sweaty. That weekend was the best I've had in ages. We must do it again.'

'Anytime,' I say.

There is a pause. 'Go on. Tell me about this job? I've got a drink. The food's in the microwave and the dog and I are stretched out in front of a fire, desperate to hear more.'

For a moment I feel a rush of some biological urge to feed and care for Finn. An image of a huge farmhouse kitchen, the smell of home cooking wafting from an Aga and me, elegant yet on trend in fabulous jeans and a pastel, cashmere sweater flits into my mind. I chase the dream away, yet the sensation remains. 'If I get the job, I'll be around for the foreseeable future. It's an opportunity to inspire children about art, not simply those who can paint or do graffiti.'

'Do you need the job to stay around?' His voice sounds concerned.

'What do you mean?'

'I'd hoped you might want to stay around for other reasons.'

I know he is hedging for reassurance. 'I wouldn't go far,' I say. 'There is nothing that would tempt me to move out of the area.'

'Good. I'm hoping that ring will be the start of something between us.'

'I'm sure it will be.' I have an idea. 'How would you like me to come over and cook after school tomorrow? I can pick up some ingredients on my way and when you finish work, there'll be a decent meal waiting?'

'I'd love that. I'll leave the key under a bucket in the back barn, the one for the hay store?'

'Perfect.'

'Tell me more about your day while I sort this microwave meal out and pour another drink.'

We talk until ten o'clock and I go to bed in a haze of anticipation and satisfaction.

****

Finn closes the call. Why is it so easy talking to Rachel? Once he's got the last drop done and he's completely legit, he'll ask her to make their relationship exclusive and formal. Perhaps she can move in? He whistles Gyp. The dog trots over obediently. Finn ruffles the soft black and white ears. 'How do you fancy having a nice lady living here? Plenty of cuddles for us both?'

The dog licks his hand in appreciation. Finn stands up and walks over to the collection of keys hanging from the board. He takes one and fixes a wooden tag. It has the word *BOSS* carved into it. She'll like that. He slips on his boots and jacket and opens the back door. Gyp follows. Once out in the fresh air, Finn shivers. There will be a frost tonight. He'll take one turn round Lower Meadow so Gyp can do what he needs to do and he can leave the key for Rachel.

Stars pepper the sky. Fewer lights shine on the hillsides. People are in for the night and the dark sky benefits. The taillights of a plane wink high above him as it crosses East to West. An owl hoots from the nearby copse. There is only one other thing on his mind. What if Rachel finds out it was him who hit her? She says she can't remember. What if her memory comes back? The thought makes him shiver. Finn wants out of this whole mess and to move on with Rachel. Should he have agreed when that man inquired about renting the field for his daughter to ride her pony? Or was he involved too? Yes, the extra cash had been very useful when he was broke. Delivering a few packages of dodgy fags was nothing terrible, was it? Things are different now. Those plastic wrapped bags were bad enough but people? All he wants is a simple life.

Two bright eyes stare out from a leafless hedge. Gyp barks. A muntjac emerges. It barks back before it heads into the undergrowth. Finn grabs Gyp's collar. 'Don't terrorise the wildlife. That's our future.'

Finn reaches the old barn. Should he check the phone? Yes. There's no harm. He pulls aside a bale and opens the small metal cabinet. The phone is safely tucked inside. There are no messages. The battery is ninety percent. For a moment he worries in case it isn't working so switches the phone from silent to sound and calls the number from his personal phone. He lets it ring three times before deleting any evidence in the call log. That will do. They'll get in touch when they're ready. There's a full moon next week. He'd better check every couple of hours. The pick-up could be within the next few days.

Once back inside the farm house, Finn throws another log on the fire and pours himself a single malt. Gyp has curled up on the mat, the firelight reflecting in his glossy fur. One more pick-up and he'll be free.

Chapter 32

Mark slows the car as he follows the track into the car park of the recreation ground. A security light shines on the kids' playground and the main entrance. There must be CCTV cameras. What might they reveal? A small figure glances up from an upturned bike. It must be Tyler. He is about to run when Mark opens the window and calls out. 'Got a puncture?'

'Chain's knackered.' He stands upright and stares at Mark. 'I'm not doing anything wrong. I've got a right to be here.'

Mark gets out of the car. 'Never said you didn't. Let's have a look.' He leaves off the hat and saunters over. 'I've had a bike since I was a nipper. My grandad taught me all he knew. Reckon I can take anything apart and mend it.'

'Yeah?' The sneer has been replaced by a gentler tone. 'Can you fix it?'

'I've got a few tools in the back. Wait here.'

'Can't go anywhere, can I?' The defiant tone is back.

'You could run and I'd never catch you.' Mark lets his words sink in.

He fetches a small tool kit from the back of his car. He likes to have a few bits and pieces as he calls them. Ever since he needed a screwdriver to prise open a car door, he's kept a kit like this. He knows what the rest of the station call him — Ever Ready Mark. He doesn't care.

'Let the dog see the rabbit,' Mark says and places the tool kit on the surface of the car park.

'What?'

''Give us space, lad. Social distancing, remember?'

Tyler springs back. 'Sorry.'

Mark crouches down and squints at the back wheel. The chain has come off the gears. 'Let me show you what to do and you'll never get stuck anywhere again.'

For a few minutes they work together. Mark shows the boy how to turn the wheel and slide the chain over the cogs. With a final twist of the pedals, the chain clicks into place. 'Cool.' He perches on the seat.

'Give it a try round the car park.'

The boy pedals and raises the front wheel in a show of defiance and bravado. 'For a plod, you're not bad,' he says.

'I reckon one good turn deserves another. Can I ask you a question?'

The lad's face screws up. 'Yeah? Such as?' The same cold tone returns.

'You're Tyler, right?' Mark would bet a pound to a penny the lad has an issue with authority. 'I've been told you're the best person to ask about what goes on in this village.'

'Who says?'

'Most everyone I meet.'

'Cool.' Tyler sits astride his bike. 'I'm Tyler. What do you want to know?'

Mark collects up his tools. He's prepared to wait. It will show Tyler he's serious. 'Unusual stuff,' he says.

'Like the cabin cruiser with the darkened windows?'

'Yeah?' Mark pretends he's not that interested.

'Yeah. *Lady Luck* she's called. Turns up most months.'

Mark nods. 'Nice name for a boat.' How much more does the boy know? 'What's so strange about people going out on a boat now and again?'

Tyler snorts. 'If you've got a decent craft like that, you'd be up on the deck, showing it off, right?'

''I suppose so.'

'You'd take your mates, your girlfriends, your family out for the day, eh?'

Mark closes the tool box and straightens up. 'Yes. I would.'

'Not this owner.' Tyler is silent. He moves back and forwards on the bike.

'Any idea who it is?'

Tyler glances around him. 'Bloke they call The Tsar. Foreign.'

'How do you know?'

'I've heard him shouting. It aint English. I know a lot of foreign languages. This sounds weird… ovich… ostovic… like that.'

'Where did you hear this?'

'That night the old geezer was killed, I was by the harbour. I saw a couple of blokes get out of an old van. They hooted the horns. Jason came out and spoke to them. They ran off along the tow path.'

'Did they see you?'

'Course not. I slipped away and went home. I know when people mean trouble.'

It's time for Mark to be honest with the lad. 'What you've said could be important. You realise I might need to speak to you with your mum and dad present?'

Even in the poor light, Tyler's eyes show his fear. He reminds Mark of a startled deer. 'He's not my dad.'

'Is he your stepdad or just an uncle?'

'He's a bastard. If he thinks I've been talking to you, I'll get it.'

'Does he hit you? You can tell me, it won't go any further, I promise.'

For a moment Mark thinks Tyler might clear off. He waits. 'What do you think?' Tyler says.

'I know my dad used to use his slipper on my bum for serious stuff, like the time I nicked some fags and when I cheeked Mum.' He hopes Tyler will believe him.

Tyler shakes his head. 'I can't do anything right.'

There's no point going further down this route. There's a potential safeguarding issue and it's taking him away from The Tsar. 'Is he one of your stepdad's mates?'

'Dunno. He came round to our house one night. It was late. Really late. He handed over a parcel. The next day we get a new car and Stacey gets a new bike.'

'What did you get?'

'What do you think?'

The moon appears from behind a cloud. The scene reminds Mark of a painting he'd seen once, all silvery light with dark buildings and trees. The light casts shadows on the ground; long shadows of a boy on a bike and a man, standing, legs apart. 'Is that why you get out of the house?'

Tyler sits upright. 'What are you, some sort of social worker as well as a plod?'

Mark needs to get him back on side. 'Just a hunch. I did the same when I was your age.'

'What happened?' Tyler is curious.

'I got in trouble with the police and look what happened to me.'

Tyler smiles. 'I'd like to be a lawyer. I like arguing. I nearly always win.'

I bet you do, thinks Mark. Why can't the school recognise a bright lad like this could go far? 'You need to work hard at school.'

Tyler shrugs. 'Didn't even come to my case meeting. Said they were too busy. Mum might have come if she wasn't scared of him.' The boy scratches at his skin. The sleeves of the sweatshirt move and reveal red marks.

'You got a rash? My kids get eczema.'

Tyler pulls the sleeves down and tucks a thumb into a hole in the cuff. 'No. It's nothing.'

He's lying. The one thing Mark has learnt about dealing with kids is they love to talk unless they're hiding something.

'Tell you what I'll do. I'll show you how to keep the chain tighter so it won't come off as a thank you for all the information and then you can get home. Deal?'

Tyler thinks for a moment, his eyes looking up, down, left and right as he searches for an answer. 'Deal,' he says.

Ten minutes later Mark is back in his car. As he'd anticipated, Tyler had to loosen his thumb in the cuff and the sleeves rolled up slightly. It was enough to tell the red marks were small and round. There were also the yellow-purple remains of old bruises. Someone is battering the kid and he has a good idea who it is.

He glances at Tyler in the rear mirror and waves. A quick call to Social Services tomorrow morning would be enough to frighten the bully off for a time and he'll tell the boss about the links with a foreign sounding man who paid a call. Knowing the boss, she'd take the house apart if she thought she was onto a decent lead that could solve the murder and perhaps point to something bigger. What Tyler described and what he'd seen with his own eyes had the marks of organised crime.

****

Ginny is making up packed lunches in the kitchen when he gets in. The house is quiet. The twins must be in bed. 'Sorry. I got caught up in a possible child protection issue,' he says and closes the back door.

She stops what she is doing and looks at him, her face a mask of concern. 'That's awful. Will it be a care order?'

Mark undoes his boots and drops them on the shoe rack. 'I doubt it, but I hope the bastard is chucked out by his wife and she takes him to the cleaners for support and money.'

'You need a beer. I'll get it.' Ginny wipes her hands on a tea towel and opens the fridge door. She passes a cold can to Mark. She is smiling. 'There was an email from the school when I got home. Mrs Cook reckons they can get some extra help for

Emily,' she says and returns to sandwich making. Her back is towards him and as Mark pulls the top of the can and gulps down the cool liquid, his gaze falls on the tight material of her skirt stretched across her thighs and hips.

He goes across and nuzzles his face on the back of her neck. 'That's excellent news.'

Ginny leans back against his body. 'I've got some good news too,' she says and pauses in the elaborate job of arranging lettuce and slices of tomato onto grated cheese in just the right amount.

'What's that?'

'You know we said about another baby?'

The chill beer hits his stomach. 'You wanted that,' he says. 'I told you I'm happy with the two we've got.'

Ginny's mouth pouts. Her lip protrudes slightly. 'We talked.'

'You talked. Tell me the news anyway.' Mark sighs.

Ginny looks up at him. Her face is shining. 'My period is late and I've bought a test. I wanted to do it with you.'

'How did that happen?' Mark says. 'We haven't had unprotected sex in years, have we?'

'Nothing is fail-safe,' Ginny says as her face flushes. 'Except abstinence.'

'We've always been careful.' Mark takes another drink. 'I don't understand it.'

Ginny turns away. 'We had a long talk and I thought you wanted what I did. You don't care what I want, do you?'

'It's not that I don't care. We have got more than enough to do to look after our two.' Ginny's shoulders move up and down. There is no sound but he knows she is crying. He turns her to face him and cuddles her close. 'Let's do the test together and whatever happens, happens.'

'If the test is negative, we can try properly this time?'

'Do the test first. I'll wait here.'

Ginny opens her bag and takes out a small package. 'Won't be long,' she says and disappears into the downstairs toilet.

Mark sits down at the counter. He cradles the beer between his hands. How had the condoms he'd used meticulously for seven years failed? He was always ultra-careful. Why had it gone wrong now when Ginny wanted a child so much? After a few minutes there was the sound of flushing. Ginny reappears with a small plastic wand which she places on the counter top.

'Three minutes and we'll know if we're to be parents again.' There is no doubting the excitement in her voice.

Mark stares at the small piece of plastic. Yes, he'd love the baby. Of course, he would and he'd do the best for it as well as the twins, but this wasn't what he'd planned. They were doing well, able to go out and about, take the kids on decent holidays and he'd just got a promotion. Until a few weeks ago, Ginny had been keen to get back to work too and do more hours. What has happened?

Four minutes later and there is no doubting the sadness on Ginny's face. 'I was so sure,' she says and blows her nose on a tissue. 'Sorry. I'm being over dramatic.'

Mark places one arm around her shoulders and draws her towards him. 'I can't claim to understand as it's not my body, but I can say I'm feeling your pain and I'd do anything to stop it.'

Muffled sobs echo through his body where Ginny's head rests against his chest. 'Thank you.'

Mark eases his body to a more comfortable position. 'How about I run you a bath, bring you up a nice cup of tea and you can get an early night?'

'That would be wonderful,' Ginny says and breaks away. She rubs a hand across her tear-stained face. Black smudges of mascara ring her eyes like a panda.

Mark is on autopilot. Run upstairs, put plug in bath. Turn on taps and add a sprinkle of Ginny's favourite bath bomb. Find two large and clean towels from the cupboard. Place them over the radiator. It isn't until Ginny is ensconced in the bath, the mug of tea by her side that he dares to gather his thoughts. They would have to have a long conversation. He doesn't want another child. He is happy with the life they are leading and the life they are on the edge of leading with a better salary. They could move house, get a decent car, have a few holidays. He's always wanted to visit Disneyland. The kids would love all the rides. They could have a great life.

Another baby would put a lot of that on hold. He'd have to work longer hours; that came with the job. The thought of coming home after a long day and looking after two kids and a new baby does not fill him with the joy that the advertisers promise. How the hell did working mothers manage? There was something else. The small amount of time he'd spent recently on his poems, or scribbles as he calls them, had made him feel alive again. He wants more of that. How on earth is he to convey this to Ginny?

Perhaps he could start the conversation about a new house? If he could have a shed in the garden that would be perfect. For once all thoughts of work disappear. He wants to be Mark Mulroney; husband, father, policeman and poet. Well, he'd thought it and the sky hadn't fallen in. Perhaps there is a chance to do and be something different.

Chapter 33

'Where are you off to in such a rush?' Tashi calls to me from the opposite side of the arts and science quadrangle.

'I'm going to unleash my inner domestic goddess.'

She crosses over the paved area, dodging a stray mask and a few empty crisp packets. I already knew the message to be conveyed to the kids tomorrow morning's online assembly. 'Who with, or is that a stupid question?'

'I'm off to Finn's house to prepare a decent meal.'

'Check out the deli or the fish stall in the Valleys Centre. It'll be open till gone five.'

She looks at me and I know what she wants to say. I get in first. 'It's okay. This is the best thing that's happened to me for ages, and I suspect it is for Finn too.'

'Uh huh. Promise me one thing though.'

'That depends.'

'Don't give up on the day job. We need you here to boot some life into art and design.' She tilts her head to one side. 'Please.'

I want to hug her. I can't. 'That won't happen,' I say. 'Another decent thing about Finn is he respects my career.'

'Which one?' A smile crinkles up the edges of Tashi's eyes.

'Both. Although I think I might take your advice and stick with endangered, rather than dangerous species from now on.'

She laughs. 'Good idea. Enjoy the meal and whatever …' She flaps a hand.

'The whatever might have to wait till the weekend.'

'Lightweight,' she calls to my back as I zip through the main entrance, remove the mask and head for the car park. The pupils have all been spirited away by the convoy of school buses. A few are still waiting for a late lift. Most will have walked home. I hope there aren't too many hanging around the High Street. I know they will all be ignoring social distancing and I don't want to be a snitch. The poor kids have had a hard enough year as it is.

I park by the police station and head down the steep street, flanked by shops on either side. At least the cafes are busy. I replace my mask as I go into the new mall. Except it isn't a mall. It's more like an indoor market. I find the fresh produce and buy a cauliflower, potatoes and some ripe tomatoes. At the fish stall I select two salmon fillets, after making sure these are not factory farmed. The deli provides olives, prosciutto and finally sourdough from the bakers makes up the meal. I'll do a starter and main. It's relaxing to have a drink and something to graze on when anyone gets home from work. I add balsamic vinegar and a decent olive oil although I'm sure I've seen those in Finn's cupboard.

By the time I arrive at Finn's it's close to five o'clock. Where did he say the key was hidden? I head for the smaller of the barns and search for a light. A single bulb sheds a dim glow on the darkened interior. Old fences are piled up. What looks like animal stalls are empty. A few metal feed troughs lie on their sides. Some have holes. There is a rustling sound. Is it mice? Or rats? I breathe in the musty smell of dust, animals mixed with a sweetness, like mown grass. I thought he said he kept sick animals here? The place is empty. Thank goodness it isn't dark outside. I'm looking for an old bucket and there it is, next to a bale of hay, or is it straw?

As I lift the bucket there's a sound, like a phone. It's coming from behind the bale. I drag it aside. What's an old filing cabinet doing in a barn? The phone is still ringing and is coming from inside. I pull open a drawer. Wrapped in a chamois cloth is a small and very cheap cell phone. The screen shows a series of missed calls and a text message.

Why are you now answering? Next delivery soon.

More animals? Finn did say he was interested in diversifying. Before I replace the phone, I scroll further but there is nothing. He must delete everything. Should I tell him about the message? I can't really, can I? He might think I've been snooping. It isn't as if it's important. There are no times or dates. It could just be a heads-up advert. Yes. I reassure myself that is probably what it is. He'll keep me informed in his own good time. I've better and more important things to do. I replace the phone, collect the house key, and unlock. The kitchen is warm. As I switch one of the lights the cosy atmosphere envelops me. I'd like a house like this. I don't want a fancy chrome and white thing. I like snugness, the feeling of hunkering down away from the outside world, as if I'm in a little burrow, all my own. I focus on the task at hand. Within thirty minutes everything is ready for cooking and the platter of cold meats and breads is covered and in the fridge. I check the time. Five-thirty. Did Finn say six?

I wander back into the lounge. TV? No. Music? Yes. Some ambient music will set the scene. I select a playlist as a mix of smooth, mellow jazz classics fills the small space. I sit on the sofa. What is it about being in someone else's house? I get up and inspect the array of books. I've done it before. It's as if I'm double checking. What am I searching for? Photo albums? Only old people have those, don't they? Except a few pictures of Finn's childhood would be interesting. I check my watch. Plenty of time. I wonder if there are any clues about his past life. I'm sure we're not sleeping in Finn's teenage room. I walk slowly up the stairs, listening for a car driving up and I have to scuttle back to safety. I can't say I was up here using the loo. There's one in the utility room.

I lift the latches of the different doors leading off the hallway. There are five bedrooms, a bathroom, and a big cupboard. The bedrooms remind me of a country cottage in a glossy magazine: pastel colours, a mix of dark, wooden dressers, chests, wardrobes and modern beds and flooring. The walls have a selection of landscapes in gilt frames. They're Victorian or Edwardian oils and in need of restoration. Who painted them? A relative? I open the door of the final bedroom which is more like a box room. As I step inside, there is a door into another room. It's slightly ajar. I creep closer, ready to spring away if I hear the sound of tyres on the gravel. I fumble for a light switch. There is one inside the door frame. It lights up a small interior space, devoid of windows. Removal boxes are stacked three high. They are sealed and, on the outside, someone has written *photos, books, university* and *school* like a filing system. This must be where Finn has stored all his personal stuff. He did say he'd lived in London, so I am pretty sure when he moved down he packed it all away and it's still waiting to be unopened. This is where I'll find out what I want. I finger the brown sticky tape that holds the two flaps of the box marked *photos*. It would be so easy to lift it off.

I can't. I feel like a voyeur. This is ridiculous. If I want to know something, why don't I just ask? Why am I being a total idiot? I turn to leave the room and stop dead. Hanging on the back of the door is a black outfit. There is a green-brown jacket with no labels, black trousers, a bit mud stained, and a pair of black boots. I run my hands over the material. I unbutton the jacket, and a black woollen hat falls onto the floor. It isn't like a beanie hat. It must cover half the face.

I drop it as a memory turns my stomach to water. He wore a hat like this, didn't he? I pick it up and hold it at arm's length. No. This one doesn't cover most of the face. There is a huge gap where the features will show through. I wish my hands would stop trembling. I examine it more carefully. This one couldn't cover the face. It's too small, isn't it? My heartbeat slows down. I stick it in the pocket of the coat and scurry downstairs. I would never have made a good detective or even a good burglar.

I slump onto the sofa. My stomach is still in free fall. I breathe deeply to calm myself. My attacker wore a full-face cover, didn't he? My head is full of questions I cannot answer. Why hadn't I switched on *Pointless* instead? Talk about curiosity killing the cat. I am still jumpy when I finally hear a car stop on the gravel outside. A door slams. There is still so much I don't know about Finn. Perhaps Tashi is right and I should take things slower? Tonight, I will ask Finn more questions about his past and I'll ask if he's got any photos. The door opens and Finn's smiling face greets me. Gyp rushes in and flops down on my feet, waiting for a fuss. I can't stop my face from breaking into a smile as he comes forward.

'Excuse me, Gyp. I get to say hello first,' Finn says and envelops me in his arms.

It is ten before I get home. Finn did show me photos of his past. It's all very mundane. Most farmers will have waterproof clothing for times when they have to go out in bad weather. Won't they?

Chapter 34

Mark wakes early. It has been a restless night. There are things that need to be discussed. How could he sleep when Ginny's muffled sobs penetrated his dreams? He had cuddled her and she had drifted off eventually. Not until the first glimmerings of dawn percolated through the closed curtains had he fallen asleep. He eases his body away from hers and climbs out of bed. She stirs.

'Shh. Get some rest,' he whispers and kisses the top of the bandanna she wears to keep her hair smooth. 'I'm getting us some coffee.' She stretches and sighs. Mark checks his watch. Six-thirty. He has some time and space for himself. An idea comes to him.

And the hands on my wrist
Touch and kiss
Once each hour

Lucky watch. He slips into the ensuite, turns on the shower and turns it off again. The noise might disturb her. He'll use the main bathroom and if the kids wake and need the loo they can go downstairs. He'd never liked the kids seeing him naked. He's old fashioned, like his dad. It's a quick shower, ears cocked for any signs of life. He dresses, selecting a plain dark grey suit, mauve striped shirt and a grey tie for his first non-uniform appearance, makes Ginny a coffee and is drinking his own when Emily's voice disturbs his thoughts. 'I've got tummy ache.'

Her skin is flushed from sleep, her dark hair flops into her face and she clutches the one eared teddy she'd had as a baby. 'Have you been to the toilet?'

'Gross. Yes. No.'

Mark nods and pours her some juice. 'Drink this and go to the toilet, even if you sit there for a while.'

She takes the glass and turns it in her fingers. 'I really, really don't feel well,' she says.

Mark places a hand on her forehead. 'No temperature.'

'Have I got Covid?' There is no fear in her voice.

He suspects another reason. 'What lessons have you got today?'

She counts on her fingers. 'Maths with Mrs Jenkins. It's shapes. In IT we're designing a logo using Paintbox, PE and English.' Her voice drops as she says the last word.

'Poetry or story? When I was a kid, we always did a poem or a story on Friday. One time we all went outside. It was blowing a gale and we wrote what it was like. I remember the birds struggling against the wind. I said they looked like old men and women and got a star for a good description.'

Emily ignores him. 'It's spellings.'

'Uh huh. Have you learnt them?'

'I learn them, but I can't remember them. Ever.' Her eyes fill with tears.

That's the reason for the stomach ache. 'Tell you what, get your spelling book and we'll go over them while we have breakfast. Get dressed first, mind, and tell your brother to hurry up or it'll be the wet sponge.'

'Really?' Her face brightens. Whether that is the prospect of her brother getting a soaking or the extra help, Mark wouldn't like to guess.

'Yep, and we can sing them if you like. I might be able to make up a verse or two.'

'Wicked.' She scampers up the stairs and he can hear Andrew's door open. 'Dad says get up or he'll sponge you.'

Poor kid. If she is trying to pull a sickie at the age of eight because of a spelling test, what would it be like later? For a moment Jason's offer tempts like a cool beer on a hot day. He can't do it. Once you venture down that route, it never lets you go. He'll find the cash they need somehow. He'd like to get that damned case sewn up. A bit of overtime on the murder would come in handy. The video from Rachel's lapel camera might have provided some openings. If only he hadn't messed it up. Perhaps he could contact her and ask to double check? He could say the files got corrupted. It was always happening with new systems, wasn't it? He makes a mental note to contact Rachel. If he could clear this case up, he would be welcomed by the murder team who were getting increasingly frustrated by the lack of progress. He's certain there is a link. If only he could discover it.

The door opens and Ginny appears ready for work. 'I'm sorry,' she says and comes forward for a hug. 'I really am a sentimental old fool.'

'That's why I love you,' he says and pulls her close.

She eases away. 'Heh, not so keen, tiger. That can be left for later.'

'Dad, Mum, you are disgusting,' Andrew says as he and Emily bounce into the room. 'I don't want a smelly little kid brother or sister.'

'Who says that's going to happen?' Mark says as Ginny moves away and fetches cereal bowls from the dishwasher.

'Everyone knows when a mum and dad start to kiss, it means sex and sex means babies.'

Emily nods. 'We learnt that in PSHCE and SRE.'

It means nothing to Mark. He glances at Ginny. 'What happened to good old biology?'

'Still the same thing under different names.' She shrugs.

Mark holds out his hand to Emily. 'Spellings.'

Emily hands her book over. 'He mustn't tell me the answers.' She points and glares at Andrew.

'Oh no. He can only spell them backwards after you have your turn. Right, first one.' He glances at Ginny. She is gazing at the two children, a strange faraway look in her eyes as if she is seeing them but isn't. They would have to talk this weekend. He looks at his family. It is as near perfect as he'd always dreamed. He doesn't want anything to spoil that illusion.

An hour later Mark is sitting in the boss's office. He has weathered the cat calls and the whistles about his new outfit from the rest of the team. There's a frown on her face as she skims through the report he's made. 'The Tsar?' She looks up and there's no mistaking her interest. 'Any more information?'

Mark shakes his head. 'Everyone was a little cagey. I think they're scared. He's the Big Shot I reckon.'

DCI Eve Fletcher tips the glasses from the end of her nose and sits back in her chair. The purple and white striped blouse has a button missing and a small coffee coloured stain is visible on the white material. 'Well? Verdict?'

What he says now could make or end his career, or at least put him back on traffic and domestics. 'If the name *Tsar* is a reference to a foreign influence, this could be for the serious crime squad. I suspect the poor woman who got hit was an innocent bystander and the perpetrator one of many. If we catch him, there will be others. He might talk. He probably doesn't know much. A tip off might scare them all away.'

'You mean off our patch? What about the murder? Not that you're expected to comment. I'm interested in your ideas.'

'Lewis Barnes spotted something and knew something. I'd like to ask Tyler a few questions. I reckon he could add some more bits to the jigsaw.'

'Excellent. The Tsar is a name we've come across before in Bristol. I'll get onto them ASAP. Any information you get from now on will be sent to me for further decisions regarding actions to be taken.'

'The lad, Tyler is a concern. I'm sure his stepfather is abusive. I plan to contact Social Services today.'

'Good idea. Otherwise, we can say the case as far as we are concerned is closed.'

'What about Lewis Barnes?' Mark can hear the shock in his voice.

Eve Fletcher shrugs. 'No clues, no evidence, no suspects so no case. It will remain open for a few more weeks pending further questions.' She splays out her hands in supplication. 'I doubt if there will be any stronger leads, though.'

'Is it always this messy?' Mark says. For some reason he'd expected more closure from detective work. It's uncomfortable and he wants justice for Lewis Barnes.

'This isn't like the stuff you see on TV. Although we do go down the pub from time to time.' Eve smiles. 'We'll keep asking questions, checking for evidence, but unless we get a decent lead, this case might remain unsolved for a long time.'

Mark shakes his head. 'Poor Lewis,' he says. Eve picks up her pen. Is she really prepared to leave things as they are? Why can't he interview Jason again, and Tyler's father would be a good starting point.

'I understand your frustration, but when we come across potentially big cases like this we have to alert the forces who've been on their tail, and I know Bristol and South Gloucestershire are both interested in a person called The Tsar. There is one thing you could do for me?' she adds.

''Yes, ma'am?'

'Check the images on the CCTV of the van rental place with that girl's video. There might be a link.'

'I didn't think she got any images except of wildlife,' Mark says.

'That was when we were looking for a person. Now we're looking for a vehicle. Focus of attention. So often we omit to look at the whole image.'

If Mark felt uncomfortable before, there was even more reason now. That sodding video he'd lost. He'd have to get in contact with Rachel again. If he was a religious man, he'd say a prayer. He stands up. 'I'll report back as soon as I get any leads,' he says and escapes.

Once back at his desk he contacts Social Services. It is all he can do. The next task is to contact Rachel Thomas. He still has her number and email. He'll send a text as she is probably in school and can pick it up when she is free.

Hi Rachel, I'm just checking to find out if I can search through the video footage from your lapel camera. New technology means we might get some clearer images. Let me know.

The reply comes back sooner than he'd expected.

Sorry. I think it's tucked away at home. I'll check later and drop it into the police station if I find it.

That was it. Case over. The chance of her finding it, unscrambling the images and matching it with the videos on CCTV was so small he was at a dead end. He wants to say it doesn't matter. He is lying to himself. He wants a neat ending. He opens the files and spreads the notes he's made on his desk.

He is deep in thought when Cassie places a coffee on his desk. 'Any new leads?'

He takes a deep breath. 'Nothing.'

She pulls a chair up and sits next to him. 'We did our best, Sarge.'

'Did we?' That's the trouble. If he hadn't screwed up that video there might be more he could do. Should he tell Cassie?'

'Mark?' It's the boss. 'Take Cassie and get down to the docks. There's a domestic and the local PCSO says you know the family. A lad called Tyler has attacked his stepfather with a knife. The whole place could kick off.'

'On our way, ma'am,' Mark says as he and Cassie head to the car park.

****

Mark and Cassie are shown into the front room of a very new house. Tyler is curled up on a red leather sofa opposite a huge TV screen. Underneath are a number of games consoles. Leaning against the door leading into the white and chrome kitchen is Mrs Chip Shop, a cigarette dangling from her peach-coloured lips.

'Thought you was Plod,' she says as Mark enters. She shows no concern for either her partner or her child. She removes the cigarette and uses it to light another one. It's a bluff; Mark knows a scared woman when he sees one. Tyler's little sister is nowhere to be seen and the partner, or whatever he likes to call himself, is being attended to by paramedics. He isn't badly hurt but he is mad as hell.

'What's been going on?' Mark says as soon as he has identified himself and Cassie.

Dave Hawkins answers. 'Little sod must have told that damned school I'd been beating him. Social Services turned up and started asking questions. When he came back, he went for me.'

'Never did. Lying bastard.' Tyler sits, head bowed, unwilling to look at anyone. He rolls up his sleeves. 'He did this to me. Look.'

Amongst the bruises are small red circles, like the ones on Lewis Barnes's feet. Mark now recognises cigarette burns when he sees them. 'All right lad, we'll take you down to the station with your mum and you can tell me all about it. Is he all right to answer a few questions?' Mark addresses the paramedics. 'I'll need to speak to the stepfather first.'

'No worries,' a voice with an Australian twang answers. She turns to Tyler's stepfather. 'If that's okay by you, Mr Hawkins?'

'Certainly is. The sooner you know what he's really like, the better.'

Mark takes Cassie aside. 'You take the car and go back with Tyler and his mum. Tell the custody sergeant we need a social worker there ASAP. I'll speak to the PCSO and get a lift back after I've finished here.' He drops his voice. 'Get me the doctor's report on Lewis's death sent to my tablet. There's something I must check.'

Mark stands back as the paramedics leave and Cassie, accompanied by Tyler and his mother, gets into the car. The PCSO remains outside to keep prying eyes away. Mark's fingers ball and he fights to keep a calm tone. The bloke is a bully, and like a bully he is about to get caught out. 'So where do you want to start?' he says and sits down on the sofa. He'll start by playing nice cop.

'Like I said, the kid went for me after all I've done for him and his mum.'

'Why would he go for you at this moment? Has anything else happened lately?'

Dave Hawkins leans back, spreads his legs wide and places his shoebox white Nike trainers fully on the cream carpet. They look out of place against the washed-out grey joggers, although if Mark is not mistaken, the logo on his top is of a small rider on a horse. He likes his designer kit.

'I admit I shouted at him when he got suspended again. He takes off on his bike and doesn't come back till late last night, so I said he'd not be allowed to play any games online for a week.' He holds out a bandaged arm. 'Don't think I deserved this.'

'Just an argument?'

'Can't stop a parent from a bit of yelling can you? It aint against his human rights, yet, is it?'

'I'm interested in the marks on Tyler's arms. Apart from the bruises which might or might not fit with the size of your fingers and hands—' He is bluffing. Dave's face blanches. He's on the right track. 'I'm interested in the small red marks which are remarkably similar to the ones on Lewis Barnes.' A ping means Cassie has sent him the report he needs. He taps on the file on his tablet and scrolls down to the image of the soles of Lewis's feet. 'Take a look?'

Dave Hawkins collapses sobbing and wringing his hands. The face he turns towards Mark is grey with fear. Either this is real or he is a damned fine actor. 'You don't realise,' he stammers out. 'If this ever gets back, he'll kill me, the wife, and kids. I know he will.' The sobbing continues.

'What will get back and to whom?'

Dave does not answer the questions. He is in his own world and information spews out. 'I tried to find out what Lewis knew. That's what *he* wanted to know, see.'

'Who?' Mark perseveres. 'Who are we talking about?'

Dave quietens his voice. 'The bloke who set all this up. Calls himself The Tsar. When I told The Tsar there was nothing, he didn't believe me. Said he couldn't leave anything to amateurs like me. The next morning the old boy is dead.'

'I need information and solid facts,' Mark says. 'In return, you'll get witness protection. It could mean a new start for everyone.'

Dave nods.

'How did you meet The Tsar?'

'I met him in the local pub with Jason from the harbour. Jason knew I was short of cash and I'd done a bit of driving for him in the past. On the side, like. Cash in hand. No questions asked. Said it was fish for the local restaurant trade. It was a few ciggies too and designer gear.'

Mark's eyes flick down to the logo on Dave's shirt. He notices. 'Ten quid to you. Looks good though, doesn't it?'

Mark nods. 'Go on.'

'Except it didn't stop there.'

Mark waits, as Dave recovers his voice. Was this how he had made enough to furnish the house, buy the house? How long has it been going on? Everything is new or nearly new. Not a mark on the leather sofa, nor on the carpets. The huge series of photos of the family, minus Tyler of course, would have cost shedloads in a studio and that was before the bespoke frames which matched the cushions. On top of this was the TV and the high-tech games equipment. Mark reckons no one would have got much change from ten grand for this lot.

'Phones next, then designer bags and watches. You wouldn't believe how many electric scooters we shifted before Christmas last year.'

'How long has this been going on?'

Dave thinks for a moment. 'I did my first drop of elvers to a restaurant in London in May 2018. By Christmas 2019 it was all sorts. I didn't ask about the packages in plastic we dumped in waste bins or dropped off at the back of nail bars but I know the smell. Dope.'

'And your cut?'

'I got five hundred in advance and another five hundred after the drop had been completed. I did three sometimes four a month and all in the South West.'

Mark sits back. This is getting big. Yet he still hasn't got a link with Lewis. He takes a punt. 'When did it become people?'

Dave looks up, eyes wide as a frightened deer. His mouth moves as if he is rehearsing a lie before he realises he's beaten. 'January this year, before lockdown. That's when The Tsar took to turning up unannounced. I reckon he was checking me out. We did a drop a month before he put me back on dope. I didn't mind. That bloke Lewis was always skulking round at night.'

'Why kill him?'

He breaks down again. 'I didn't know anything about that. The Tsar comes round one night and wants to know if I'd grassed him. There was a report in the paper about that woman who got herself beaten up. The Tsar was scared. Said his boss wanted answers. Word had got back that the police were sniffing round here and someone was enquiring about the boat we sometimes used, *Lady Luck*.'

Mark's stomach lurches. Had his enquiries contributed to Lewis' murder? 'That doesn't explain these marks. How did

Lewis get them?' The darting, piggy eyes told him this little runt was about to squeal all the way to the prison cells.

'All I told him was Lewis was often out at nights and he might be the source. We went down there together and The Tsar tied the old bloke up, made me burn his feet. Just twice like a warning. He then orders me back home. I left him to it. The next day I found out Lewis was dead.'

'You'd better come down to the station.' Mark stands up. 'David Hawkins, you are under arrest on suspicion of assisting the murder of Lewis Barnes. You do not have to say anything, but it may harm your defence if you do not mention when questioned something which you later rely on in court. Anything you do say may be given in evidence.'

'I know the drill. I want a lawyer though and I want to know my family will be okay.'

'We'll do all we can to protect and support them.'

'I'm a dead man,' Dave says and buries his head in his hands.

Mark speaks into his phone. 'Tell the boss we've got someone in connection with the murder of Lewis Barnes. She might like to send round a search party for incriminating evidence.' He'd bet a pound to a penny Dave Hawkins managed to secrete a packet or two. Cutting a bit of dope with grass clippings to make up the weight was a trick all dealers knew well. It would explain the lavish lifestyle more than a few hundred quid from a few dodgy driving deals. The boss was right, though. This was organised crime on a big scale. They had only touched the tip of the iceberg, and he'd also bet the next drop would go ahead as planned if this was all kept very quiet.

Chapter 35

Hi Rachel, I'm just checking to find out if I can search through the video footage from your lapel camera again. New technology means we might get some clearer images. Let me know.

I read the text again and my reply. Was I too quick to assume it had all got lost? What if there was a chance the face could be identified? All that eye recognition used in passports must have a spin-off elsewhere. Or perhaps the police don't have access to such high-tech stuff? No. I'm certain they do. Wasn't there a case recently when some MP got his wife to say she was speeding when it was really him? Wasn't that revealed by CCTV?
I send another message.

Hi Mark,
Sorry if that sounded a bit abrupt. I promise to have a search round when I get home but I'm certain the camera isn't on the jacket any more. In fact, I thought it had been kept for evidence. I've seen the TV programmes when they open huge boxes of evidence, all neatly labelled.
Rachel Thomas

I click send. Funny how I still add my name to messages although the person knows who sent it. Must be all the English lessons when it was drummed into us; Dear sir or madam needs yours faithfully, Dear friend, needs yours sincerely and so on. Funny I haven't thought about that in years. We hardly ever teach it.

I place the phone back in my bag. It's never good practice to be seen with a phone in your hand, unless it is one of the school ones which Tashi insisted should have some luminous sticky tape on the back so everyone knows it's official.

After the weekend with Finn, we had a long conversation. As we're semi-official and in case another lockdown looms, we're preparing to spend more time together, sharing the houses. It means I need to go home tonight and do some serious organising. A trip to Dunelm Mill won't break the bank. I can't see Finn being over interested in thread counts and sheet colours, but I don't want him to stick his toe through the threadbare duvet covers I've been using since the ex and I split and he took off with the fixtures and fittings for his new love nest. The bastard! I stop. No. Thank goodness he spotted we were incompatible, or we'd be married and I wouldn't be as happy as I am at this moment in time.

I check my timetable. No meetings tonight so I can nearly beat the kids out of the gate and get on the road. I spend the rest of the day in between teaching and crowd control wondering how I can create a desirable residence from my two bedroomed terraced cottage. I google the term *shabby chic.* Most of the ideas are shabby, chic and way over my budget. I'll do the best I can. At least if it's snug, cosy, and welcoming with decent food, I'm sure Finn won't mind. All the same, I'd like to have the place clean and tidy with the new cream bedding and the pale-yellow towels. I can feel the house saying 'about time too.'

We've planned a picnic this weekend with Tashi and her family. I know she's desperate to put him through the third degree. I hope she doesn't scare him away.

With Finn spending more time at my place it's time to give him space. A spare toothbrush stuck in a jar on the bathroom window ledge hardly says 'I love you.' And I'm not convinced he hasn't been using my shaver when he's stayed over for more than one night. I open the bathroom cabinet. I pick up one half-empty pot of miracle cream after another. I only need one. Not that any of these have done any good. I survey the faint tracery of lines around my eyes, like a Medieval cathedral ceiling.

I keep the fullest, toss the rest in the bin and wipe the shelf with a spare tissue. That's better. One whole shelf to himself. He's not like plenty of guys I've met before, spending more time than me getting ready and with an army of clothes and products. Besides, he doesn't seem to mind neither of us is in the first flush of youth. Makes it easier somehow. I've always wanted to find someone I could just be with. Less *Where are we going tonight? Who will we see?* Not that anyone has had a scintillating social life recently. More *Which do you fancy, Netflix? Sky? Britbox?* as one of us opens a bottle of red wine and searches for clean glasses. Note to self; get dishwasher fixed.

I glance round the bathroom. Clean towels? Check? Spare loo roll? Check. Sanitising hand wash? Check.

Now for the bedroom. The phone rings. 'Tashi? What's up?'

'Don't ask. Soroush has been sent home with a high temperature and a slight cough so we're all stuck here for the next fourteen days or unless he tests negative. We've been allocated a test centre an hour's drive away.'

'How is Mamaji?' The virus is worse for older people. I hope she will be all right.

'Sitting at the top of the house in regal splendour with her phone on auto call for cups of tea and biscuits. I've a good mind to buy her a kettle and fridge and she can keep her own stock up there.'

'It won't be for long,' I say and hope I sound reassuring. 'Do you need anything from school?'

'No. The temperature may be the start of a feverish cold, but I want to warn you we might not be able to do the park picnic after all,' she says. 'And I was so looking forward to seeing you and Finn.' There is a pause. 'It is still on, the Rachel and Finn thing?'

'Yes, of course,' I say and can't stop the warm glow running from head to heart before taking refuge somewhere in the lower part of my stomach.

'I knew it was, or I'd have had a very sad lady on my staff. Oh, that reminds me, the interview will be over Zoom next Wednesday afternoon instead of in person. Too risky with all the virus circulating at the moment. The head says to take the call in the art room and if you have any ideas or want to show some work, you've got the opportunity.'

'Thank you. I'm looking forward to it. It makes my whole life seem more settled for the first time in years.'

'It's serious with you and Finn, isn't it?'

'I suppose so,' I say and the glow sets off on another race round the veins.

'As I always said, you stopped looking for a man and a decent one turned up. Just be careful.'

'Why?' The glow cools to warm.

'I don't know.' There is a pause again. I imagine Tashi walking round her immaculate kitchen, phone tucked beneath her chin, her forehead furrowed. 'I suppose it's because everything happened so quickly. You know…'

'You mean I haven't been able to parade him in front of my well-meaning and very inquisitive friends, colleagues and family like a prize dog in the ring at Crufts?'

There is a short burst of laughter. 'Yes and no. I suppose it's just me being-'

'A worrier? The big sister I never had?'

'Cautious. That's the word.'

I push clothes along the rails to make some space. What about shoes? Finn can't leave them in the kitchen all the time. I look down at the floor of the wardrobe. It's crammed with boxes and carrier bags.

'Are you still there?'

'Yes. Sorry. Must be a bad connection.' I'm lying. I want to escape the interrogation.

'Well, as I said, be cautious and I'll call you when we've got more details of the tests and quarantine.'

'Take care,' I say and ring off. The phone is nearly out of power. I go downstairs and bring the charger with me in case Finn calls. I plug it in and go back to the wardrobe. I pull out an old pair of heeled boots, a pair of dance shoes when I was taking Zumba and three boxes of high heels in ridiculous pastel colours, mementos from someone's wedding and totally unsuitable for my working life. They can go to the charity shops when they need new stock.

I stop. In the corner is a crumpled-up plastic bag. I know what it is. Why hadn't I seen it before? Or perhaps I had, and my brain was obliterating any reminders of that… incident to protect me. Why haven't I used the word attack? That's what it was after all. I take a deep breath. If only Finn would call. We could do this together on Saturday afternoon. It would help having him here with me.

I'm being silly. I know what's in it. All I have to do is drag the bag, pick it up and take everything down to the communal bin outside, lift the lid, drop it in and hey presto. All memories will be removed by the binnies next Tuesday morning. Yes. That is what I will do, and afterwards I'll call Finn and have a glass of wine to celebrate while he tells me all about his day.

I sink to the floor, stretch out one hand and grab at the plastic bag. The contents spew out as it splits. I don't need to look. I know what is there; brown trousers, walking boots, thick cable knit socks, pull on green hat and thermal top. Everything I was wearing when he attacked. On the top is my green jacket with the small camera still attached to the lapel. How could I have forgotten that?

'The rest can go but not you,' I say and pull it free. I take the bag into the kitchen and dump everything into the bin for non-recyclables. The camera I place on the counter top. I switch it on. Of course, it has no power. I remove the SD card and insert it into my laptop. Was it switched on when I was attacked? Is there any footage of him? No. The police would have checked, wouldn't they? I hold my breath. Is this the information I need to get the bastard once and for all?

The screen blurs. Black and white images of trees and bushes emerge from the mess. It blurs again. I must be walking backwards. A figure looms closer. Light from a torch dazzles the screen until it is raised high. I shiver, remembering the moment when the torch hammered down onto me and I lost consciousness. I flinch and force myself to open my eyes and look back at the screen.

I glimpse a face, partly obscured by a mask. The eyes stare at me. A strangled scream pierces the silence of the kitchen. I recognise those eyes. I've seen them watching me as we have a quiet drink, hold hands in a secluded restaurant and as they search my face when we are making love.

I freeze. My mouth twists. I swallow hard and run to the sink. I vomit and turn on the tap with one hand while grasping a bottle of bleach with the other. There is very little to swill away. The ammonia stench of the bleach catches the back of my throat. I retch, and sink slowly to the floor, resting my head against the kitchen unit. Finn is the man who attacked me. Finn? What was he wating for? Poisoned food? Wonky electrics? Or perhaps a fatal accident on a holiday? I want to hate him. I can't. Perhaps I should go round there now and kill him before he kills me.

Have I been duped all along? Isn't that what some killers used to do in the past? I've memories of a story I used to tell the children about revenge when I took lower school English. Thuggees. That was it. The bands of robbers, cheats, and swindlers in the India of the past who would travel alongside their victims, gaining their confidence before murdering them and disposing of their bodies. Is this what Finn has been doing all the time? When would he have made the final move? How would it have happened? I shudder at the thought of hands round my neck, squeezing the life out of me as I claw and scratch to stay alive. Or would it have been more subtle? A drugged drink and the slow descent into oblivion? What would he have done with my body? A strangled cry makes me jump. It is my own again. I must stay strong.

I want to tell someone. Tashi is the obvious choice, except she has concerns of her own. My parents are stuck in Spain. They'd only worry. What do I want? I want the truth. Except if I come out and ask him, what would he say? 'Oh yeah. It was me. Fair cop.'

Cop? Mark Mulroney. Hadn't he texted me already today? I stagger to my feet and clutch at the edges of the counters. My legs are reluctant to move and when they do, they tremble as if they are made of cotton wool. I edge my way towards the stairs. My phone is up there. I clamber up, taking each step like a baby would. I crawl to my bedroom. The new covers make it look welcoming. Who for? For a moment I want to pretend it hasn't happened. I want to believe it's all in my mind. Perhaps it is. I want to return to the excitement of new bedding, planning meals and not face the prospect of utter betrayal. The police will help. They'll know what to do.

I pick up my phone and re-read Mark's text.

Hi Rachel, I'm just checking to find out if I can search through the video footage from your lapel camera again. New technology means we might get some clearer images. Let me know.

I text a different reply.

I have found your video footage.
Rachel

I want to tell him to come over, now. For a moment I am scared, really scared Finn may turn up at any time. What would I do if he did? Could this be the moment he gets rid of the only witness to what he did? And why did he do it? He had plans for his farm. How did a man like Finn get corrupted? Tashi was right all along. I don't know him after all.

I creep downstairs and switch off the lights. I lock the door and pull all the curtains. The computer will show a blue light if anyone is hanging around outside. As everyone leaves their gadgets on, that won't mean I am inside. I want to go over to the laptop and replay the video. I daren't. Part of me is clinging to the hope I'm mistaken and all I have is a suspicion it's Finn. More than anything I want that suspicion to be smashed. I am too scared though in case a second viewing says I am right. Another part of me is screaming for the truth. For once, ignorance truly is bliss.

I stay hidden on the floor, away from the light of the laptop so no one, even if they peered into the room through the thin curtains, would see a shadow. I curl up, my phone clamped in one hand. Please pick up the message, Mark. Please.

Chapter 36

I have found your video footage.
Rachel

Relief floods Mark's body. Tomorrow he will meet Rachel and go through the video footage with her. For the moment, there's enough from the cameras on the motorway bridges and the entrance to Able Cars and Vans to check. There must be more than one link. Unless he's looking for a second vehicle or perhaps even more. Like a drug's mule at customs will often be a decoy for the real smuggler who breezes through unhindered. Is that the case here? Everyone except The Tsar appears more like the petty criminals who do the dirty work and are expendable. There is something niggling him, however, and he can't work it out.

He texts back.

Come to the station tomorrow with the camera and we can run it through the systems, unless you want me to check it out first on my own?

Another text pings back immediately.

I think I recognise the face and I'm scared.

If there's definite facial recognition, it's all the evidence he needs and Rachel might be in danger if The Tsar is as ruthless as Dave Hawkins claims. He replies.

I'm on my way. Pack a bag for a short stay. We'll find you a safe house if necessary.

How can he explain this to Ginny?

No. I reckon I'll be all right. I'll see you tomorrow at nine.

She is a tough kid. Although she doesn't know the extent of what is going on. Perhaps he should be more scared too.

If you hear or see anything, get on the phone. I'll alert the local patrols to keep an eye on you and your house.

That's the best thing to do. With cases like this any unusual activity can scare everything underground. Pretending life is normal is the best way to lull everyone into a false sense that nothing has been uncovered. While he waits for Rachel's confirmation of her address, he calls the desk sergeant and alerts her to the situation. The sight of a patrol car is enough to make any criminal lie low for a while, at least.

****

Mark is at the station well before nine and has booked the Covid secure IT and investigation suite. It's always cold in there and the pale blue paint does nothing to make it feel more hospitable. He sniffs. The smell of sanitiser lingers in the air. The comfy chairs are covered with plastic. At the wooden desk there are four upright wooden backed seats at intervals. He removes one and places it at the side of the room. The other two he places opposite the lone chair and makes sure it's facing the door. 'Why the sudden interest in the video? I thought we had a copy?' Cassie says as she ensures the chairs are at a recommended distance. The last thing Mark needs is for them all to go down with Covid.

Should he admit his mess? If they're to work together, it's important they realise neither is perfect and each are prepared to watch the other's back, if needed.

Mark holds out his hands. 'I screwed up. I checked the tape and forgot to save it. Shit, I'm not even sure I checked all of it.'

Cassie's face freezes. She's still innocent enough to believe superior officers are infallible and reliable. She has a lot to learn. 'Does that mean we could have identified the smuggler ages ago?' Her face takes on the shock of another realisation. 'Does that mean we could have saved Lewis?'

That thought has tortured Mark all night. Logic had won in the end. 'That was part of a bigger plan. We might not even have linked the two unless we'd done all the investigations. This fella who attacked Rachel is probably only one of a dozen, and he won't have any way of tracking down the big boys unless we had that information already and could ask the right questions.' He wants to sound confident. It does nothing to take away the bitter realisation that Cassie might be right.

'How do we play it?' Cassie perches on the edge of the desk. Her uniform trousers flap over her thin legs. Her white shirt is dazzling and even the small pips on her shoulder epaulettes shine. She is proud to wear the uniform. He hopes she'll stay that way.

'Routine. More information has come in. We might not have to explain anything. Rachel Thomas recognises the man or thinks she does. That is one hell of a good start.'

On cue the custody sergeant opens the door. 'Miss Thomas is here,' she says.

Rachel hovers in the entrance. A mask covers part of her face. Her eyes show she hasn't slept much that night.

'Come in and sit down. You may remember DC Cassie Turner?'

'We haven't met,' Rachel says as she takes the seat opposite Mark's paperwork.

'As this isn't an interrogation there will be no recordings made, but DC Turner will ask a few questions to clarify what we may or may not see. Do you understand?'

Rachel nods. 'I'm very certain I know whose face is on that tape,' she says with only the hint of a tremor in her voice.

'Shall we get going?' Mark points to the desktop computer he has set up. It has a variety of attachments that means it could read the Dead Seas Scrolls if they turned up.

Rachel nods and opens her bag. She pulls out a small memory card. 'It should read straightaway.'

Mark inserts it into the first reader. There is the reassuring clunk as it registers on the system. He scrolls through using the mouse and opens the files. 'Which file are we looking at?'

'Cat sightings autumn 2020.'

Mark frowns. 'Why the odd labelling?'

Rachel gives a half smile. 'The value of a video of one of the fabled big cats of Gloucestershire could be worth a fortune and make me very famous.'

'I understand.' He hits play and beckons Cassie to stand beside him. He turns the screen so it faces them both and is away from the dazzle of the lights.

Rachel's hands grip the table and she leans forward in her seat. 'It's about ten minutes in,' she says.

'If there is anything even remotely useful, this new device will find it,' Mark says, turning so he can glance at Cassie. 'Isn't that right?'

'Yes, boss,' she says and he relaxes. She understands.

Mark scans through the images. He remembers some. 'When you get past the ducks and the geese, that's about the start of the night time sections,' Rachel says.

She's right. The images of Canada Geese flying up in the air is followed by darkness and pinpoints of light. He slows the video to one quarter of normal speed, his finger hovers over the pause button. A shadowy figure moves slowly towards the screen. It must be the man who attacked Rachel.

'That's him.' There is no mistaking the fear in her voice.

Mark slows the video even more and frame by frame they watch as the figure, in slow motion, like a dream sequence, advances. His hand raises above his head. He comes closer. Mark freezes the video. The face is half obscured by a balaclava. He remembers them from school days before caps and beanies took over. The eyes are clearly visible. The hair is tucked away and the lower half of the jaw is covered. There may be enough to scan the image onto their data base unless he's got a clean record. 'Can you do a definite recognition?'

'That's the trouble.' Rachel twists the cuffs of her sweater and pulls them over her hands. Her voice quavers. 'I'm ninety percent certain. I can't be sure though.'

'Do you know this man, personally?'

'He's my…' She falters as if wrestling with what to call him. 'He's my boyfriend. He's called Finn Driscoll.'

Mark glances at Cassie. 'Run a check on him through our system.'

'I'm onto it, boss,' she says and leaves the room.

Mark stops the video and minimises the screen. Rachel relaxes slightly. 'How long have you known this man?'

'Only a few weeks. He got my name from the article about the attack and wanted to ask me about the photos I took.'

'Go on.' Mark lets her struggle to find the words she needs. He knows not to prompt her.

Rachel loosens one hand and tucks a stray wisp of hair behind one ear. 'It does seem a bit weird… him finding me… like that.'

'Has he shown any interest in what happened that night?'

Rachel shakes her head. 'No.' The answer comes too quickly.

'Are you sure?'

'He asked me about it a couple of times. I thought it was out of compassion. He did want to know if I could recognise the person who hit me.' She clamps a hand over her mouth. 'Do you think he deliberately tried to find me?'

Mark doesn't want to lie. It's exactly what he suspects the man was doing. Cassie comes into the room and he's spared any further explanations. She sits down. There is a printout in her hand.

'Finn Driscoll has led a remarkably crime free life. There are a couple of speeding tickets along the M4, and he must have lived in London at one time as there is an incident at a party in a flat in the Barbican which led to a breach of the peace five years ago. The whole thing came to the attention of the press because of the involvement of a minor royal and a member of the Middle Eastern glitterati when a gold Lamborghini was trashed.' Cassie places the papers on the table.

Finn isn't rich,' Rachel says. 'He's a farmer. He inherited his dad's farm or two.'

'He might be if he worked in the city. Then again, he might have debts,' Mark says.

'Credit check?' Cassie says.

'Run him through the usual line of enquiries and that includes phone calls.'

Rachel jumps like a startled deer. 'He does have two phones, I think.'

Mark signals for Cassie to wait. 'Tell me more.' From his experience most criminals have a variety of the cheap and cheerful, throw it away phones and no questions asked when a job is over.

Rachel gets out her phone. She taps it and shows it to Mark. 'This is the number I use.'

Cassie makes a note and leaves again. 'I'll see what I can find out,' she says. The door closes behind her again.

Mark leans back in the chair. He needs to take this very slowly. Rachel seems to be struggling with her memory, or perhaps it could be her feelings. How involved is she with this man? 'Tell me about the other phones.'

'Phone,' she says with a trace of relief. 'I was going over to his house to cook a meal and he told me where he'd leave the key. I was in the barn when I heard a ring tone. There's a metal filing cabinet and rolled up in a canvas bag was this phone.'

'You didn't answer it, did you?' His eyes fix on her face. Her eyes are wet. This is not fear.

'No. I picked it up and a message came up on the screen. It wasn't protected or anything so I read it.'

'What did it say?' Mark speaks as quietly as he can. He doesn't want to frighten her.

'It said, *next drop soon.*'

'Any idea what that might mean?'

'I assumed it was about animals. Finn was always telling me about his plans to have more unusual animals on the farm. I don't mean lions or elephants, more like rare breeds of sheep or goats. I assumed it was something to do with that.' Rachel's face crumples. 'It is him, isn't it?'

Mark pushes across a box of tissues. All his instincts are to reassure her. 'We need more evidence,' he says as an idea pops up. 'Would the phone still be there?'

Rachel looks across the table at Mark. This is the part of the job he hates most. It's the moment when loss, of a friend, a family member, a pet or even a livelihood sinks in. There's nothing you can say to take away that moment of utter desolation. 'I can go and find it for you if it's still there. Finn's always out in the fields in the mornings.' Her voice is firm and calm.

Mark knows this is risky. Finn may be lurking around. Rachel may be in danger. If the phone has gone, Finn will know someone's onto him. 'Could you take photos of the messages?' It's a hunch that might pay off.

'Unless they've been wiped. I'd still be able to get the number though,' Rachel says.

'That would be good. The messages would be better.'

Rachel shrugs. 'I'll give it a go.'

Mark hesitates. He can't condone going onto someone else's property like this, can he? What the hell. He'll cover his tracks later. With this new lead he'd be justified in going over there. 'Cassie and I will follow at a distance. If you feel frightened in any way, call us. You can set up my number on speed dial.'

Rachel stands up. 'I'll go now. Finn's often back at midday.'

'We'll follow. Don't leave until we've cleared it with high up.' He calls Cassie and asks her to wait with Rachel.

Mark knocks on the glass partition where the boss is studying the screen. 'I'm off to Finn Driscoll's farm. Rachel Thomas reckons he might be her attacker. She isn't sure though.'

The boss looks up from her screen. The black and orange striped shirt makes her look like a giant cat. Her eyes fix on Mark. 'Serious Crime reckon this is either part of the same organisation they've been trailing for months or a copycat. Get as much information as possible. If we can be there at the next drop, it'll be one for us and our country ways against the big noises in the metropolis.' Her top teeth nibble at her lower lip and her head wobbles like a nodding dog. 'Yeah. One for us.'

By the time he gets down to the car park, Rachel is sitting in her small run-around. Cassie has been allocated an unmarked Hyundai. The boss must reckon they are onto something big. 'Are we ready?'

'She's a brave girl,' Cassie says and signals for Rachel to move away. 'I hope this works.'

'So do we all,' Mark mutters as Cassie puts the car into drive.

Chapter 37

While I wait in the car, I call school and say I'm not feeling well so will go and take a lateral flow test and call back later. That will stop any well-meaning inquiries. I have a spare one in my bag from the start of term when we were all supposed to be trained to test the kids. I text Finn.

> *Could have Covid. I've a spare lateral flow test to save the bother of getting one done at a test centre Will drop it off in our hiding place for the keys. Don't come near till we both get the all clear. I doubt I'm infected but we can't be too careful.*

I should add love or some kisses. I'm in a daze. I don't know what to do. I add a couple of emojis, the crossed fingers and a heart will be enough, and press *send.* What if I come across Finn? My head says I've got a good reason to stay away and be there… After all, I'm simply being a good friend, aren't I?

I can't believe I'm doing this. Shouldn't I be in a heap on the floor or sobbing still? Perhaps the crying was exhausted last night? It must be shock. Somehow, I've got energy coursing through my veins, not blood. There's also a bit of anger in there, and humiliation; others were right not to trust him. Why was I fooled? I spot Mark in the mirror. He waves. I drive off and turn right to follow the hill into town. If anyone sees me, I have a perfect excuse. I'm going to get a Covid test. No one dares argue with that.

I slow at the roundabout and turn left. In the car behind are Cassie and Mark. Only Cassie is in uniform, but you wouldn't realise unless you looked carefully. I follow the road out of town and head up towards the common. I'm gripping the wheel so tight my hands ache. Mark and Cassie have stopped to let a bus go past. They're probably used to this. I continue at a slower pace until the road narrows and the traffic is sparse. Cassie and Mark are behind me again. I brake at the approach to Finn's driveway. Their lights flash as they pull into a small turn with the sign for some holiday lets. I continue on my way, alone, checking in all directions in case I spot Finn's Land Rover. My phone pings. I pick it up.

Poor you and poor us! Never mind, out here in the upper fields I'm so socially distanced I'm practically a recluse. Thanks for the test. I'll be back this afternoon. No point going home. These goats are demons for escaping. They won't like a short sharp electric volt though. Speak soon. XXX

I let out a sigh. There's plenty of time. I pull up outside the house. I must be crazy. It can't have been Finn in that video. We've had such a great time together. Why would he go to all this trouble? The thought he might really care for me dawns. Perhaps he did and does. Perhaps he's doing this for the money, nothing more. I must find that phone. I close the car door and walk over familiar territory. The screech of the peacock in the apple orchard makes me jump. There is the familiar bleating of the Jacob's sheep and Finn must have let the hens out as some cute ones waddle on their flat feet, leg feathers flapping like wide leg trousers, occasionally stopping to peck at the ground. What if I found the phone, ditched it, and told Mark and Cassie it wasn't there? Could I get to Finn first and stop him?

What could I say? I know who you are? Self-doubt is clouding my judgement again. He can't care for me. Except all of this began before we met. What if he went down this route to get the cash he needed? The last few months have been desperate times for many.

I stand in the entrance to the barn and breathe in the warm, musty smell of animals, hay, and feed. Where is the metal filing cabinet? I take a step forward. Wasn't it behind those bales? There is a crack, like wood splitting. I stand still, hold my breath, and listen for any more sounds. One foot sinks. I look down. I'm standing on a rotten plank. Time to get on with the job and get out. My heart is pounding so hard, it must be heard for miles. I take several deep breaths. My hands are quivering and my knees feel as if they are about to collapse. What will I do if Finn turns up? Damn! I've left the test in the car. I poke my head outside the barn, fearing he'll change his mind and be back sooner. I scurry out, grab one from my car and place it where Finn once left me his keys.

That's when it hits me again; it's so unfair. I force back a sob. We'd had such a wonderful time, or was I still deluding myself? What if everything was fake? I shake myself. I intend to find out. First, I need to do as Mark has asked. Light from the outside filters through the holes in the roof of the barn. The place is fast falling apart. No wonder Finn needed money. Once, there must have been an upstairs gallery for storage. The floors are crumbling and there is no wooden ladder like you see in films, leading to the secrecy of the loft space.

What would I do if Finn returned? I'd have to keep him at arm's length. I smile. Social distancing means I won't get near him. He's hardly likely to tell the Covid Marshalls there is a woman breaking quarantine. If he's really involved in this filthy business, he'd keep a low profile. I stand in the barn doorway and turn round slowly. Where is that damn cabinet? I circle again and venture deeper into the gloomy interior. If he needs access to the phone, it won't be in an inaccessible place. I look over at the pile of bales of straw again. Were they all here last week? I get closer. There's an odd assortment of bales piled on end, like a wall with one balanced on top. I grab the top bale and it collapses onto me as the others fall forward. Jesus they are heavy. I squeeze my way out and there is the cabinet.

I open the top drawer. The phone is wrapped in canvas as it was before. I take it out and check the screen. There's still power and it isn't locked. Is that a new message? I photograph it and others with my own phone. Mark wanted the number, didn't he? I scroll to settings. *About phone* should do it. The kids showed me how to do this once before. It's weird how some things you never forget, even if you haven't had to use them. I take another photo of the number and wrap the phone back in the canvas. How was it folded? No one will remember that will they? I slide it into the drawer and close it. The bales are easy to stack round, like the standing stones at Stonehenge. The one on the top is harder. I place my hands under the twine keeping it in a cuboid shape. If Finn had used plastic covered bales, I'd never do it. I heave. The bale lifts slightly. The twine cuts into my hands. One more go.

With all my energy I lift. It budges and I shove it on the top as the twine comes away in my hand and straw spills everywhere. To my eyes it is obvious someone has tampered with it. It'll warn Finn. I collect up some of the spilled straw and place it in what I hope resembles a cuboid. The string hangs loose. If Finn pulls at it, the whole thing will fall to pieces as it did for me. All I need to do is make it look as if it hasn't been tampered with. I place the twine around the bale and twist it at the back. It's a bit baggy. So what? I've done all I have to do.

I escape back to the car and drive off. Even if I meet Finn, there's a good explanation. I can bluff that. Mark's car flashes its lights as I pass. It's time to head back to the station. It's only after I've handed all the information over to Mark and Cassie and they let me go home that I realise what has happened. I slump over the steering wheel in the car park. An elderly woman in a floral mask walks past, trundling a shopping trolly behind her. She stops and looks my way. I can see her face. I can't draw attention to myself. I fake a sneeze, followed by another and scrabble for a tissue. I blow my nose hard. The woman hurries away. She probably thinks I'm infectious. No darling, I want to call out. Where there's snot it's not. It's a phrase the kids like to use. I'm being cruel. It isn't like me. The poor old lady has probably been sheltering most of the year. She might even have lost family and friends. I drive home. It is only when I arrive back inside and can close and lock the door behind me that the enormity of what I've done and the sadness at what I may have lost hits me. I make a hot water bottle and curl up in bed, fully dressed, my phone by my side switched to flight mode. I don't want to see or hear from anyone ever again. Why won't life give me a break?

Chapter 38

Mark needs to see the boss. He's already requested permission to track Finn Driscoll's phone for calls. What he has done was not strictly in the true line of investigation; more of a hunch and Rachel has played along beautifully. If only she'd gone to a safe house or even arranged to stay with friends. But she's tough and stubborn. Even so, he makes a note to let the Duty Sergeant know of a potential vulnerable woman who is alone. The Night Angels patrol that area too. They'll help.

DCI Eve Fletcher is leaning against the partition separating her small office from the open plan space they all share. She would be aware of the request for a phone track. Her team reckon she knows stuff before it happens. 'In a rush, are you?' She swipes a hand through the dark hair with more than its fair share of grey showing at the roots.

He suppresses a smile. He knew she knew he is on to something and it's time to come clean.

'I've uncovered something of interest.'

'I'll be the judge of that. Grab a coffee and meet me in my office in ten.'

As Mark waits for the machine to regurgitate a strong cappuccino, he checks Rachel's images from Finn's phone have come through on his tablet. They are perfect. For a while he worried they might be a blurry mess with too much hand wobble and fuzzy focus. These are good. No surprise, really. She is a photographer, after all. With any luck, the phone record will show contacts around the time of the sightings. The text message is different. They must take action and fast.

'Any luck?' he says as he places a cup of strong black coffee in front of Cassie.

'Give us a chance. The request went in a few minutes ago and you know it can take up to an hour.'

'We might not have the luxury of time,' Mark says and waits outside Eve's office as she speaks on the phone. She glances at him and beckons him to come in and sit down.

She stops the phone call with a curt, 'When it's on my patch, I deal with it.'

Mark remains silent. If there's something going on, she'll let them all know about it when the time is ready.

Eve slams the phone down. 'What have you got?'

'Some information from Rachel Thomas about Finn Driscoll.'

'Yes?'

Mark leans forward and scrolls down through the messages till he finds the most recent, dated today and sent at 8.30 am.

> *Next stock delivery today. Collect from Portishead. Deliver before midnight. Money can be collected from box as usual at 9 am tomorrow.*
> *382863 206786*

'I think this shows the details of the next smuggling incident.'

'People or something else?'

'People seem to be the cargo of choice at the moment although I reckon some other substances have been available at other times.'

Eve nods. 'We found traces of cocaine in Hawkins' garage and in the back of his fancy, new BMW.' She smiles. 'He'll be helping police for a while.' She leans back in the chair. 'I reckon he'll squeal.'

'And this?'

'Pity it isn't a pick up from Blake Point, although with the amount of time you two have spent down there recently, I'm not surprised they've done a bunk.'

Mark hangs his head. 'Sorry.'

'No. Don't be. You might have stopped a few others getting involved. In these times there are a lot of people who will be tempted by the promise of easy money.'

Did she know of Jason's half-hearted attempt at bribery? 'The rest of the message is a bit unusual. What might it be?'

'Did you do Geography at school?' Eve tilts her head to one side and looks at him. Is she enjoying this?

'All I can remember is Oxbow lakes and where the deserts are in Russia,' Mark says and scratches his head. 'Wait a minute. grid references.' He slaps his thigh with one hand. 'Could they be grid references?' He is about to jump up when Eve holds up one hand.

'We have a time and possibly a place. It means we need to have a team in wait for the delivery. That costs. The last thing I want is to look a fool if this turns out to be a fake. You've two hours max to go through any messages, check for dates and times. Is there a pattern and…' she pauses, 'Get the grid references for all the other places where there have been sightings. I've put the best team on standby. If there are any Covid parties today, they can have a good time on us.' She picks up her phone. 'Well, go on.'

Mark tries to look cool as he slides into the desk next to Cassie. 'Overtime for a few lucky sods tonight,' Todd calls out.

'Try explaining that to the missus,' another voice chimes in. 'Still, she's more understanding if it's serious and not some yobs getting stroppy or a bunch of teens sniffing hippy crack.'

Mark ignores them. Everyone likes the idea of a sting. This isn't likely to be armed but they'd have a few tasers and plenty of energetic lads and lasses to catch the poor sods as they run off. The driver would be an easy touch and if he told all, they'd be onto something. He moves closer to Cassie. 'What do you know about grid references?'

Cassie speaks without looking away from her screen. 'Six figures with the first three being the square and the division into tenths for the eastings. The northings are the second group of three numbers. They're always separated by a space.'

'Impressive,' Mark says.

'Merely the product of my very thorough, very traditional, Catholic girls' school education,' Cassie says. 'The best place to start is Grid Reference Finder. It's far more efficient than scrabbling round on the floor with huge crumpled Ordnance Survey maps.'

'Pity,' Mark says as he logs on. 'I used to quite like maps.'

The site is easy to find, once he'd bought some credits to use. He types in the numbers he'd seen on Finn's phone. 'What the hell?' He slaps his forehead. This can't be right. The place identified is close to where Rachel had been attacked. 'Cassie, check this for me, will you?' There are times when he distrusts his own eyes. This is one of them.

'What's up?' She leans over his desk. Mark can smell her perfume; sharp and lemony.

'If and this is a big if, the six figures we found on Finn Driscoll's phone are typed into the grid finder here, it comes up with a place close to the spot where Rachel was found. I remember the name of the wood.' He vacates his seat. 'You try.'

Cassie reads through the screen. 'Eastings… northings,' she mutters. 'Here goes.' She taps each number, reciting it to herself. 'Check I haven't made a typo?' She looks up at Mark.

'That's the same one I used.'

'Right, here goes.' She presses enter. The screen is replaced with a map. She scrolls round. 'Just searching for something familiar.'

'Such as?'

'Close by the place Rachel was found was a pathway leading to a farm. The pathway is on National Trust land. That should be labelled. Yes, here it is. And if I'm not mistaken this road is the B road leading to the A46,' she says with a note of triumph in her voice.

'I am right?'

'Yes. Our courier has chosen the same drop off point.' She pauses. 'Why would they do that?'

Mark gets up and perches on the wide window ledge. The old 70s building has low windows overlooking the town. It's a place where he likes to sit and think. Today the ideas come quickly. He turns back to Cassie. 'It's more common than you'd realise. Some criminals reckon the police won't think anyone would go back to the scene of a crime.' He shakes his head. 'It happens all the time.'

'Interesting. Like the idea that lightning never strikes twice in the same place. What now?'

'Can you check if there are any more six figure references like that on the phone record and do they by any chance tie up close to sightings we've got registered?'

'Will do.' Her eyes swivel back to the screen.

Mark stands up. 'I need to run all this past the boss.' Tonight, if Eve Fletcher has her way, a group of police in an unmarked van and a helicopter will be close by the drop off point. Other cars will be stationed to watch out for a van on the roads leading to the drop off point. There aren't many choices. This is an area of country lanes. Manned surveillance cameras along the M5 will be on the lookout for a transit van passing through. The driver might take a back route. It's doubtful. From what he'd worked out and from the information Dave Hawkins provided, the usual plan was to collect the cargo, drive to the drop off point, let them go and get the hell out of the place. The poor devils had to fend for themselves after that. There were never any niceties. It was quick and highly profitable.

'It could be a long night,' he says as he heads towards Eve's office, whistling.

Chapter 39

I must have drifted off to sleep. When I wake it's mid-afternoon and I know I must do something. I can't stay here, like a wet lettuce. I've never been a quitter and I won't start now. I switch my phone off flight mode and check on any updates from school. More and more kids and staff are going off sick by the hour. I'll go back tomorrow; they need me.

What should I do about the messages I've photographed? I read through them several times. Finn must be involved in something weird, or he had been. What if I tipped him off about tonight? Except what could I say? My phone rings. It's Finn. I ignore it. I can't trust myself to speak to him. Sure enough a small ping tells me there is a voice message. I listen.

Hi Rachel,
Thanks for the test. It looks complex. I'll give it a go later today. I suppose we can't see each other for a while or until we both get the all clear. If you do test positive or get any symptoms, call me. I don't want you to be alone and I can sort some food. If we're both positive, we ought to hole up together? It's a thought. I'll be working on the barn this afternoon and probably late into the night so text me rather than call as it's a bit difficult to have a decent conversation half way up a ladder.
Speak soon. Finn xxx

How convenient. For a while I wonder why I'm not feeling anything. Yes, it hurts to hear Finn's voice. This time I reckon he's telling so many lies. How many more has he told? Was I going to be one of those poor women who gets conned into giving away all her money? Tashi had warned me. I'm the one lying to Tashi. I must let them know it's all okay and I'll be back tomorrow. I'll claim I got the chance for a special lateral flow test at the centre. I email school. These lies turn my stomach. It's necessary. What is it about humans and our ability to switch from truth to lies in a nano second?

I check the texts from Finn's phone again. Why those figures? I get a piece of paper and scribble them down. Is it a code? Why the groups of three? There would need to be more if it spelt out a series of words. I search online for things to do with six-digit numbers. There are maths worksheets making the largest and smallest numbers, a link to a pornographic website and how to create ID numbers using six digits. I'm certain it isn't a code. Could it be a place name?

I type again; *6 digit number to identify location.* Still more on place value and bank codes. It isn't one of those. They have six figures in three groups of two. I scroll further down. Global Location Number is from the USA. Is there a system in the UK? I type *how to write six figure locations* and the first suggestion in dear old Google's drop-down list is *how to write six figure coordinates.*

Could it be a coordinate? Jake would know. He's a maths teacher and does geography with all age ranges. Could I text him and ask? What's my excuse? A sighting? He knows of my love of wildlife. What was it my grandmother used to say? One lie leads to another? She was right. What if I get to the place where Finn is and tell him…What can I tell him? The police think they know the time as the text clearly says the same time as before. I reckon it must have been about eleven-thirty. The time on my camera was wrong. It was an hour later as that was one thing that never worked properly. I'm sure it even had the wrong date on it occasionally too.

My mind works overtime. All fatigue has gone. I'll get there, tell Finn I know all about it and tell him either to give himself up or deny he was there and I'll be his alibi. I open my phone ready to call Jake. Why am I doing this for Finn? I like him. No. I suspect it's gone beyond like. I love him or I'm in the process of falling in love with him. The effect is the same; alternate bouts of exhilaration and anguish and the overwhelming desire to protect the beloved at all costs.

I text Jake.

Sorry to disturb you. I've just had a tip off about the big cats seen somewhere round here. I think they've used a grid reference. Any ideas where I'll find out where without buying an OS map of the planet?

Test is neg. I feel such a fraud. Back to work on Monday. I owe you a drink.

Rachel

Does it sound creepy? Over friendly? I want the tone to be friendly and informative, nothing more. Friends do each other a favour from time to time, don't they?

I decide I am no use wallowing in misery. If I'm correct and it is a place close by, I'll go early and wait. That's one thing I'm good at. What if Jake doesn't get back to me in time? I leap off the bed. Adrenalin flows through my body. I'll start the search myself. I feel like Frodo when he says, "I will go to Mordor though I don't know the way."

I'm making a cup of coffee. It's late afternoon. Habits die hard. All teachers need a caffeine injection at this time. I'll start work on the OS references after this.

My phone pings a message.

Hi Rachel

Good to hear you're OK. I'm still at school. Send me the reference and I'll access the data base we use here. It shouldn't take me long. J

I text him the six numbers and wait. He is as good as his word. The results sicken me. I know the place well. Has Jake realised the grid reference is the same location I was attacked? No matter. I am certain my hunch to get there before the police and speak with Finn is the right one.

> *You are a diamond. That drink is on me. Monday after school? Will see you anyway around and about. Have a good weekend.*
> *R*

His next message comes by return.

> *I know I can't tell you what to do but please take care. J*

Does he think I'm still after the cats? This time, there is bigger prey and I want to rescue him.

> *No worries. I'm sticking to moles, sheep, and blue tits from now on but the info makes me feel more certain I WAS on the right track and I can alert a fellow spotter. They can be famous.*

He returns a smiling emoji.

My next task is to while away the hours until it is time for me to leave. It'll be dark by seven which will give me plenty of time to be in place by nine. I need to get out my winter wear clothes. Rain isn't forecast but if it's a clear night, there will be a frost. I check the forecast. It's nearly full moon. With a clear sky, it's harder to remain unseen. I'll need to cover part of my face with a scarf. I go upstairs and lay out what I need; thick black socks, walking boots, green padded trousers, thermal long johns, thermal vest, fleece, and waterproof jacket. I search out the camouflage scarf I got from the last Secret Santa and makes sure I have gloves, a head torch and a bottle of water. My phone is charged. All I have to do is wait.

The time passes slowly. I flick between different TV channels. There is nothing I want to watch. I turn on a film channel. I start one and give up. I can't follow the plot. My head is elsewhere. In the end I watch the shopping channel, marvelling at how someone can enthuse for twenty minutes over a grill pan or a pair of winter boots.

I must eat. Soup and toast will do. I can't risk fainting from hunger or my stomach making noises at a crucial moment. I do switch on the news. From the way the pundits are talking, we're in for another lockdown except the children will still go to school. It won't work. It's impossible to prevent children and young people from getting too close; it's in their DNA. I suppose I ought to work out what I'm going to say to Finn. I prefer to let the moment dictate. I'm usually the most planned and organised person imaginable, constantly mentally rehearsing lesson starters, interview questions, date chat-up responses. This time I hope the right words will come at the right time.

At eight o'clock, I leave the house. I plan to drive to the car park below the woods and walk along the bridleway to the rendezvous point. I'll keep off the main track. There are plenty of places to hide under the holly trees or amongst the piles of scrub left behind when they replanted a section of dying ash trees.

By eight forty-five I am in place, nice and snug. The moonlight intermittently illuminates the area. Am I scared? No. Last time I didn't know what was happening. This time I at least have a say in the outcome. I settle down on the soft leaf litter and wait.

Chapter 40

Mark eases his body in the confines of the seat and checks his watch. Nearly eleven. If the van is coming through on time, it should be within sight at any moment. He nudges Cassie. 'Keep a watch out.'

She yawns and scratches her head. 'Is he late?'

'Not really. It depends which route he took; the ring road or through town.' As if on cue, a plain white van comes into sight. 'This should be him,' Mark says.

Cassie looks down as the van passes them. The driver wouldn't have taken any notice of a couple sitting in a car in a pub car park. 'That's definitely the one, Sarge,' she says. 'He's turning left. He must be taking the back route up through the estate and into the village. It's a straight run from here.'

'Right. Here goes.' He puts the car into drive. 'We've sighted the van heading North. We're following,' he says into the radio.

A disembodied voice barks back. 'All crews ready and on standby. Head to rendezvous as planned.'

Mark follows the van at a distance, eyes straining to keep it in sight but not so close as to raise suspicions. The other members of the team will be heading that way and the helicopter is scrambled. It is all going beautifully to plan.

****

The cold earth is making its presence felt. I wish Finn would hurry up. Unless he's changed his mind and it's all over. Perhaps he said he wouldn't do it. We can get his life back on track and everything will turn out fine. I'm kidding myself of course. Life isn't like that. Headlights glint through the trees. Is this him? I ease myself away from my hiding place. If the lights go past, it can't be him, nor if it's a car. I'd cross my fingers except they are too cold and I'm past relying on fate. The lights slow as the vehicle pulls into the turning space where the buses used to wait. Usually it's full of dog walkers. Not tonight. A figure emerges from the driver's side and goes round to the back. He slaps on the side of the van. 'Out,' he calls. I know that voice. It's time.

****

Damn stupid driver. Mark hits the blue lights and hoots the horn as some poor devil reverses into the lane. He sees Mark's face and the blue lights and waves his apologies. The car lurches back up the driveway.

'Have we lost him?' Cassie says.

'No. not yet.' Mark pushes his foot down hard on the accelerator and switches off the blue lights. The less attention they draw to themselves, the better.

'I can see the van,' Cassie says.

Mark slows and switches off the headlights. He pulls into the entrance to an old manor house. An upstairs curtain twitches. If the owners get upset who cares? This is police business. 'We do the rest on foot,' he says as he and Cassie get out of the car. Mark checks his taser. 'This way,' he says as they keep to the shadows and creep towards the van.

****

I watch as the door at the back of the van opens. Dark figures leap out. 'Across the road, take the left and run,' Finn shouts.

'Where are we?' One of the figures comes round to where Finn is waiting.

'The end of the road. Out.'

'We were told you'd take us to the city centre,' the man says. A few of the others sense there could be trouble and stand back, watching. The rest do as Finn says and they are gone in the darkness.

'They're my instructions,' Finn says. 'Go.'

The man sizes Finn up. He looks at the others. 'Take us to the city,' he says. 'Or we'll take the van.'

They are advancing on Finn. He can't stand up to them. They'll kill him.

I leap out and run forward. 'Finn, let them have the van.'

He turns. 'Rachel? What are you doing here?'

****

'Bloody hell, that's Rachel,' Mark says. He stands upright, the taser resting on his hip. 'You are all under arrest. Lie down and put your hands flat on the ground. All of you.' He motions for Cassie to train her taser on them.

A second squad car arrives in a blaze of lights, followed by a backup van and a K9 crew. 'Run,' the man screams as the group disperse and head off, chased by the officers as the unmistakable sound of a helicopter gets closer.

'I said get down and that includes you, Mr Driscoll,' Mark calls out. 'Cassie, check if Rachel is all right.'

The slight figure of Rachel is caught in the beams of the headlamps. For a moment she and Finn stare at each other. 'Please, Finn. Do as they say. We can work it out.' Her voice rings out in the night air.

Finn backs away. Does he think he can outrun us and a helicopter? Who does he think he is? Superman?

'Stay away, Rachel,' he calls out. 'Stay away.' He runs into the darkness.

Cassie fires a taser and it falls far short.

'After him,' Mark shouts. His voice is cut short by a scream. It is followed by another. The scream is human. The next sound is animal. It is a long, piercing yowl, a wail, a cry like a huge cat.

'No,' Rachel sobs and falls to her knees. 'No, please not that.'

Cassie bends down and places her arms round her.

'Stay where you are,' Mark says as the officers fall back. He takes a flashlight and a taser and walks towards the sound of the scream. He has not gone further than five metres when he sees a foot sticking out of the undergrowth. The body is covered in blood. He backs away as he hears a snarl and green eyes stare at him. He shoots the taser. It misses. The eyes disappear. Mark moves closer. 'Get a medic here ASAP,' he speaks into his radio and kneels by the inert figure of Finn Driscoll.

Chapter 41

Smuggling ring smashed

Mark re-reads the headlines. It's a good result. The Met now had a decent lead on the Tsar and nearly all the last group of people had been caught. Bristol and Avon were whining they'd been eclipsed. Seems the smuggling ring had worked most of the south coast. So much for police sharing information. They'd get the ring leader, eventually. Jason Carter had squealed about all the smaller smuggling jobs and Tyler's stepdad, Dave Hawkins, would be put away for a good few years for his part in the drug smuggling. The lags wouldn't like a child abuser either. He was in for a tough time.

It was a pity they couldn't pin the murder of Lewis Barnes on anyone, yet. It was still under investigation. He'd liked to have questioned that Finn bloke. Although by the way Rachel spoke about him, he was just tempted by easy money. The last time he spoke to her, she said she was okay. She'd helped his brother arrange the funeral. She was still at the school but now in a permanent, full time teaching post and continuing with her photography. The brother had liked the images she'd taken of the farm, introduced her to a few of his friends and she'd several exhibitions planned for the summer months.

He puts the paper away and checks his watch. Time to go home. Ginny is waiting.

Acknowledgements

I would never have attempted a detective novel like this without the expert guidance from the wonderful tutors at Swanwick Summer School for Writers and the tutors at Curtis Brown Creative.

As always, thanks go to my fellow writers at Catchwords, the staff, and students on the MA in Creative and Critical Writing at the University of Gloucestershire, and neighbours who have been intrigued by the idea of a crime series set locally.

It goes without saying that the patience of long-suffering family and friends are essential in the process from original idea to finished product and I am more appreciative of them than any words can convey.

About the Author

Write books? Me? Never! That was for people who did English Literature degrees or had famous relatives who already wrote or published. However, as a teacher, I was tempted to write for children, so I began to experiment with short stories and completed an MA in Creative and Critical Writing in 2016. I realised what I really enjoy is the psychological interplay between characters and the relationships between them, using my knowledge of psychology and over ten years of studying personal development. My first full-length novel, *Virgin at Fifty,* a poignant and funny feelgood novel about starting over, was published by Black Pear in 2018.

With my husband, I co-authored a book on happiness, called *Finding Happiness after Covid 19,* which was published in July 2020 and followed by *How to be Happy* in 2021. I may yet get round to writing a children's book.

I've won several short story competitions, taken part in Stroud Short Stories on two occasions and the Cheltenham Poetry Festival in 2017, judged competitions, including children's writing competitions, and am an active member of several writing groups.

My website www.pamkeevil.com will tell you more, including how to keep in contact.

Follow me on Twitter and Instagram and message me if you are interested in finding out more or join my mailing list for regular updates.

Enjoyed the book?

Please help all authors by posting a review of this book. It really does make a difference!

And it doesn't have to be long and complicated; a star rating will be enough.

If you can add one or two words, that would be fabulous!

Other books by Pam Keevil

Just what do you do when you've got no job, no family, no friends, and the world you are plunged into is unfamiliar? This is the challenge for Angie Jarvis. As Sister Ruth, her warnings about Father Benedict's unhealthy interest in his young parishioners have been brushed aside for years. She loses her faith in God and humanity and finally leaves the safety and comfort of the convent she joined as a young woman over thirty years ago.
In her quest to create a new life for herself, there is one certainty, she plans to have sex and plenty of it. Except she soon discovers it is not just relationships that are a challenge. She is a virgin in more ways than one.

https://www.amazon.co.uk/Virgin-at-Fifty-Pam-Keevil-ebook/dp/B07CRGF675

When unconventional American Mona flees an abusive relationship for the healing peace of the English countryside, she meets Sheila, whose life has followed a more traditional pattern. Will their friendship withstand a disaffected husband, a jealous ex, a potential love interest, the suicide of a friend, and the threat of developers despoiling the village or will they inspire in each other the courage to make the changes they need?

https://www.amazon.ca/Wild-Girls-Pam-Keevil-ebook/dp/B0BJFM9YMB

With romance, mystery and murder, set in a village where pagan rituals exist beneath the veneer of the modern world, Mayflies is a world of intrigue, jealousy and resentments. Alice is a newcomer, lonely, running from past unhappiness. Ruby is a single mother, resenting that her own mother disappeared from her life when she was a small child. Luke is a failing city financier. Their lives are inextricably linked when the skeletons of a mother and child are discovered; a discovery which threatens to unravel all their dreams.

https://www.amazon.com/Mayflies-Pam-Keevil/dp/1838467416

Coming soon…

From The Gloucestershire Chronicles, featuring Detective Mark Mulroney.

Who Pays the Piper?
The discovery of the body of a young man from an eco-community reveals a web of lies and deception in both the community and the village in which it is set.

A Fair Exchange
A severed hand leads to a grooming gang, but will anyone dare to give evidence?